THE
ARMAGEDDON
FILE

Center Point
Large Print

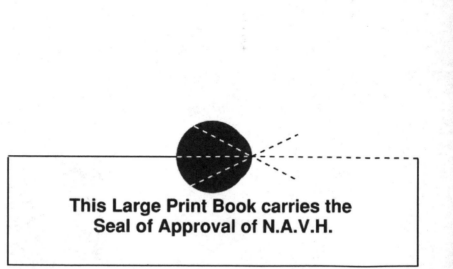

**This Large Print Book carries the
Seal of Approval of N.A.V.H.**

THE ARMAGEDDON FILE

STEPHEN COONTS

CENTER POINT LARGE PRINT
THORNDIKE, MAINE

This Center Point Large Print edition
is published in the year 2018 by arrangement with
Regnery Publishing.

The text of this Large Print edition is unabridged.
In other aspects, this book may vary
from the original edition.
Printed in the United States of America
on permanent paper.
Set in 16-point Times New Roman type.

ISBN: 978-1-68324-671-8

Library of Congress Cataloging-in-Publication Data

Names: Coonts, Stephen, 1946- author.
Title: The Armageddon file / Stephen Coonts.
Description: Center Point Large Print edition. | Thorndike, Maine :
    Center Point Large Print, 2018.
Identifiers: LCCN 2017050421 | ISBN 9781683246718
    (hardcover : alk. paper)
Subjects: LCSH: Presidents—Election—Fiction. | Conspiracies—Fiction.
    | Politcal fiction. | Large type books. | GSAFD: Suspense fiction.
Classification: LCC PS3553.O5796 A87 2018 | DDC 813/.54—dc23 LC
record available at https://lccn.loc.gov/2017050421

To my friends
Dale A. Mayer and Sandra J. Hyer,
who were there when the first egg was laid.

DISCLAIMER

This is a work of fiction, peopled by and involving foreign and domestic companies, institutions, organizations, and activities—private, public, and government—that are products of the author's imagination. Where actual names appear, they are used fictitiously and do not necessarily depict their actual conduct or purpose.

CHAPTER ONE

Over the Christmas holidays Callie and Jake Grafton invited some of Callie's academic colleagues to their condo in Rosslyn for dinner. Callie had been a part-time language instructor at the university for many years and since she was a gregarious, intellectually curious person, made it her business to meet interesting colleagues at the faculty club and make friends.

After dinner Jake invited Professor Giovanni Mezzi to his study for a cognac while the other guests, including Mrs. Mezzi, visited with Callie. Jake knew from his wife that the scholar smoked a pipe whenever he could, so when they were in the study, Jake told him to light up.

After a pro forma objection just to be polite, the professor loaded his old pipe with a blackened bowl rim and set the tobacco afire with a lighter whose flame could have cut steel. He achieved ignition and exhaled clouds of pungent smoke, which quickly formed a haze that rose toward the ceiling.

Mezzi was a professor emeritus who taught only one course to grad students and busied himself with research in his field, which was political science. He had unruly white hair that he wore rather long and favored bow ties and

British tweeds with elbow patches—tastes the professor had picked up when he was a Rhodes scholar at Oxford. He was comfortably plump and his clothes were rumpled.

Grafton, on the other hand, the director of the Central Intelligence Agency, the CIA, was an inch or so over six feet, lean and trim, with graying, thinning hair combed straight back. He was wearing slacks and a tan shirt this evening, his usual at-home attire.

"Were you surprised at the outcome of the November election?" Jake asked casually. Vaughn Conyer had beaten Cynthia Hinton decisively in the Electoral College by winning five key states that the polls said were going Democratic: Pennsylvania, Florida, Ohio, Michigan, and Wisconsin. In January, Conyer would be inaugurated as the nation's forty-fifth president.

"Like everyone," the professor said seriously, and emitted three short puffs of tobacco fumes. He gestured with his pipe. "Lacking any private data, I accepted the polls as an accurate reflection of the mood of the electorate, which didn't turn out to be the case."

Jake nodded encouragingly and said, "I believe the pollsters were spectacularly wrong about Brexit last June."

"Polls are art masquerading as science," the professor said. "To have any pretension of being an accurate reflection of the public mood, one's sample must be large enough to accurately weigh all likely voting groups and one must carefully construct the questions. Then there is the fact that some voters will change their minds after talking to the poll-taker and, human nature being what it is, some of them lie, either to make themselves look good to the poll-taker, to tell him what they think he wants to hear, or simply for the satisfaction of lying. Then there is the problem of people who don't normally vote coming out of the woodwork for an election. Turnout is notoriously difficult to predict accurately."

His tobacco had apparently gone out, so he fired off his blowtorch again and attended to it.

"Almost all the polls said Hinton had a comfortable lead and the media took them as gospel, even though unbiased observation showed that Vaughn Conyer was riding a groundswell of public approval that had carried him through the primaries against fifteen seasoned politicians. He was brash, a non-politician, and he pounded on the jobs issue and immigration, which proved to be key issues with the electorate. Hinton represented the political establishment and promised more of the same policies that huge numbers of people, the so-called 'white male' voters, rejected."

"How did they miss all that?" Grafton prompted.

"When the media and public get the results

11

of polls, we are faced with the problem of confirmation bias, which is the human tendency to favor evidence that confirms our pre-existing beliefs while ignoring evidence that we might be wrong. I suspect there was a lot of that leading up to the election."

"What about all the post-election charges that the Russians interfered with our election?" Jake asked the question casually, but he leaned forward in his chair for the answer.

"The Russians hacking the Hinton staff's emails?" Mezzi smiled. "That may or may not be true." Two more puffs. "Political professionals regard the electorate as sheep to be herded and sheared. The emails stated that graphically and crudely, but that isn't news. Elections aren't held in a vacuum. Everyone influences an election by the things they say and don't say. The world isn't static and the news cycle rolls on relentlessly like a giant asphalt roller. People comment at home, at work, on social occasions, all the time. Also now on social media. All these things, or any one of them, can cause people who aren't firmly committed to change their minds right up until they fill out the ballot."

Jake took a tiny sip of cognac, and holding the glass between his hands to warm it, asked, "When you are looking over the election results, do you get any little suspicion that there might have been some fraud?"

The professor smiled, sipped cognac. and puffed contentedly. "The term 'honest election' is an oxymoron," he said. "Election fraud, or voter fraud, call it what you will, is as old as elections and is everywhere, ubiquitous. Public office is a plum that often provides a large salary, prestige, influence, the opportunity for graft, and, of course, that ultimate aphrodisiac, power. Not everyone who runs for office is a scallywag, but many of them are, so a lot of brains are always trying to game the system."

Mezzi went on between sips of cognac and leisurely puffs on his pipe. Slipping money to politicians was a practice as old as the pyramids, he explained, yet even if illegal, it was not election fraud. Plain and simple, election fraud meant attempting to steal an election by allowing ineligible people to vote, miscounting the votes, buying votes, or by some other method.

The smaller and poorer the voting district, the greater the temptation and opportunity for a politician to give the electorate a dishonest nudge his way. In the old days politicians stayed in power in poor counties for generations by buying votes for a half-pint of whiskey. The first person into the voting booth brought out a blank ballot, which he exchanged for a bottle. The second man took the marked ballot inside and put it in the box, and brought his blank ballot out to trade for a bottle, and so on. Political machines stuffed ballot boxes in the big cities—Truman's defeat of Dewey with the help of the Chicago machine was legendary. Chicago politicians routinely waited until Illinois districts downstate had reported their totals so they knew how many votes they needed to manufacture, then they did it. That went on for decades.

Chicago was old news, yet even in our modern era big-city fraud seemed alive and well. "The press reported that in thirty-seven percent of the precincts in Detroit during the last election there were more ballots cast than voters registered. Amazingly, Democrat candidates were always the beneficiaries of these electoral miracles, so some people took that as proof that God was a Democrat."

Grafton smiled, which was apparently the response Mezzi wanted.

"In 1993, the Pennsylvania Attorney General charged a state senate winner with vote fraud, and a judge overturned the election and gave his seat to his Republican challenger. One lovely comment was that the Democrats didn't commit voter fraud all the time, 'They only steal elections when they have to.' "

Mezzi continued, "Absentee ballots have always been open to fraud, but now any voter can request a mail-in ballot, so the vistas for cheating have expanded exponentially. County officials never have the funds or means to systematically purge voter rolls of dead people. Voters who have moved out-of-state and registered to vote elsewhere are still on the voter registration rolls in many counties nationwide. Voting your dead relatives' mail-in ballots happens nationwide. In some places if a voter allows the sheriff or one of his deputies to mark an absentee ballot and mail it in, the voter can earn a little money, a bottle of booze, or have a misdemeanor traffic violation dismissed.

"The lack of laws that require voters to identify themselves with a photo ID while registering or at the polls was a boon for organized efforts to bus people around to vote the graveyards or the people retired in Florida or Arizona. Then there are illegal aliens voting: best guess was that there were thirteen or fourteen million illegals in the country—no one knows how many voted. The Democrats in California legitimized the scam by passing a law making it legal for aliens in the state to register and vote in violation of federal immigration laws, thereby diluting the vote of California's American citizens, not only in state elections but in federal elections. These illegal voters would, the California Democrats hoped, help them stay in power. Of course, in Mexico only Mexicans with a government-issued photo ID card are allowed to vote."

Grafton muttered, "As everyone knows, California isn't Mexico."

A flicker of a smile crossed Mezzi's face. "The

entire election system in America is a patchwork antique that desperately needs an overhaul, yet politics raises its slimy head whenever the subject is raised. Those politicians who think they benefit from crooked elections resist change with all their might. The federal government doesn't run elections; counties do, supervised by their state governments, and they lack funds to change the system, even if they had the will."

Complicating the whole matter were various southern states' systematic efforts for a century after the American Civil War to deprive minorities of the right to vote. The federal government had successfully put an end to that, but politicians and judges opposed to voter ID reforms in the second decade of the twenty-first century still waved the bloody flag and fought tooth and nail in federal courthouses to prevent it.

The shift from paper ballots to voting machines with computer chips in their innards opened up a whole new way to cheat. In other words, new ways to deprive the American people of the right to rule themselves. Anyone with the money and organization, domestic and foreign, could get in the game.

"Can the election system be cleaned up?" Grafton asked.

Giovanni Mezzi shrugged. "People are people," he said with a sigh. "If you plug one leak the dike starts leaking someplace else."

"What do you think of the suggestion that this past election was rigged?"

"Not much. The voting machines and tabulating machines are not on the internet, so it would take an organization to fix a national election, lots of people."

Grafton bored in. "How many?"

Mezzi looked thoughtful. "Maybe it could be done. All you have to do is get the swing states to go your way."

"What if the polls were right and the results were doctored somehow? What if the election was stolen from Cynthia Hinton?"

"There's no evidence of that," the professor objected. He glanced into his pipe, which had gone out, and placed it in his pocket. "That said, the farther one gets away from the precincts, the cleaner elections look. One needs to be close to see the dirt."

Grafton smiled and stood. "Perhaps we should join the rest of the guests," Jake said.

Professor Mezzi agreed and led the way out of the study. Jake followed him out and firmly closed the door to keep the room from polluting the rest of the apartment.

CHAPTER TWO

Junior Sikes was a pedophile. He knew he had a dangerous obsession that might get him into serious trouble, but he couldn't help himself. He was too frightened of possible discovery and arrest to attempt physical contact with children, so he satisfied himself with kiddie porn that he downloaded on his computer. It was a poor substitute for the real thing, but if he could keep his appetites under control by merely watching movies of men screwing little girls, he could avoid ruin, and the abyss.

He had attempted therapy for his problem on two prior occasions. The therapists made him talk during session after session about the domineering women of his youth, none of which did him any good. The past was past, may his aunt who raised him roast in Hell, and today he was who he was, a bald-headed little guy with a big chin and too much forehead that the girls in high school and college had never noticed.

These days he downloaded kiddie porn on his laptop and watched when he couldn't think of anything but sex, which was several times a day. Even a few minutes was enough of a fix to hold him until he could get home to his big-screen computer. Junior spent at least three days a week traveling for his job, so he never downloaded porn on his office desktop. Sure, it was password protected, but everyone in the office was a nerd and hacker, so he didn't want to run the risk. That nosy bitch in the next cubicle, Rosa, had her own hang-ups and wore men's clothes and a butch haircut. She hated him and would cut off his cock if she had the chance.

This morning he was looking at some new porn he had downloaded at home last night when he heard footsteps coming down the hall, quickly. The footsteps of a group of people. He hit the escape button and the porn disappeared from the laptop screen. In its place was some code he was working on.

The office manager came into his cubicle, followed by two policemen in uniform.

"Back away from that laptop," the manager said gruffly. She was a hefty black woman. She placed her hand on his shoulder and jerked him, chair and all, back from his desk so he couldn't reach the computer keyboard.

"He was watching it, Miz Williams," Rosa crowed as she elbowed her way around the two policemen who were blocking the opening to the cubicle. "I saw it. Filthy stuff."

Junior Sikes stared at her.

How?

She saw the question on his face and a smirk of triumph crossed hers. "I cut a hole in the cubicle

19

wall, you slimy little pervert!" She ripped down his calendar on the wall behind him, and there it was! A hole about the size of a quarter. She must have moved the calendar with a pencil eraser while his back was turned and looked through the hole.

"I'm afraid I'll have to place you under arrest, Mr. Sikes," one of the policemen said.

To Junior's amazement, he found his voice. His world was crumbling, he was so frightened he was shaking, but he got it out. "Do you have a warrant?" he asked the policemen.

"I saw it!" Rosa said. "Men fucking kids. It's on that laptop."

"You need a warrant," Junior managed.

"We have one," the black policeman said, and handed Junior the sheet of paper. He tried to read it. It was dated yesterday. Based on a sworn affidavit. Rosa had sworn to it.

"We'll take that computer too."

A ray of hope peeked into Junior's world. "Not without a search warrant," he protested.

"They don't need one," Ms. Williams said flatly. "That computer is company property and I'm turning it over to the police."

Junior stared at Rosa with hate in his eyes. "You goddamn filthy, cunt-lapping dyke!"

The policemen stood him up, cuffed him, and one of them took him away. The other stayed behind to sign a receipt for the laptop.

• • •

When they took him in front of a judge that afternoon, Junior Sikes said he couldn't afford a lawyer, so one was appointed for him. A public defender.

The lawyer came to see him the next morning. He was a rumpled, overweight man, about forty, with a Van Dyke goatee and a ponytail dangling from thinning hair. The sleeves of his sports coat were frayed and shiny. His crooked tie had a spot on it that looked like mustard.

"My name is Dillworth," he said. He settled himself comfortably on a chair across the glass barrier in the lawyer-client room. He got out a legal pad and pen from a ratty, gray, plastic, soft envelope. Uncapped the pen and inspected the tip for leaks. Apparently satisfied, he asked, "Your full name and address?"

Junior told him and Dillworth wrote it down.

"Age?"

"Thirty-four."

"Got a criminal record?"

"No."

"Man, I want to know if you've even been arrested for jaywalking."

"No."

When he had all the information he wanted, Dillworth said, "They found kiddie porn on that laptop you had at work and are executing a search warrant on your apartment this afternoon. Do you have a computer there?"

"Yes."

"Got kiddie stuff on it?"

"Yes."

Dillworth sighed and made a note. Like he was making a shopping list: milk, eggs, bread, and peanut butter. It wasn't his life that was circling the drain.

"Are you any good?" Sikes asked. A good lawyer, he meant.

Dillworth didn't look up from his pad. "After I finished my stint as clerk for Chief Justice Roberts, I turned down a professorship at Yale Law so I could be a public defender, spend my working days visiting clients in jail. I like the smell."

"Can you get me out on bail?"

Dillworth eyed him critically. "Where are you going to go?" he asked.

"Home."

"You're lying, Sikes. You may think you can outrun the law, but I doubt it. You don't look as if you have what it takes to be a fugitive."

"That's none of your business. I want out."

"They all do."

"I have a *right* to get out. Innocent until proven guilty."

Dillworth sighed. "If I had a dollar for every innocent man I've defended, I couldn't afford a Happy Meal."

"I didn't shoot or rape anybody."

"They haven't charged you with those crimes," he said dryly. "Can you afford bail? Gotta pay ten percent in cash to a bail bondsman. Ten grand on a hundred-thousand-dollar bond. The judge will go at least that much for kiddie porn, maybe more since you're a dangerous pervert. Your arrest made the local news section of the morning paper, the tweeters are twaddling, and he's up for re-election. You got that kind of cash?"

"Well . . ."

"If you do, you can afford to hire your own lawyer. I defend indigent clients, the oppressed, the under-privileged, the downtrodden, you know the bullshit. So . . ."

Junior Sikes rubbed his large forehead. Jesus, he was neck-deep in the shit. Now or never. He pretended to think for ten seconds or so, then played his ace.

"I want to talk to the FBI," he said.

If Dillworth was surprised it didn't show. He made another little note. Jelly for the peanut butter. "What about?"

"I'll tell them."

Dillworth looked him over and nodded slowly. "Like the feds come trotting whenever I give them a call. You're going to have to give me enough to elevate them off their asses at the federal courthouse or you can forget it."

Junior Sikes wiped his forehead. And his eyes, which were leaking a little.

"I work for American ElectTech. We make and sell voting machines. The company has been rigging them so they change votes."

"Are you shitting me, Sikes?"

"The last election and the next."

"You were involved in that?"

"Yes."

"How involved?"

"I helped write the code—it varied from jurisdiction to jurisdiction—and installed it on ElectTech machines around the country when they had us in for a pre-election function check and certification of the machines."

"The company knew that you were doing this?"

"They told me what races to fix and what percentage the various candidates were to get. After Hinton lost the election anyway, they started doubling down on the next one. Getting more sophisticated. I'm working on the software now."

"And they called the cops because you had porn on your computer? You expect me to believe that?"

"It was that dyke, Rosa Caputo. She's on the software team too, but she's a moron. She called the police and swore out a complaint. The company probably didn't know about it until the cops showed up."

Dillworth's eyebrows went up and he examined Junior's face, his skepticism obvious. Then he gave that up as a waste of time. With his lips screwed up, he made another note, longer this time. He put his legal pad and pen back in the plastic envelope and stood. "I'll see what I can do," he said. "Don't hold your breath."

The attorney walked out.

Junior Sikes had a cell to himself. The cells up and down his row had inmates, usually two, and they talked back and forth. Junior didn't say a word to anyone. He was so depressed he stretched out on the bunk, closed his eyes and didn't move. He began thinking about suicide, how easy it would be. Not in here, of course, but outside.

Poof, and it would be all over, the obsessions, the shame, the hopeless future. He tried to shut out the world, the sounds, the smell, the situation, all of it.

That evening he roused himself to pee, then sat on the bunk with his back to the wall and his eyes closed. Concentrated on breathing, on counting his pulse, on trying to just turn off his mind.

How would he manage to survive in prison?

When the deputy brought a tray for his dinner and slid it through the slot in the cell door, Junior didn't even glance at it. He wasn't the least bit hungry.

One of the guys in the next cell tried to talk to him, but Junior ignored him. Then Lights Out came and Junior curled up in a fetal position on the bunk. The light was on in the corridor; it never went off. Still, the forty-watt light in the cell was off and that afforded him a bit of privacy. For the first time in hours, tears leaked from the corners of his eyes.

He would never survive prison. He was a small man, never worked out, and would be physically abused. He would probably end up as some tattooed, biker drug-dealer's butt boy. The FBI was his only hope. Testifying against the people at ElectTech in return for probation. Those people were guilty of felonies, as he was, but the first to turn state's evidence could perhaps get leniency. Maybe even immunity.

He thought about the ElectTech crowd, the dyke Rosa, that bitch LaVerne Williams, both of whom threw him to the wolves. He was perfectly willing to put his co-workers in prison if he could stay out. After all, Rosa with all her kinks had been absolutely delighted to rat him out for kiddie porn. Her perversion was socially acceptable and his wasn't. Junior told himself Rosa and LaVerne deserved whatever was coming.

Junior was asleep when he heard the rattling on the cell door. It was the deputy. "Wake up, Sikes. You got a visitor."

"What time is it?"

"Jail time, idiot. Get your flip-flops on and I'll unlock the door."

He put them on as the door swung open.

"I'm going to leave the cuffs off. Behave yourself or you'll wish you had."

He walked ahead of the deputy and asked over his shoulder, "Who is it?"

"FBI."

They were amazingly early. He didn't expect them for a couple of days. Or never. His heart leaped. Oh man, if he could only cut a deal!

The deputy took him to a well-lit interrogation room. One man was in the room, a middle-aged, fit, clean-shaven guy in a business suit, wearing a tie. A small recorder sat on the desk. Four chairs were arranged around the desk.

Without preamble, as the deputy turned to leave, the man's hand came up and Junior saw with a start it held a pistol with a sausage on the barrel. The man pointed the gun at the deputy's back and pulled the trigger. The report was just a small *splut*. The deputy fell forward onto the floor.

The pistol turned in his direction. "No . . ." Junior said, lifting his hands as if pushing away the gunman. "No . . ."

He didn't see the flash or hear the shot. The bullet smacked him in the forehead and plowed through his skull into his brain. Junior was dead as he began to fall.

CHAPTER THREE

My name is Tommy Carmellini. My boss Jake Grafton, director of the CIA, had me on temporary assignment with an FBI task force investigating election fraud. When the call came in from the task force Special Agent in Charge, Margaret "Maggie" Jewel Miller, that a voting machine technician was in jail in Pennsylvania for kiddie porn and ready to talk about election fraud, I saddled up and drove from Washington.

Last November we had had one hell of a presidential election, the final face-off between the liberals, or "progressives" as they liked to call themselves these days, and everyone else. Representing the liberal establishment in a baggy pantsuit made in China or Bangladesh was Cynthia Hinton, wife of a former president, and herself a former U.S. senator and secretary of state. In the other corner was a billionaire businessman, Vaughn Conyer, who had never held an elected office, not even as a city councilman.

Hinton was the establishment candidate, promising more of the same. Conyer was a populist candidate, against everything the establishment stood for, and the huge underdog. In the summer of 2015, if you had gone to Las Vegas and plopped your savings account on Conyer's nose, you could have gotten odds of twenty-five to one from the casinos, and everyone, including your spouse, would have thought you were certifiably nuts. That summer Hinton was an even bet in Vegas. Right up to the election, and even on election day, the pollsters, media, and odds-makers trumpeted that Hinton was going to win. But on election night when the votes were counted, the spavined dark horse that the pros said didn't have a chance won, to the horror of the liberals and amazement of everyone else.

With that presidential election only four months past, the rumors of election fraud were still giving off smoke and heat, as they did in every election. I was on the FBI task force because unhappy Hinton supporters suspected, without evidence, that foreign governments might be involved. If they were, I was supposed to inform my boss so that the awesome power of the CIA could be harnessed to crush the guilty bastards and make them keep their foreign fingers out of our ballot boxes. As a cynic might say, Americans had been rigging elections for centuries and didn't need foreign help.

In Pennsylvania I found a suburban motel and dropped into bed. A phone call from Maggie woke me up at seven in the morning.

She told me there had been a shooting at the jail, and the snitch that was going to rat out

American ElectTech was dead. She would meet me there.

I showered, shaved, draped my manly form, put on my shoulder holster, and slid my Kimber .45 into it. I left my stuff in the room. Outside a gentle rain was falling from a solid slate sky and the air smelled of spring, a faint, sweet aroma of fertile earth. Bulbs in the motel's flower bed were sending up shoots.

I fired up my ride, a 1974 Mercedes 450SL convertible in robin's egg blue, and steered it to the filling station next door. I asked the counter person where the jail was as I paid for a large cup of coffee. She gave me a hard look, said she had no idea. I typed it into the map feature of my cell phone, and it popped right up. Google knows everything.

Maggie Miller was tall for a woman, with a long nose and a wide mouth. She had frown lines around her mouth, hard eyes, and salt-and-pepper gray hair. She wore no make-up that I could see. I thought she was in her mid-forties, but maybe it was just the job.

She was certainly stressed this morning. "They took the hard drive out of the jail monitoring computer system and shot everyone who saw them. Four men dead, one of them the snitch. The others were deputy sheriffs, jail employees. All were shot with what appears to be a silenced nine-millimeter pistol. Or two or three of them."

The crime scene scientists were still photographing bodies, but I didn't watch. I had seen too many bodies as it was, and I certainly didn't need a gander at four more. In addition to the scientists, there were four FBI agents, a half-dozen city policemen, two state troopers, and six deputy sheriffs, all trying to stay out of the way. The sheriff, whose jail it was, was almost incoherent with rage.

I was in the intake room where prisoners were photographed and outfitted with a jail coverall and flip-flops when the crime scene investigators laid out Junior Sikes's stuff on a table and began going through it. His wallet was there.

After they had emptied it, I bent over the table and examined without touching the three credit cards it contained. A Visa, a Mastercard, and an American Express card with the company's name on it. His driver's license was there too. I photographed the lot with my cell phone.

I looked through the rest of his stuff, which didn't seem of interest, and asked, "Where's the computer this guy used for porno action?"

"It was supposed to go to the crime lab this morning," Maggie said, still frowning, "and was being held in the evidence locker. The lock is broken and it's missing."

"Did it have kiddie porn on it?"

"The sheriff's deputies did a quick check yesterday and said it did."

31

"Did they have his password?"

"An ElectTech rep gave it to them. They owned the computer, they said."

"Ain't security wonderful! What about ElectTech?"

"We're getting a search warrant. We've surrounded the place and aren't letting anyone in."

"I'd like to go in for a look when you get the warrant."

"Fine."

"I'm going to get some breakfast. Call me, will you?"

She nodded and I beat feet.

On my way back to the motel—a free breakfast went with the room—I called Jake Grafton. Got him at home. I had worked with him on and off for years and knew him fairly well. He was a retired two-star admiral and if he had any nerves, I had never seen any evidence of them.

After I filled him in, I ventured an opinion. "It looks like a professional hit. Clean, fast, deadly. No clues to speak of, although maybe the scientists can come up with DNA or something. Forget fingerprints."

"How about a search of the would-be snitch's apartment?"

"FBI is getting a warrant." I told him about the credit cards. "I'd like to send the photos to Sarah and let her see if she can hack into the credit card company's records. Be nice to know where this guy has been for say . . . the last year or so. If he was doctoring voting machines, maybe Sarah can go look at one."

I needed Grafton's permission to ask Sarah Houston to do some illegal searching. If the CIA were ever called to account for illegal computer hacking, Grafton would take the heat. Sarah was the best hacker and data miner east of Shanghai, and my girlfriend. We tried to keep business and pleasure separate, but that didn't work very well, so our relationship occasionally got messy.

"Sure," he said.

We said goodbye and broke the connection.

Sitting in the motel's parking lot with rain splattering on the car windshield, I diddled with my phone. Every few seconds I would pause to scan around the lot, seeing who was moving. I didn't realize I was doing it until I found myself looking behind me. I had assassins on the brain.

Five minutes later the photos were on their way to Sarah along with an email detailing what I wanted.

I went into the motel and surveyed the breakfast bar. Lots of carbs from various boxes, probably from Costco. I ended up with two hard-boiled eggs, yogurt, and another cup of coffee. Ah, the fast, glamorous life of a CIA spook.

I idly examined my fellow breakfast diners, wondering if any of them had been out doing evil things during the night. They looked like the usual half-awake tourists, civil servants, businessmen, and specialty construction workers, all about to pull stakes for another day in the work-a-day world.

As I shucked the eggs I wondered what I had gotten into this time. Assassins who smacked four guys in a county jail and waltzed out with a computer from the evidence locker seemed a bit heavier than a county clerk planning to stuff a ballot box. Be that as it may, the jail hits weren't my problem. Election fraud was the FBI's bailiwick, and assassins belonged to the cops. I was looking for a foreign connection. I had not the slightest clue how I would identify one unless I ran into a guy named Raskolnikov.

Two weeks ago this gig had looked like a nice break from the Washington grind, but now I wasn't so sure. Bodies lying around made it something other than a routine voter-fraud case. Some heavy hitters were doing some shooting: it was enough to give you pause.

The coffee was pretty good, better than the stuff at the filling station, so I had another cup and settled in with a copy of the motel's free newspaper, which was chock full of political news and sports.

The political, media, and financial establishments didn't see Vaughn Conyer's upset victory coming. The new president had now been in office a couple of months and was trying to fulfill campaign promises while, predictably, the establishment elites pushed back hard, street thugs rioted, and his political enemies howled. None of the twenty-some celebrities who had promised to leave the country if Vaughn Conyer won had actually done so, to the disgust of those who backed the winner. The American cultural divide, more like the Grand Canyon, yawned wider and deeper than ever. Another congressman was being prosecuted for graft, the Middle East was erupting again, European voters were giving their establishment some hard licks, Puerto Rican bonds were back in the news, and another big bank was in trouble with its regulators.

When I had my fill of politics, I turned to the sports pages. Baseball was in spring training in Florida and Arizona, and, according to one sports writer, had some strong young arms. I wondered if I could have made it in the major leagues as a pitcher. I hadn't thrown a baseball since college but I could chuck a pretty good grenade. I decided that baseball was another opportunity on the road of life that I had missed. Oh well, a man can fantasize.

Maggie called at ten o'clock. The FBI had found a judge and gotten a warrant. I used my iPhone's map feature and drove over to the ElectTech building. The agent at the door was difficult, so I phoned Maggie and she came down and got me.

I ignored the door dude and strolled in out of the rain behind her.

They were taking the place apart. The executive who ran the office was a woman named LaVerne Williams, and she wasn't there. Actually, none of the employees were there. I stationed myself in her office and watched the agent and deputy sheriff—local law had men and women on the scene—and saw one of them turn out a drawer full of her personal stuff. An insurance bill had her address. I read it and left.

In the parking lot the rain was almost a mist. The drops caressed my cheeks as I walked to my ride. Safely in the driver's seat, I typed the address into the map feature of my cell phone.

The house was ten miles away in a middle-class, mixed-race neighborhood. The yard was beginning to show traces of green through the winter detritus. Not a cop or agent in sight. I had gotten there before them. I reached under the seat, extracted my pack of lock picks and a pair of latex medical gloves, and pulled the gloves on.

The paint had worn off years ago on the area of the porch where people walked, and several of the boards were rotten. Still, it was a nice, modest house, just needing some maintenance. I pushed the doorbell and heard it dinging inside. No one came to answer it. After knocking repeatedly on the door and hearing nothing from within, I tried the doorknob. It turned.

I glanced around to see who was watching—apparently no one. It was a workday and kids were in school. Still, a journalist might arrive at any moment. I touched my shoulder holster before I realized that I had done it, then opened the door, stepped in, and pushed the door shut until the latch clicked.

"Hello. Anyone home?" I called loudly.

Silence.

I knew nothing about LaVerne Williams, whether she was married or living with someone, whether she had an elderly relative at home or lived alone.

I looked through the rooms on the ground floor—living room, kitchen, dining room, a half bath—then opened the door to the garage. Her car was in there, plus a lawn mower and some other stuff.

So where was she?

I had made it to the ripe old age of thirty-four by being careful, so I pulled the Kimber .45 from my shoulder holster and stood listening. The house was quiet. The silence was interrupted by a tinkling as ice fell into a tray in the refrigerator freezer.

I went up the stairs with the pistol in hand. My subconscious was trying to tell me something. No one around, the car in the garage . . .

She was in the master bedroom, or at least the big one. On the bed.

"Miz Williams?"

I took a few steps closer and got a good look. Her mouth was open and she had a bullet hole in the front of her head. Her eyes were open, frozen. Not much blood, which meant she had probably died instantly or within seconds.

I put my naked wrist on her bare arm. She was fairly cold. I'm no expert but I've seen my share of corpses. She had been dead for hours, shot sometime during the night. A small pocket pistol lay near her hand on the bed. Perhaps she awoke when she heard noises, someone climbing the stairs. She heard the noises, grabbed the gun, the door opened . . . and *bang*. I thought it doubtful that a suicide would hold the pistol up to her forehead and pull the trigger with her thumb. The scientists would definitely answer the question of suicide by comparing a bullet from the pocket pistol with whatever they could find in her head or buried in the mattress.

I checked out the bathroom, the guest bedroom, and the closets. Took a deep breath.

LaVerne Williams knew too much. Like Junior Sikes. Too bad for her.

Perhaps the scientists could find something in that house that pointed toward the killer, but I didn't bother looking. On the porch, with the door closed, I called Maggie Miller on my cell. "That woman who ratted out Junior Sikes—do you have her name and address?"

"Sure. Rosa Caputo. Why?"

"I'm over at Miz Williams's house, and someone killed her during the night. The front door was unlocked. I want to check on Caputo. You'd better send someone over here."

Caputo lived in an apartment complex, a fourth-floor flat. It was a newer building and had skinny trees in islands in the parking lot, which was only about a third full. A sheriff's car sat at the entrance with the emergency lights flashing. A uniformed deputy sheriff and an FBI agent were in the lobby talking to the superintendent when I walked in.

I knew what was upstairs . . . just *knew*.

The FBI agent glanced at me, said "You're Carmellini?"

I nodded.

He motioned for me to come with him. My feet felt like they weighed twenty-five pounds each as I walked onto the elevator behind the three of them. On the way to the fourth floor no one said anything. The super had a master key, but he didn't need it. The FBI guy turned the knob and I followed the law in. The super stood in the hallway, twisting his hands as a little dog circled his feet and yapped madly. Looked to me like the pooch was desperate to get out to answer nature's call.

Rosa Caputo and her live-in female companion were both dead. Rosa was in the living room near the door in her pajamas and the companion was in bed in the only bedroom. Both had bullets in their heads. Their bodies looked helpless, pathetic. What a waste!

I went down in the elevator and stood a while in the rain. A van with the call letters of a local television station drove up and disgorged a female reporter and a male cameraman. I unlocked my car and climbed in as the super came out with the dog on a leash.

I gotta get in another line of work. Sooner rather than later.

Seven dead people, four of them in the county jail—there was no way on God's green Earth to keep the murders under wraps for a few days.

Interviews with the local sheriff, an infuriated, balding career cop, were also on the air. No, he didn't know the motives behind these murders—"assassinations" he called them— but law enforcement investigations had been launched. The voters could rest assured that no stone would be left unturned until the guilty party or parties were brought to justice. In fact, the FBI was also investigating.

The natural question was why the FBI, which only investigated federal crimes, was involved since murder was a state crime. So a television reporter asked it as the camera captured every dancing pixel: "Why the FBI?"

40

"The Election Fraud Task Force," the sheriff answered, as if that fact was unimportant. After all, the FBI was the FBI.

Some of the victims worked for ElectTech, a local company that made voting machines and sold them nationwide. Now that the FBI Election Fraud Task Force was involved . . . the story went thermonuclear. Within minutes it was all over local radio and television, then the networks. The next morning it was front-page news coast to coast. I read it in my motel's free newspaper while I ate two more boiled eggs and yogurt.

We were in a conference room at ElectTech going over what the task force had uncovered in the files when Maggie Jewel Miller got a call. She looked at the number on her phone, then left the room to talk. When she came back in, she wore a scowl. Everyone looked at her. "We're off the case," she said. "Justice Department's orders."

Everyone around the table tried to talk at once. Miller spoke and her voice carried through the hubbub. "We're to turn the case over to local law enforcement and go back to Washington."

They sullenly chewed the rag for a while, but they were pros and weren't going to buck the boss. I went outside and called Jake Grafton at CIA Headquarters in Langley. Didn't get him, but got an executive assistant whom I knew well.

Grafton called back in ten minutes. The

conversation was short. After I gave him the news, he said, "Come back to Washington. We need to talk."

The new FBI director was a man named Robert Levy, who had started out in Army Intelligence, then went to a high-tech firm that sold lots of stuff to Army Intelligence. From there, somehow, he got into law enforcement. The previous FBI director left immediately after the new president's inauguration, resigned as an alternative to being publicly fired. So here Levy was on the job as the nation's chief cop.

Levy refused to come to Langley for lunch, so Grafton refused to go to the Hoover Building downtown. Instead they met at a picnic shelter in Rock Creek Park. Six FBI agents were scattered around the perimeter of the picnic area, joined by Grafton's two bodyguards. Five guys and three gals, all packing serious heat and wired with radio microphones and receivers. A gentle rain dripped off the shelter roof.

Grafton and Levy sat at the picnic table with a pizza in a box. "Seven people dead in Pennsylvania and Justice called you off," Jake Grafton said. "How come?"

"You could have asked me that on the telephone."

"I wanted to see your face, Levy." Grafton took two pieces of pizza from the box and put them on a napkin. He licked his fingers. "People say that when you're lying you can't look anyone in the eyes."

"What son of a bitch told you that?"

"Reem Kiddus." Kiddus was the new president's chief of staff.

"Consider the source. What did you want to make this secret powwow about, anyway?"

"Why did you call off the Election Fraud Task Force in Pennsylvania?'

"Because Kiddus told the AG to talk to me. I would have told you that on the phone."

"Any explanation?"

" 'The election is over,' he said, 'and the president wants to move on.' "

"So now the FBI is taking orders from the White House?"

"Don't give me that shit. I just got this job. The last guy about sank the agency. Morale is in the toilet. This agency investigates federal crimes. Do you know of any federal crimes we aren't investigating?"

"No."

"I am not going to waste time and assets stirring the cesspool on the off chance one will surface. If you find one, give us a call." Levy got up and walked off. His bodyguards tagged along.

Jake Grafton picked up a slice of pizza and got busy chewing and swallowing.

Back in his office, Jake sent for Sarah Houston,

his computer guru. She was tall and had long, dark-brown hair, almost black. Her nose was thin, not too long, and she had dark brown eyes set wide apart and a square jaw. When she smiled she showed a mouthful of beautiful white teeth.

"I have a project for you," he said after she was seated, erect in a chair beside his desk, her knees together. "I want you to do a spreadsheet on the counties in six states: Michigan, Wisconsin, Pennsylvania, Wisconsin, Florida, and Ohio—the swing states that went for Vaughn Conyer. I want you to compare the presidential election results from 2012 to the county-by-county results in 2016."

"Okay."

"What I am interested in is how many counties actually swung their states from Democrat to Republican."

"Election fraud?"

"I want to examine the possibility. You read the newspapers?"

"I do."

"The interesting fact about presidential elections in America is that we have the Electoral College, which makes each state a winner-take-all proposition. The College was the great political compromise that made ratification of the constitution possible back in 1788. The little states didn't want the large states to decide elections. Yet the large states wanted more of a say in who got elected. The Electoral College forced political parties to campaign nationwide and have national platforms. Arguably, the Electoral College is one of the reasons that the United States has lasted from 1788 until now, 229 years, even though the nation has changed dramatically from a few states with agricultural economies strung along the east coast to the richest nation on Earth with over three hundred million people spread across the continent."

Sarah remained silent. She was used to her boss talking out loud, a bit like a college professor preparing the ground. Or, she imagined, a navy admiral defining the problem for his staff.

"Consequently," Grafton continued, eyeing her, "it isn't necessary for a candidate to win the popular vote nationwide. He or she only need win the key states by a simple majority. One more than half. The amazing thing is how slim the majority can be, if it is in states with significant numbers of electoral votes. A few percentage points in key precincts or counties can do the trick."

He paused, his eyes on hers. She nodded, indicating she understood.

"I want you to identify the counties that swung the states. We may or may not look at precincts later. Right now I want you to concentrate on counties."

"Yes, sir."

"How long will it take?"

"Not long. The numbers should be easy to obtain. I should have the spreadsheet for you tomorrow."

He nodded and wiggled a hand, signifying the interview was over. Sarah rose and left the office.

I checked out of the motel and got on the road. The rain had stopped but the clouds were low and visibility was perhaps two miles at most. Traffic threw spray from the road and I had to keep the wipers in constant motion. The road was full of trucks rolling fast, a never-ending stream, like blood in a big artery.

I automatically checked the mirrors now and then, looking for a tail. If I had one, he or she was hanging well back. Not that I expected a tail, but with seven bodies back up the road, it never hurts to be careful.

I had worked for Jake Grafton on and off for years. He had been the Pentagon's go-to troubleshooter until he retired. Retirement for him lasted a year or two, then he went to the CIA, my agency. His prominent nose looked like an oversized after-market item that somebody glued on when the original manufacturer's equipment wore out. It was the thing folks noticed when looking at him for the first time, but his gray eyes soon captured everyone's attention and they forgot about that nose.

The eyes were hard and cold and stayed on you. Used to be that those eyes kinda intimidated me, but not anymore. They were the perfect advertisement for precisely the kind of man he was: extremely competent and a fierce, ruthless warrior. I don't know that I really liked him, but I respected the hell out of him. He was a man you always called "sir."

It was late afternoon when I was admitted to his office, which had the usual trappings of a government big shot: flags, carpet, original art on the walls, a nice desk, and comfortable chairs. The only item of personal memorabilia in sight was a framed eight-by-ten photo of his wife, Callie, which sat on his desk.

"Tell me about it," he said after he shook my hand and resumed his seat. He didn't shake hands with everyone, but we had been through so much together that perhaps he thought I merited one. Or he had something planned for me that he knew I wasn't going to like. Or both.

I told the tale in a few sentences.

"What do you think?" he asked.

"Somebody in Washington doesn't want the dirt shoveled."

Grafton rubbed his hand over his head and tugged at an earlobe. "No one has told me not to look for a foreign connection, if one exists."

Oh, man.

I'm not the brightest bulb in the box, but I

began to suspect where this was going, straight into a snake pit. "The killings are going to be investigated by regular law enforcement agencies," I said, repeating the obvious. "Maybe that was the best Mr. Influence could get."

What the hell?

I decided to say it: "As you are very well aware, by law the CIA is forbidden to operate inside the U.S. of A. That means investigations and interrogations and all the rest of it."

He grunted. "If I kept you on it, do you think you could find out anything?"

There it was, out in the open.

Can I call 'em or what?

"Was ElectTech fixing voting machines? We don't even know that. That was the question the task force had to answer first to establish jurisdiction. Since the FBI got called off, we don't know."

"Assume that they were."

"Someone with more brains than I have needs to look at the software program in a rigged machine. Or that missing computer that Junior Sikes used for porn. That might answer the foreign source question right there."

"I doubt it. Even if it appears to have Russian programming, that won't tell us if the Russian government is involved."

"At least it'll give us cover," I insisted. "I want to know if ElectTech rigged software in the last election or was getting set to do it in the next one."

I shifted around in my seat. I had to make him understand. "If I go stomping around in this mess, I don't want to find out that those killings were about smuggling drugs or jewels or running whores or filming child porn—things that have absolutely nothing to do with the CIA. If it comes down that way, the FBI will have my ass on a skewer for obstructing justice. Yours too. It's gotta be foreigners fucking with our elections, or nothing."

He didn't seem perturbed. I had a sneaking suspicion we weren't on the same sheet of music.

He was, I thought, being purposefully obtuse. "There is no way to prove a negative," I remarked. "To find out who doesn't have their fingers in this pie we will have to determine who does."

He flashed a smile, or as much of a smile as you were likely to get with Jake Grafton, and it was gone in about a second. He asked, "If I give you the green light, how would you go about it?"

Well, he was the boss and I was just a grunt. If I got in trouble he would be in deeper, and I knew he wouldn't evade the responsibility. Jake Grafton didn't operate that way.

I raised and lowered my shoulders. "Best way would be to just go up the ladder. Williams had a boss, and he or she had a boss, and so on."

"It's all corporate spaghetti," he noted, toying with a paper clip. "Everyone will deny responsibility for telling anyone to do anything illegal. You know that. And you won't have FBI credentials to scare the crap out of them and induce them to talk. You don't have anything to trade. On the other hand, with assassins out there permanently shutting mouths, one suspects that today there are a handful of people in corner suites crapping their pants."

"The cops will be talking to those people."

Jake Grafton adjusted himself in his swivel chair. "The assassins were an interesting move by Mr. Influence, or X, or whoever. That changes the whole dynamic. The interesting thing is that it happened so quickly."

I thought about it for a moment. Someone, either at ElectTech or in law enforcement, no telling who, made a telephone call. That started the snowball rolling downhill, and, yes, it arrived quickly.

That implied an organization, tightly controlled and ruthless. They wouldn't stop at seven bodies. They would be perfectly willing to put Tommy Carmellini's name on the list of victims.

Oh, what the hell?

Finally I said, "I'll need some help. A couple of guys, at least, and research by Sarah." Research by Sarah Houston was bureaucratic obfuscation. If she couldn't get into a computer system and ferret out its secrets, no one could.

"So you are willing to try it?"

The corpses of Junior Sikes, LaVerne Williams, Caputo and her companion crossed my mind. Whatever they were up to, they didn't deserve to die like that. Still, my hard little heart didn't bleed for them. You do the crime, you take your chances. The three jail deputies were just victims, collateral damage, in the wrong place at the wrong time, like traffic accident fatalities. Shit happens. Still, apparently pro hitters did the work. The cops would probably never get 'em.

"The feds have powerful weapons, including prosecutions for lying to the FBI. I wouldn't have that. No one will talk to me."

"Hmm . . ."

"Those killers might come after you, admiral."

He nodded and held his tongue.

"Okay," I said. "If you can stand the risk, I suppose I can. Even though I'm a lot younger than you are and have more good years left."

The corners of those gray eyes crinkled and he looked mildly amused. "I'll think about it and get back to you in a day or two."

I went off to my little office to see what had piled up on my desk during my absence.

The next morning Jake Grafton went to the Eisenhower Executive Office Building for a confab with all the heads of the American intelligence services, all seventeen of them, and the director of national intelligence, the DNI, and the new director of the Department of Homeland Security. Chairing the meeting was Vaughn Conyer's new chief of staff and his national security adviser. Two months into the new administration and the players were still getting acquainted.

The agenda was long, with a look at all the world's hot spots and problem areas. The chief of staff, Reem Kiddus, kept the meeting moving along. Still, it lasted three hours with only one potty/coffee break.

Election fraud wasn't mentioned. When the meeting broke up, Grafton stayed behind for a private word with Kiddus.

"Mr. Kiddus, I understand you told Justice to have the FBI pull the Election Fraud Task Force out of that ElectTech investigation in Pennsylvania."

Kiddus's eyes went around the room to see who else might be listening. "Who told you that?"

"Robert Levy."

"Murders aren't federal crimes."

"Election fraud is."

"There is no proof of any fraud."

"There might be, if a thorough investigation was done."

Kiddus took a deep breath and exhaled. He examined Grafton's eyes. "The president wants to put the election behind us. Raking though the ashes diverts media and political attention from his programs."

Grafton said, "I am going to have my agency look into the possibility that there was fraud with a foreign connection."

"I'm subtly hinting that the president doesn't want the cold, dead ashes stirred. Do I need to draw you a picture?"

"And I'm telling you, Mr. Kiddus, we'd better find out once and for all if a foreign power engaged in election fraud in an American election. If they did, they can do it again."

"You're in a minefield, Grafton. There are statutes. Politicians who would love to do you and us."

"Understood. But I run the CIA. Foreign intelligence is what we do. We don't just cross our fingers and hope that the world is a wonderful place and everyone is as honest, trusting, innocent, and naïve as we are."

"Do I have to tell you to drop this?"

"I don't think you're that stupid, Kiddus. If I'm wrong and you are, put it in writing."

Grafton turned and walked away.

Apparently Grafton made his decision over the weekend because he called me in on Monday morning and announced that we were going to find out if the recent election was fixed. Of course, he didn't tell me that the White House chief of staff had told him to lay off—I didn't find out about that until several weeks later. If he had shared that little love pat with me that morning, I would have probably laid an egg right there. We had defied the White House on one occasion before and it had nearly cost us our lives and our country. I wouldn't have been willing to go there again for all the money on Wall Street. But he didn't say a word about Kiddus's warning so I went along like a pig to the slaughterhouse.

We discussed it a while, maybe a half hour, then Grafton called in the executive assistants and dictated a couple of memos to get the ball rolling for me. When that was accomplished I wandered away and strolled the halls.

A powerful organization, with assassins and influence.

After a bit I found myself at the hardware section in the basement. Since my real job was a technician—which meant I broke and entered professionally, burgled places, cracked safes, installed listening devices and monitored them, and so on—the guys in the equipment department knew me well.

The guy on duty was Jasper Cerullo, a black guy with an Italian name, like mine. He was about as Italian as I was.

"Hey, Carmellini," he said, and examined my ID anyway. Then he compared it to the badge dangling from my neck, and held it up to compare it to my face. All this was overkill for show, of course. "Man, the facelift didn't do a thing for you. They cheated you, Carmellini."

"It's my trusting nature."

"Yeah."

"I need to check out a radio-spectrum scanner."

"Portable, plug-in, or what?"

"Portable."

Jasper went down the aisles and came back with one. He plunked it on the counter and pointed to a stack of forms. "You know the drill."

I took the thing out to the parking lot and turned it on. The green light came on, as advertised, and the back-lit signal-strength meter. I walked toward my car. The needle began to twitch. Standing beside it, the meter showed a good strong signal. I hit the button to let the thing scan the wavebands. It bingoed twice on the same frequency. The signal seemed strongest from the front of the car.

I turned it off and unlocked the trunk. There was an old blanket in there. I got it out and started with the wheel wells, looking. The beacon was under the front bumper, and I found it after checking the front wheel wells. It was held in there by magnets. I looked it over, then put it back in place.

The damn thing was probably installed in Pennsylvania. So whoever put it there knew who I was and what I drove. And precisely where I was at this very moment, at CIA Headquarters in Langley, Virginia.

If someone you don't know wants to kill you, someone whom you have never even seen, unless you are protected by the Secret Service the odds are pretty good that he'll get it done. He can pick his time and place and achieve total surprise. *Bang*. As I thought about that I realized I was touching the butt of my Kimber .45 in my shoulder holster. A little chill ran up my spine. I am not brave and I am not bulletproof. Just a mortal blob of protoplasm.

Raindrops hit my face as I put the blanket and scanner in the trunk of the car. Spring. It meant crocuses and cherry blossoms before a segue into the steaming hot, miserable summer of the mid-Atlantic. Why George Washington wanted the national capital here was a mystery. Maybe he wanted a short commute.

I scanned the parking lot for anyone who might be watching as I walked back toward the main entrance of the building. Didn't see a soul paying any attention to me. But then, if the killer was any good I might not even see him before he pulled the trigger. *Adios*, Tommy.

Back inside I went to find my on-and-off girlfriend, Sarah Houston, if she was still here. It was after six o'clock. She and I were on just now, or were when I left for work this morning, so I was hoping for a friendly smile and maybe even a kiss. I got both after she answered my knock on her office door and admitted me, so I dropped into the chair in her cubbyhole and stared between the computer screens on her desk at the woman herself.

The tip of her nose was a trifle too long to make her a candidate for the cover of *Vogue*, although it wasn't a schnozzolla like Grafton's trophy. Her smile was dazzling, and I really enjoyed seeing it aimed at me; it rarely was when she was working, as she was now. Flirting at the office wasn't one of her smirches.

We made a few private remarks, then she passed me a sheet of paper. It was a list of the late Junior Sikes's trips. Over two dozen in the past year. Beside the names of the cities, she put the counties and states they were in.

"I figured this guy was a computer geek," I said, "and you'd have a devil of a time cracking his passwords."

"I thought the same thing," she said, "so I didn't even try. I've been in the credit card companies' master databases for years, so I went there first, got his passwords, then pretended I was him."

I scanned the list. The closest city was in suburban Virginia. I said the name aloud.

She said crisply, "Junior Sikes went there last September, before the election. It's the seat of a swing county, one that's been known to go either way. It went solidly Democratic this past November. In fact, every county on the list is in a swing state and is big enough to generate a lot of votes and help carry the state. Any candidate who could carry those counties has a good chance of winning that state."

I read the list. Florida, Pennsylvania, Michigan, Wisconsin, Texas, Virginia, and Colorado. Swing states with lots of electoral votes.

Sarah continued, "Every one of those counties that Junior Sikes visited went Democratic in the last election, but the Republicans carried the states anyway, except for Colorado."

"So the margin was really bigger than it appeared," I mused.

"*If* the voting or the tally machines were rigged. Were they?"

"I don't know. Let's go to Virginia tomorrow and find out. Can you print out the software of a voting machine and see if it was diddled with?"

"The malware might have erased itself after the election."

"Would there be any evidence of that, if it happened?"

"Perhaps." She shrugged. "Depends on how sophisticated the program was. But how are you going to get us access to voting machines and scanners?"

"We're investigators from the Federal Election Commission. The alias folks are ginning up credentials as we speak and will have them ready tomorrow morning."

"Don't get your hopes up, Tommy. I'll have to download the software, if I can, and try to figure out if it's honest or not. It may take me a few days."

I shrugged. She was the only soldier I had, and the people I was after weren't going anywhere. They would still be there when I got around to them.

Sarah continued, "ElectTech is a subsidiary of Allegheny Corporation, which has a main office in Pittsburgh. They make machines that contain computers." She didn't consult her notes.

"Who is the vice president who supervises ElectTech?"

"That isn't clear from their federal filings. Allegheny is a public corporation with a market capital of two billion dollars. Listed on the NASDAQ. Sixty percent of the stock is owned by a Delaware corporation, privately held, that's thought to be one of the investment vehicles of a hedge fund. That vehicle is Red Truck Investments."

"So who is the principal of the hedge fund behind Red Truck?"

Sarah leaned back in her chair and caressed the keys of her computer. "Anton Hunt."

I tried to keep a poker face. Anton Hunt was the King of Chaos, a man who made billions shorting stocks and currency. I knew of his activities, everyone knew of his activities, which had been the subject of numerous newspaper and magazine articles throughout the years. A native Austrian, he was famous for shorting the British pound during a banking crisis some years ago, a crisis that he was accused of making worse, and pocketing billions on the deal. He was wanted in Indonesia for manipulations of its currency; the Indonesians had put a $10 million bounty on his head, so it was doubtful that he vacationed in Jakarta. Amazingly, as a youth during World War II, he had been a soldier in Hitler's SS, and now he was a "progressive" who gave big bucks to left-wing causes all over the world, funded demonstrations, and hung out with the Democratic elite here in the States. He was old as dirt, in his late eighties.

Somehow it all fit, if ElectTech did indeed dabble in election fraud on behalf of Hunt's good friend Cynthia Hinton. And the answer was way too easy.

"Write up a report for Jake Grafton."

"I already have."

Actually, the corporate chain meant nothing. Even if Allegheny or Red Truck were owned by Mellon Bank or Kellogg's of Battle Creek, that didn't mean the owners knew what the little warts way down the line were doing. No one was going to drag the president of ElectTech into a police station and accuse him of dealing in kiddie porn just because Junior Sikes liked it. Even if we could indeed prove that ElectTech employees were up to their eyeballs in voter fraud, we had no proof that the officers of ElectTech, Allegheny, Red Truck, or the hedge fund, or Anton Hunt, even knew about it, much less directed it.

Sarah locked up and we went to dinner in a little Italian restaurant we liked near her apartment. Took a bottle of Chianti back to her place and finished it before bed. Man, it was nice to be home.

After she was asleep I lay there in the darkness thinking about things. Maybe the best way to smoke these guys out and learn who was pulling the strings was to just bull in and stir up a lot of dust. The problem with that approach was that it was a one-shot weapon.

I really wanted to know if we were sure enough that this was an election fraud conspiracy before I started making people run for cover. If I raised too much dust before I knew what was really going on, I would have nothing to give Grafton to fend off the political types who wanted to befriend Mr. Influence, whoever in hell he or she was.

I was thinking about assassins, corpses, and a beacon on my car when I drifted off to sleep.

CHAPTER FOUR

Our election commission credentials worked like a charm. The county clerk, a porky glad-hander who looked as if he had made a career of courthouse politics, said, "The feds, huh? This is the first time any of you guys ever visited this office."

"We normally just deal with the secretary of state in Richmond," I said easily. "But with all the newspapers full of stories about possible fraud in our kerfuffle last November, we thought we oughta drop by a few counties for a look. Can't do them all, of course—nowhere near enough people."

The clerk had an opinion about fraud and unburdened himself of it while Sarah and I listened politely and nodded occasionally. Then he summoned one of his flunkies and told her to take us to the storeroom.

It was in the basement of the courthouse. It was half full of simple machines that punched holes in paper ballots and the scanners that totted up the results. The entire back of the room contained cardboard boxes labeled "U-Haul" stacked six high. A patina of dust and grime coated everything. Well, the election had been in November and this was late March . . .

The scanners were medium-sized machines that ran through a stack of ballots at several hundred a minute and tallied up the votes. When a ballot box had a certain number of ballots in them, one of the clerks took the ballots out, got them stacked neatly and precisely, and put the stack into a scanner. After tallying them, the scanner spit them out. Secret, covered LED windows constantly displayed the totals.

The clerk who had unlocked the door to the storage room was a large woman who waddled when she walked. She told us to call her Sally.

After superficially inspecting the machines— perhaps two dozen scanners and three hundred or so hole punchers—I asked, "What if a ballot hangs up or doesn't go through the precinct scanner?"

"Then we tell them to run it through again."

"What do you do to ensure the machine didn't read the ballot twice?" Sarah asked.

"Oh, there's a button on the back we push to erase the tally of the previous ballot. And we make a note of it in a ledger, so we can audit the process."

"So if the ballot is inserted twice, it will be read twice?"

"Right. The machine can't tell one ballot from another."

Sarah continued, "And if the clerk is distracted or forgets to push the button, the totals will be off."

The clerk cast a baleful eye on Sarah, who was now Suzanne Shapiro, according to her credentials. The name was alliterative and I liked it. Sarah didn't, so I planned to use it as often as possible.

"Miz Shapiro," the clerk said in a voice with an edge on it so that we would know we were treading on dangerous ground, "our election personnel are *very* professional."

"Are the ballots saved?"

She gestured at stacks of cardboard boxes labeled "U-Haul" in the back of the room, taking up about half the floor space. "In case of a recount."

"And the number of ballots is compared to the number of voters who signed in at each precinct?"

"Not unless there's a recount."

"This recount, if there is one—do you folks run the ballots through the scanners again so you can check the totals against the precinct count from the first time around?"

"Of course. And the ballots the machines kick out because they can't be counted—for whatever reason—are hand counted."

"Hmm . . ." I said.

"We seldom have recounts," the clerk said dismissively. "An election every two years, or occasionally one a year—that's about all the democracy the county budget will allow. And why have a recount unless you have a statistically significant chance of getting a different result?"

"I wouldn't know," I muttered, then regretted my choice of words. What I knew about federal and state election laws would fit comfortably in your eye without impairing your vision, yet today I was a federal election geek, and, of course, they knew everything. Ignoring my faux pas, I motored right along: "Now if you don't mind, Miz Shapiro and I want to check out several of your scanners."

"I *suppose* you can . . ." she said, and pursed her lips as if thinking deeply.

My fake Miz Shapiro smiled condescendingly and pointed to a machine on the counter. "We'll do this one first. Thank you for your time, Sally."

Dismissed, the clerk waddled for the door and pulled it shut behind her.

"I hope she doesn't lock us in," Sarah said, and plugged the scanner into a nearby socket. While it warmed up she removed her laptop from its carrying bag and sorted through her collection of cables.

I went over to the stack of boxes and inspected them. Each was marked with a number, which I assumed was the precinct where the ballots were voted. From the look of the dust that coated the tops, the boxes hadn't been opened since they were stacked here.

I played with a hole punch a bit, then wandered

back to watch Sarah. It was kinda chilly in this basement, and my jacket felt good. I wondered how long the ballots would last before they mildewed.

Three minutes after Sarah had everything up and running and the two machines were connected with a six-foot USB cable, the machine was vomiting its code onto her screen.

I was wondering how large the program was and how long it would take to download when it stopped.

"I've got it," Sarah said.

"That didn't take long."

"It's a short, simple program. I thought it would be longer."

There weren't any chairs, so Sarah stood and scrolled through the program line by line.

After about a minute and a half, she said, "This thing is rigged, all right." She pulled a legal pad from her computer case and began taking notes.

A little flutter ran over my biceps. "Who wrote the program? Can you tell anything?"

"Not in a quick examination. I'll save this program for the wizards to examine, but we should have a couple more program samples. Select another scanner, Tommy, and put it up here on the counter. We should check at least three, I think."

"How about five?"

"Okay."

When Sarah finished with the last one, I went

out into the hallway and along to the janitor's office beside the furnaces. He or she wasn't there, probably upstairs polishing a courtroom floor, so I helped myself to some cleaning rags and a squirt bottle of window cleaner.

As Sarah packed up her stuff I wiped off all the scanners and rearranged them so that anyone who inspected them couldn't tell which ones we had checked. Okay, so I'm paranoid. Those assassins had gotten my attention.

We stopped by the clerk's office, thanked the elected one and all his visible staff, and after rescuing our umbrellas, went across the street to a pizza joint. The rain was steady, a real spring soaker, and the gutters were running full.

It was only after we were ensconced in a corner booth in the back of the place well away from curious ears that Sarah read me her notes. "Each scanner was set up to deliver a majority to the Democratic presidential candidate. The majorities ranged from 58.1 percent to 61.7 percent. Those totals are about three or four percentage points above the historical norm for this county."

"How do you know that?"

"I did some homework when I had Sikes's itinerary."

We ordered lunch, and I sat thinking about things. The inflated totals from this county would help overcome Republican votes in the more rural counties.

Sarah had a printout of the Virginia figures for the last election, county by county, which she passed to me. Out of 3,750,916 votes cast, the Democrat, Cynthia Hinton, had won the state by 212,030 votes. In other words, she got 52.8 percent of the votes statewide and won Virginia's thirteen electoral votes. The inflated numbers from this county apparently helped. Had all the typically Democratic counties in northern Virginia bedroom suburbs had their vote totals inflated, or was it just this one?

"Did Sikes visit any counties in Virginia after the election?"

Sarah had her mouth full of salad when I asked, so she nodded. When she had disposed of her mouthful, she named it. The adjacent county.

We went there after lunch. Like the previous courthouse, they had a security checkpoint complete with a metal detector that all visitors had to pass through to get into the courthouse. Fortunately I had left my pistol under the front seat of the car today. There were two security cameras mounted so that everyone passing through the metal detector was photographed. In the county clerk's office we displayed our credentials, which the county clerk inspected with narrowed eyes. Was she suspicious, or did she have something to hide?

"Well, Mr. Wilson, Miz Shapiro"—I was James B. Wilson today—"I'll have a man take you all to the warehouse where we store our election equipment."

"All right."

A male assistant clerk drove his own car to the warehouse and we followed in our sedan with U.S. government plates. He unlocked the door and turned on the lights. More huge stacks of boxes full of ballots plus not only hole punchers, but scanners and hundreds of white voter privacy booths along one wall.

The clerk watched Sarah check three scanners. I watched her too, trying to get a fix on whether she thought the scanners were rigged. I couldn't tell a thing from her facial expression, and I am sure the observer didn't.

As she checked the last one, I counted scanners and stopped to chat up our guide. "What company checks and maintains your voting machines?"

"You mean the functionality checks?"

"Yeah."

"An outfit in Ohio, I can't remember the name. They sub out the work, I guess, because we get different guys here from time to time." He had an ah-ha moment and snapped his fingers. "American Voting Inc."

"Incorporated?"

"Yeah. American Voting. When I get back to the office I can look up the file and give you their address and phone number, if you like."

"They're in our database, but I would like to

know when they were here last." Actually, our database was the internet, which knew everything these days, except that little fact.

An hour later I had my dates. A certain Edwin P. Riddenhour, a technician for American Voting, had worked on the machines in October and again in January. Mr. Junior Sikes of ElectTech had been here in September and in late January. "American Voting has the contract but they sub out some of the calls about broken machines and so on to ElectTech," the lady clerk said.

"Do they call you before they come?"

"No. We're open five days a week except for legal holidays, so they just drop in. We do call them before an election, however, and make sure we are on their list."

I nodded sagely and thanked her for her cooperation today. We government guys gotta keep the voters happy.

On our way back to Washington Sarah said, "I think the machines have been reprogrammed. They're clean."

"Maybe Sikes died before he could get the other county's machines cleaned up."

"There was no hurry. He didn't know he was going to die."

"It was just a freak accident," I mused, "a little bump in the road of life, a bullet in the brain."

Just today we had learned enough to stimulate an investigation by the FBI's Election Fraud Task

Force, if they hadn't been warned off. A start, that's all.

But there was something sinister behind this, something more than counties reporting rigged election results. There were bullets and blood.

Rain fell all the way back to Washington and traffic was heavy. Jake Grafton was impassive as he listened to our report at six o'clock that evening in his office at CIA Headquarters in Langley. He looked at the printouts Sarah had prepared of the scanner programs—if he could understand all that he was better educated than I thought he was—and glanced at me from time to time. Finally he sent Sarah out of the room and looked at me.

"I've got a couple of guys to help you, and we'll give you a fake ID and all the rest of it. If it is the Russians or Chinese or whomever, I want to know."

"It could be anyone, anyone at all," I said. "That county we looked at with the rigged machines—what if the totals were fixed not to inflate the Democrat vote, but to make sure it was no larger?"

"One or the other," Grafton said. He got out of his chair and wandered over to a window, a triple-pane affair equipped with a vibrator to foil laser-listening devices. I could see rain smearing the glass and trees whipping around outside, but I doubted if he noticed.

After a bit he came back to his desk. "Brief your guys tomorrow morning and get busy."

"This may be the biggest chunk you've ever bit off," I said.

He took a deep breath and met my eyes.

"Maybe too big to chew," I added.

He didn't say anything.

"Do you want a briefing before we sally forth?"

"No. Don't get caught."

That has to be the mantra of our age. Don't get caught. I wandered out, wondering what the hell I had gotten myself into. The stakes were enormous—the presidency of the United States. Seven corpses already—whoever was behind this was playing for keeps.

I dropped into a chair in the outer office—the receptionist, Robin, she of the big hair, was still there, busy typing—and stared at my toes. Whoever was pulling the strings at ElectTech was buried deep behind layers and layers of people, none of whom really knew anything. Only one or two people at the very top knew who the string puller was, the money man. American Voting might be involved, as well as many of the other companies in the election machine industry.

The hitters who had whacked Junior Sikes and the deputies in the jail certainly didn't know anything except the name of the man paying them. I kinda figured I would be visiting with them before long.

The first item on my agenda was to see LaVerne Williams's boss, whoever he or she was. More than likely police had interviewed him or her, and gotten precisely nothing. I was going to have to get more.

I thought a while on how to do it, then eased myself out of the chair and on out of the director's suite. Robin was still typing.

Jake Grafton gave me two covert operators to assist me. I had past dealings with both of them, although I was a bit surprised to see Armanti Hall sitting in the conference room. He was a big black man, as tall as I am but thicker through the shoulders and chest. His hair and beard were long and unruly, wild tangles, which made him look like a rock star or professional football player. An expert in unarmed combat, he had taken French leave from the agency last August after a few questionable killings in Syria.

"I thought you were on permanent leave," I said.

He shrugged. "Here I am."

"Still in trouble with the powers that be?"

"Not with Jake Grafton. He and his wife drove over to West Virginia one weekend a month ago and suggested that maybe I should come back to the agency. The old lady I was living with, Mrs. Proudfoot, passed away this winter and the orphan, Sarah, went to live with an aunt and uncle who came out of the woodwork. So I was alone."

"When I last saw Mrs. Proudfoot she looked mighty healthy to me."

"An artery in her brain burst. She was in a coma for a couple of days and died in the hospital without regaining consciousness. That beating those thugs gave her last year . . ." He paused and swallowed hard. "Anyway, here I am."

I made noises about how sorry I was.

Armanti Hall shrugged again.

The man beside him was Travis Clay, who had done some extensive campouts with me in Africa and other places. A former Special Forces guy, Travis was white and in his late thirties. He was whipcord lean, strong as an ox and a crack shot with a rifle. He didn't have a sniper's skill level, yet he was very good, better than I was.

Both of them were damned tough men who had survived combat on three continents. Neither would hesitate to pull a trigger if it were necessary, and they had good judgment, which was an absolute necessity in the spook business.

I told them everything I knew about the assassinations in Pennsylvania.

Travis cut right to the chase. "How many shooters at the jail, do you think?"

I had already considered that. "No more than two or three. Two probably. Subsonic nine-millimeters with sound suppressors. All head shots."

"All seven?"

"Yep."

Armanti and Travis looked at each other, then back at me.

"How come the FBI is backing off?" Travis asked.

"I'll ask my White House source next time I see him. How the hell would I know? Politics!"

"Maybe someone in the White House is behind this. Someone who just moved in on January 20."

"The rigged machines were set to deliver a majority to the Democrat candidate. The guy in the White House beat her."

Travis Clay leaned forward in his chair. "Don't be naïve, Tommy. You're smarter than that. What if the rigged machines were designed to keep her majority in that county *down?* What if she actually got seventy-five or eighty percent of the vote?"

That was certainly a possibility and Travis had hit right on it. It had taken me about fifteen minutes to see it, but I always was a trusting soul. Still, I wanted to minimize the possibility, keep the home team brave and unafraid and pulling their oars. "We'll keep it in mind," I said.

"Oh, horseshit, Carmellini," Travis said, his body tense and his eyes narrowed. "If it went down that way, we'll have the FBI and Homeland and every cop in the country after our asses. This set of political hypocrites ain't any better than the last set."

I took a deep breath and let it out. "Grafton wants to know the truth."

"Apparently the White House doesn't. You and Grafton better think about *that!*"

I didn't say anything. What was there to say?

"What if the pros that smacked the guys in that jail were FBI?"

"We'll find out."

"Talk about leading with your chin," Travis Clay grumped, and waved a hand dismissively.

"You want out?" I asked.

"Maybe. I'll keep you advised."

I shifted my gaze to Armanti Hall to see how he was taking all this. Calm and collected, as always. "So what's your plan?" he asked conversationally.

I told them.

CHAPTER FIVE

Another week passed while we Knights for the American Way prepared for our electoral truth offensive, with Sarah Houston's help, of course, and the help of the covert equipment warehouses and fraudulent document artists at the CIA. There were now eight of us, counting Sarah. I persuaded Grafton that the more the merrier if we ran into shooters, and he had to agree. We certainly didn't need any friendly corpses.

The corporate parent of ElectTech, Allegheny Corporation, had its executive offices in Pittsburgh in the heart of the city, a tower overlooking Mellon Square. If you are a connoisseur of American urban downtowns, Pittsburgh has got to be high on your list of cities to admire, about a hundred places up the list from Detroit and Cleveland. Since World War II the Pittsburgh city planners have urban-renewed like they meant it, although traffic is a little squirrely in the big triangle between the rivers. Andrew Carnegie wouldn't recognize the place.

We opened our Pittsburgh campaign by breaking and entering a house in the suburbs that belonged to a fellow named Kurt W. Lesh and his wife Rosamery. Kurt was a vice president of Allegheny, made $182,000 a year, had a 401K with the company matching up to six percent of his salary, and drove a company car, a Honda Accord only one year old. Blue. Rosamery was a licensed nurse practitioner and also made over a hundred grand a year. Neither had a concealed carry permit. They lived in a house that had a fair market value of about $754,000, according to the county assessor's office. Three-car garage, one bay of which contained a big Harley. Their kids were grown and the youngest was a senior at Penn State. Kurt's mother lived in a nursing home in a suburb of Pittsburgh; his dad was dead. Rosamery's folks lived in Spain. They had no siblings, uncles or aunts in the eastern United States. Kurt had a married cousin, a female, living in Allentown.

As Armanti Hall stood guard outside, Travis Clay and I tapped the Leshes' telephone landline and bugged the house—office, living room, kitchen, and bedroom. The bugs were the latest and greatest, teeny tiny and sound-activated so the batteries would last quite a while. The bugs radiated to a repeater that we installed on the soffit under an eave where it couldn't be seen from inside the house. The repeater rebroadcasted the audio to a cell tower and sent it on to a computer at CIA Headquarters in Langley, in real time. The bugged telephone's intercepted signals were also sent to a transmitter on the outside of the house, then to the repeater and on to Langley.

Our van parked on the street could also listen to the raw audio from the telephone and audio bugs. The whole installation was wireless. No amateur was going to stumble across this system unless they knew what they were looking for. We hoped to be long gone by the time anyone got around to looking, if anyone ever did.

When we finished the job we ensured the house was again locked, climbed into our van, and motored off to another house, one belonging to the president of Allegheny, Nora Shepherd. She was married to a realtor and had two kids, both in college. Her house had a dog. It didn't sound like a big one, but you never knew how territorial it was. Turned out that it wasn't interested in taking a bite out of me, for which I was grateful. As it barked, I opened the back door and let it out in the enclosed yard. He, she, or it went willingly.

We got busy bugging the phone, living room, master bedroom, and the kitchen. Sarah already had Nora's cell phone number and Kurt Lesh's, so that was taken care of. She would record the conversations on those phones at Langley.

When we finished at Nora's and I had the dog back inside, we headed downtown. That night we went into Allegheny and bugged Kurt's office and tapped his landline telephone. Then we did a thorough search of his files, just in case he carelessly left a memo there from Vladimir Putin detailing the Russian Foreign Intelligence

Service's evil plan for world domination. If he ever got it, Kurt didn't file it. Kurt W. Lesh was a notetaker. He had legal pads, at least four, full of notes from telephone conversations. The notes were fairly cryptic, but occasionally he noted who he had talked to, often just an initial and a date. Studying all these would take more time than we had, and we weren't looking for evidence.

We also bugged Nora Shepherd's office, tapped her private phone line, and flipped through her files. We found nothing incriminating, nor did we expect to. There was a photo on her desk that I took to be Nora, along with a portly, balding man with a wimpy smile. She was in her late fifties or early sixties and spreading out a little too.

Sarah had already hacked into Kurt's computer, so we didn't have to touch it. His password was his first name and birthday. She had given us many tidbits about Kurt and his place in the corporate hierarchy, but none of them addressed the key question of who controlled the programmers at ElectTech. We hoped to encourage Kurt or his boss, Nora, to tell us. They were about to have very bad experiences.

My blue '74 Mercedes with the beacon under the front bumper was parked in the parking garage beside our downtown hotel. We had installed a surveillance camera to watch it on the off chance that someone might decide to steal it or put a bomb in it after we had a chat with Kurt and Nora. Those assassins were on our minds.

Since they had beaconed my car when I was swanning around looking at ElectTech corpses, they must have known me already. So at ten o'clock the next morning I dropped into Allegheny to call on Kurt.

"Do you have an appointment, Mr. Wilson?" the receptionist asked, looking at my business card. She was a couple of years younger than I, wore a sweater that emphasized her charms, and had lipstick that reflected the overhead lights. I could almost see my smile reflected back towards me.

"No. I was in town and had a few free minutes this morning."

"I'll see if he's in."

She muttered into the telephone, "Mr. James Wilson from the Federal Election Commission."

After she hung up, she said, "He's free now. Third door on the left." And she smiled. Her lipstick didn't crack.

Kurt Lesh stood to shake hands. He was about fifty-five or so, a few inches under six feet, with a ready smile and clean-shaven. He was going bald on top. He wore a sports coat but no tie, dark gray slacks, and leather loafers without socks. Right out there on the cutting edge of fashion. As he motioned me to a seat in a little sitting area on the side of the room and joined me, I handed him my card.

He glanced at it and put it in his shirt pocket. He was seated across from me, relaxed. He crossed his legs and smiled.

"The Federal Election Commission," he said. "This is a first. I've never seen any of your people here before."

I shrugged, put my attaché case on my lap, and opened it. "Those murders at ElectTech a couple of weeks ago," I said. "We learned that Allegheny owns that company and you are the late LaVerne Williams's contact here."

His smile was gone now. I doubted if it would be returning anytime soon.

"You were her boss, were you not?"

"ElectTech is our subsidiary, but there are various people here within the company that—"

I waved that away. "Oh, we aren't worried about bean counters."

He looked as if a cruise missile had just missed taking off his head. "Well, of course, I . . ."

He looked down as I removed a subpoena from my case—a beautiful fake—and offered it to him. "I am serving you. We will do the interview in the federal courthouse, Room 412, at the date and time specified." I pointed to the thing. "This subpoena requires you to bring various documents and records with you to the hearing." I smiled perfunctorily, closed my attaché case, and stood.

"Well . . . really—" He scanned the list of

documents stapled to the back of the subpoena. "What can you . . . ah . . . tell me about this?"

"Election fraud is a serious crime, as you well know." I shrugged again, just a civil servant doing his job. "We'll put you under oath and get your testimony next week. Is there anyone else here that you think we should talk to about this matter?"

He merely stared with his mouth partially open.

"Where is the president's office? I have a subpoena for her too."

He pointed to his left, my right. I shook his limp hand and departed, leaving the door open behind me. I found the president's corner office, right where it was last night, smiled at Nora's private secretary, and was admitted. Nora Shepherd was a matronly grandmother type wearing better jewelry than most grandmothers ever see. The diamond bracelet and four-carat pendant were genuine or my name isn't Tommy Carmellini. I gave her a subpoena as she gazed blankly at my handsome face, then hit the road.

By the time I got back to the van in the parking garage adjacent to the building, things were already popping in Allegheny's offices. Kurt and Nora were in conference in her office. "Oh, my God!" Nora exclaimed, over and over and over. "Ohmigawd, ohmigawd, ohmigawd!"

"What are we going to do?" Kurt Lesh asked insistently. At least he was still coherent.

"We can't go down to the federal courthouse and give sworn testimony—" Nora wailed.

"Why not? Get some lawyers, take the fifth and give 'em the finger."

"Are you nuts? You read about what happened to the people at ElectTech. Do you want to be next?"

"Are you going to call Schlemmer?"

Nora began sobbing.

Travis Clay was also wearing earphones and ensuring the computer was recording the feed digitally. Now he caught my eye and winked.

I closed my eyes and concentrated as Nora managed to pull herself together. "My God!" she whispered. The fidelity of the bugs was remarkably good.

"The question," she said, "is how we get out of this alive."

Kurt must have nodded at that. Staying alive was probably high on his priority list. Mine too, for that matter.

"We could call this James Wilson," Nora said tentatively. "Tell him everything we know and demand protection."

"He's a goddamn paper pusher," Lesh said disgustedly. "The Federal Election Commission, for Christ's sake! If someone stuck a pistol in his face he'd crap his pants."

Obviously I hadn't impressed him. He continued, "We might as well go down to the post office and demand the protection of one of the tattooed window clerks with a Mohawk. Get a grip, Nora."

She sobbed some more, then asked so softly that I almost missed it, "So what *are* we going to do?"

"I don't know," Kurt admitted. I could hear the worry in his voice. The little wart.

I took the headphones off and massaged the sides of my head. Then I stepped outside where Armanti Hall was sipping a twelve-ounce cup of coffee.

"Where'd you get that?"

He pointed. I headed that way. Low clouds and a breeze, but it wasn't raining just then. The trees were budding. Another few days, I thought. I passed a little bed of crocus with flowers about eight inches tall.

I got my coffee and came back to the van. As I stood outside the door I called Sarah on my cell. "You ever heard of a guy called Schlemmer?"

"It's a gal. Heiki Schlemmer. Big banana in Red Truck Investments. You want all her particulars?"

"The usual. I'll call you back in an hour or so ready to copy."

"Everything going all right?"

"So far so good. And you?"

"I miss you, Tommy."

I smiled. I missed her too, and told her so. We

whispered boy-girl stuff for a minute, then I put the phone in my pocket and got back to thinking about the business at hand.

Ten minutes later inside the van Travis said, "They called Schlemmer."

"Heiki Schlemmer," I said, just so he would know I was on top of everything.

"Want to listen to it?"

"Why not?"

It was a fairly accurate, factual report. Schlemmer just said yes and no. Only a couple of questions. Unlike Nora, Heiki didn't go into melt-down mode.

When the conversation was over, Travis said, "Nora and Kurt discussed the fact that Heiki Schlemmer is fairly new on the job. Her predecessor committed suicide in December."

I got on my cell phone, called Sarah, and gave her a new assignment. "Schlemmer's predecessor. Suicide in December. Give me everything you can find out."

"Aye aye, sir."

Sarah has a sick sense of humor. The suicide angle raised a lot of questions, but until we knew more, it was useless to speculate.

"Let's see what Kurt and Nora talk about when they get home after work," I told Travis, who merely gave me a look. He knew as much about this as I did.

Kurt didn't talk about the subpoena at home.

What he did was get into an argument with his wife, who apparently wanted a new car. Her ride had 49,000 miles on it and was four years old, she explained. They argued about that for a while, then Kurt got into the booze.

Nora turned on her television to a news show. The audio from that wiped out the family room audio and we couldn't hear what she was doing. She didn't make any telephone calls.

It was a long, slow evening. I amused myself by checking the video of my car, still parked in a garage by the motel. Although people cycled through the garage from time to time, no one was interested in it, which frosted me a little. It was a cool car, a collector's car even. No one even glanced at it twice. The paint job didn't show off its sensual charms, I mused, not for the first time. Maybe I needed something eye-catching, perhaps fire-engine red.

Travis Clay went home for the night and Jose "Joe" Casillas took over on the earphones. Joe was a techie, like me, not a covert warrior. He was balding, overweight, and liked to munch potato chips. His long face wore a perpetual frown. It wasn't that he was unhappy; his face was just made that way. He made it worse by wearing a mustache that drooped around the corners of his mouth.

Around midnight the Shepherds turned off their television. Joe motioned for me to listen. I put on a set of earphones in time to hear Nora say, "We have to get out of here, and I want to go tonight."

"Are you nuts?" That was her husband Fred, the realtor. "Just because you got a subpoena?"

"It's that ElectTech thing. Seven people dead. We may be next."

"Oh, for Christ's sake! If you don't show on Thursday the feds will be after you. Get a grip! And where are we going to go? What are we going to use for money? We can't just abandon everything and become fugitives. And I have a client tomorrow who wants to see four houses."

"I am really, really scared, Fred." She sounded it. And she sounded as if she had had a few drinks. "Damnit, *you*'re the one who insisted we take the money! *You*'re the fool who thought this would be an easy score. Now *I* have a target on my back." She began sobbing. I heard the clink of ice cubes.

I glanced at Joe. His eyebrows were up and his mustache down. He caught my eye and went back to checking the digital recorder, ensuring we were getting all this.

"You don't know a damn thing about anything," Fred insisted to his wife. "You can deny anything and everything and no one can prove a damned thing. Don't panic."

Nora again: "When the ElectTech pervert got arrested, it was LaVerne Williams who called me. And I called Heiki Schlemmer. Less than forty-eight hours later someone murdered the pervert in the jail, killed some deputies, and then killed Williams and some other employees of ElectTech. Less than *forty-eight hours!* And you sit there like a fool telling *me* I have nothing to worry about! *We* have nothing to worry about!"

That's what a guilty conscience will do: force you to connect the dots.

"Why'd you call Schlemmer when you got the subpoena?" Fred demanded.

"As if I had a choice. If I hadn't called and she found out, maybe read it in the newspaper, we were as good as dead."

"Well, you did call. She knows you're playing it straight."

"Right. I can hear her talking to whomever . . . 'Shepherd is playing it straight, but why take a chance?' "

"I can't believe this shit is happening to us!" Fred wailed.

"*You* were the one that wanted the money," Nora said accusingly.

I heard a smack. Someone had slapped someone. I suspected Fred did the slapping. "You didn't seem to have any trouble spending some of it on that goddamn bling," he roared.

I felt like a voyeur and a bit embarrassed. Pushing people is a bad way to make a living. On the other hand, Nora and Fred had gotten themselves into this hole with no bottom, and they had done it for money. How much, I wondered. Was it in cash? Sarah could hack their bank accounts, but it was doubtful if they had plunked serious money, probably cash, into their regular accounts, leaving a clear trail for the IRS if they ever got audited. Not that we were after evidence that would stand up in court. This conversation was proof enough for me that Nora was up to her eyeballs in something slimy and knew it.

They argued about it for a few minutes and slowly Fred gave in. "We can clear out of here for a little while," he said finally. "Maybe we should, just to be on the safe side. Maybe we could take that vacation in Canada you've been talking about for years."

"Cold up there in the spring," Nora objected. "I wanted to go in the summer or early fall."

What could you do with a woman like that? Fred had apparently reached the limit of his patience. "Fuck, we can go to Mexico," he shouted. It's a wonder the neighbors didn't hear that, if they were still awake. "I don't give a shit! Cancun or Cozumel or something. Look at a few fucking Mayan pyramids. Figure out what the fuck we're going to do with the rest of our lives, assuming we live long enough to care."

At three in the morning they locked up, carried suitcases to the car, and departed. They took the dog. The house became quiet.

Everyone seemed to be asleep at the Lesh household. Apparently he had drunk himself to sleep. I could hear him snoring.

No one appeared to be interested in my old Mercedes.

I left the van to Joe Casillas and took a government sedan back to the motel. I needed some sleep too.

Too bad about Kurt Lesh. Tomorrow was not going to be one of his better days.

CHAPTER SIX

I wondered if Nora Shepherd would call the office to explain why she wasn't coming in today, and darn it, she did. Had a bad cold and was going to take a few sick days, she said. She didn't sound sick to me, and no doubt the receptionist thought so too, but if the prez wanted a day off . . .

We sat in the van outside the building, me, Travis Clay, and Armanti Hall, as we waited for Kurt Lesh to arrive. He did, finally, at 9:30. We waited to see if he was going to call anyone. Maybe he was on the internet, checking his emails, planning another big financial coup for Allegheny Corporation, like submitting a tender offer for Apple or Microsoft.

I looked at Armanti. "I want to scare him badly. That's all. You'll know we're getting there if he craps his trousers."

"Got it."

We climbed out of the van and left Joe Casillas to record our reality show. Trooped inside, took the elevator up, and presented ourselves to the receptionist.

"Mr. Lesh. We don't have an appointment but I'm sure he'll want to see us."

She eyed Armanti. With his long, kinky hair going in all directions and his Muhammed beard, he was quite a sight. "And you gentlemen are with . . . ?"

"Red Truck Investments."

I doubted if she believed that since I had been here as a loyal civil servant of the Federal Election Commission yesterday, but it was remotely conceivable I had changed jobs during the night. I was betting on the fact that she surely knew that Red Truck was the parent of this company.

She picked up the phone and murmured into it while she kept her eyes fixed on Armanti.

"We know the way," I told her, and went down the hall, shoulder to shoulder with my muscle.

We walked in on Lesh. I closed the door as Armanti went over to the desk and took out his pistol. He popped out the magazine and examined the cartridges, then reinserted the thing in the handle of his shooter with an audible click.

I went around the desk and spun the chair so Lesh was facing me.

"It's time to come to Jesus, Kurt. Nora Shepherd has hit the road. She thinks the hit men are coming for you and her since she called Heiki Schlemmer, just like they did for the ElectTech crowd. I think she might be right."

His face was a study. All the blood had drained out and now he was as white as toilet paper. "Who . . . who are you?" he whispered.

"That's rather beside the point," I told him. "My

friend and I are here to get some information, straight, and if we don't get it, we'll leave you to the heavy hitters who want to shut you up permanently. They should be here in a couple of hours."

"You are with the government . . ."

"Wrong. That was a little white lie. We have a few simple questions, then we'll leave you to see if you can get away from the hit men."

"I'm not—"

I slapped him. A gentle love pat.

"You're wasting time. We're muscling in on your racket. There's a lot of money to be made in election fraud, as you well know. How much did they pay you for your part in the last one?"

He thought about a lie, then Armanti Hall tapped the barrel of his pistol on the desk and Lesh looked at him. I have never seen a bigger, uglier man than Armanti Hall. He would have scared the crap out of Mean Joe Greene.

"How much, you little fucking wart?"

"A hundred grand . . ."

"See . . . this is easy." I jerked him out of the chair and carried him by his shirt and coat to a chair in the corner, where I deposited him. A stain began spreading on the crotch of his trousers.

"Are the computer codes that ElectTech used on your computer?"

"Ah . . ."

Armanti stuck the barrel of his pistol in the

94

guy's ear. "Man, if this goes off they'll scrape up your brains with a spoon."

"No. No, no, no. You can have the damned thing, but the codes aren't on there."

"Where are they?"

"Harry Tanaka brought them with him on a laptop. He's the guy. He's the guy you want. I don't know anything."

"Horseshit. What did they give you a hundred grand for if you don't know anything?"

"I—I supervised the installation."

Armanti removed the pistol from Lesh's ear and stood holding it in his hand, where the guy could see it. His eyes were on it, as if it were a rattlesnake coiled to strike.

"You lying sack of shit," I whispered, my face inches from his. "Look at me. Right in my eyes." I tapped his cheek again with the palm of my hand. "Tell it to me straight or I'll just throw you out the window. It's only four stories down. You might even live through it."

"I—I coordinated things, scheduled the visits to the county courthouses, ironed out little problems."

"I'm going to have this guy with me iron you out in a minute if you keep lying."

"I'm not lying."

"You son of a bitch. I invented lying. I know more about lying than you'll ever know. You're lying."

"They had to tell me." He was whimpering now. "I was LaVerne Williams's contact. Nora Shepherd and I had to be in the loop."

I stood up and looked around. He had a laptop on the edge of the desk and a regular PC in front of him. Was it worth checking the hard drives?

I pulled the Kimber and stuck the barrel in Lesh's mouth. "Take the laptop and the PC box," I said to Armanti, who didn't hesitate. He jerked wires and had the two devices under his arm in about thirty seconds. I nodded and he left.

I put the pistol away and pulled a chair over so I was right in front of Lesh. He looked so pale I thought he might faint. "Those hit men show up here, what are you going to do?" I kept my voice low and smooth.

His mouth worked but no noise came out.

"The ElectTech crowd was killed by bullets in their brains. Easy way to go, all things considered. No lingering diseases, pain, operations, nursing homes, daytime television, adult diapers, bedpans . . . none of that. *Bang,* and you're on your way to the hereafter. Is that the way you want to go out?"

He voiced *No* with his lips; no sound came out.

"Maybe you should tell me the truth. Maybe then I can do something for you."

Lesh tried to wet his lips. "Honest to God, it was Harry Tanaka," he said. "He was the tech guy who had the computer codes and the results they wanted. He talked to Williams and Sikes and Caputo. Shepherd and I had to know because we were in charge of ElectTech's business, and if they were screwing off and not making money, we had to crack the whip."

"I see." I looked thoughtful, leaned back in my chair, and crossed my right leg over my left knee.

"So who was giving Harry his orders?"

"Somebody in corporate. Harry committed suicide in early December and Schlemmer got his job."

I smiled and eyed him, man to man. "Come on, Kurt. You gotta do better than that. Some clown kills himself in December, so you blame him for trying to fix the election of the *president of the United States*. Do I look that stupid?"

"No. But—"

"Those people at corporate—is that Red Truck Investments?"

"Yeah."

"Those people at corporate knew that all this shit was going down at ElectTech and you were cooking the books a little—" I was taking a chance here, but there had to be a reason to pay this fool or they wouldn't have bothered "—and so everything was perking right along. Did anyone else from Red Truck ever talk to you about any of this?"

"No, everything was business as usual." He didn't bother to deny that he was cooking the books.

I uncrossed my legs and leaned forward so our noses were only about six inches apart. I could smell the stale liquor on his breath. I lowered my voice to almost a whisper. "Tell me what you think. Was Harry Tanaka taking money from some unknown evil schemer and screwing his employer, or were the folks at Red Truck telling him what to do and how to do it?"

"I don't know—"

I slapped him, hard. He about fell off the chair.

"Don't give me shit, Kurt. After Harry was out of the picture this Heiki Schlemmer moved right in. You got a call about that, didn't you?"

He bobbed his head a few times and tried to swallow. His Adam's apple jerked up and down. Finally he got it out: "Nora did."

"Who called her?"

"I don't—"

"*Don't* tell me you don't know! Nora told you. Who made that call to tell her the bad news about ol' Harry Tanaka and the good news about Schlemmer's promotion?"

He thought he wasn't going to tell me, but his resolve melted away. "The CEO of Red Truck, Nick Liszt." He whispered the name, so no one else would know that he ratted out Liszt.

"Why did Tanaka kill himself?"

"How would I know?"

"Allegedly kill himself?"

Kurt Lesh shook his head and didn't say a word.

"Don't get all constipated on me, Kurt. We got a relationship going here. You and Nora talked about this. Maybe you even talked about it with Heiki Schlemmer. Maybe she dropped a hint."

His head was going from side to side. "She didn't."

"But you and Nora didn't need any subtle hints, did you? You and Nora suspected you knew the reason, didn't you?"

Now his head was bobbing up and down.

"Didn't you, Kurt?"

The way he looked at me was pathetic. I was his buddy and was going to save his ass from the bad guys with guns.

"The wrong person won the election," he whispered.

I left him in the office and went out into the hallway. There was an open conference room across the hall and Armanti Hall was sitting there with the laptop and computer box on the desk.

"I got it," I said. "The CEO of Red Truck called Nora. They're all in it up to their eyes."

Armanti jerked his head at Lesh's office. "What are we going to do about him?"

"I dunno," I said and stretched. "Tell him to run and see how far he gets, I guess."

"Don't give me that shit, Carmellini. You aren't that much of an asshole."

I was in a foul mood. "Wanna bet?"

99

What we did was get Joe Casillas to drive Kurt and his wife—and the computers—back to Langley to give sworn depositions. Then his fate would be in Jake Grafton's lap. He got paid the big bucks; he could figure this out.

Needless to say Rosamery didn't want to go. Joe called me while she was shouting and wailing at Kurt. I told Joe to put them in the car and take them regardless.

We got pizza at a takeout joint and settled down to wait at Nora's house and Lesh's. Meanwhile we kept a wary eye on my '74 Mercedes, which was right where I'd parked it and beaconing nicely.

Evening came slowly, then darkness. The neighborhoods settled down. I had Travis Clay and one guy at Shepherd's house turning on lights and the television, while Armanti Hall, Doc Gordon and I camped out at the Leshes' place. We turned out the lights at eleven and settled down to wait.

Waiting is hard. If the hitters came, they would be ready, willing, and able to shoot someone, and we didn't want to get shot. On the other hand, sweating them to find out who sent them and anything else they knew would be a worthy objective, if we could take them alive.

I wasn't very optimistic. They had nothing to lose if the shooting started, and none of us wanted to get shot. Or die.

Needless to say, I fretted. Doc Gordon watched some television. I paced. I would have liked to have had two guys outside, but didn't think we could be out there 24/7 and not have some neighbor call the cops. So we were inside, with one man upstairs asleep and two awake and alert downstairs.

Once or twice I called Travis, just to check in and hear his voice. I didn't want him or his two guys hurt either.

It seemed to me that we had to get the shooters off the board, and I didn't know of any other way to do it. Of course, Mr. Influence could always get more shooters—it seemed as if the world had an endless supply of people willing to do mayhem and murder for money—but that would take time.

But what if they didn't come tonight? How long should we sit here waiting? Another night? Two? At what point do you decide that they aren't coming?

I left those decisions for another day. Tonight we waited.

I dozed for several hours in a chair while Doc watched, then Doc dozed while I watched. At midnight Doc went upstairs to bed and Armanti came down.

We waited as the minute hand on my watch crawled.

Dawn came slowly. I wasn't sleepy, so when

the sun was fully up, I fixed eggs and bacon from the Leshes' refrigerator. There was even toast with butter and jam. Then I went upstairs to sleep while Doc and Armanti bored themselves to tears downstairs. At noon I was downstairs again.

The day oozed along. I turned the television on and off a dozen times.

Armanti asked me at one point in the afternoon, "You think they'll come at night?"

"If they don't come during the day."

At about six in the evening rain started falling, just a gentle shower. The sky turned black and the rain fell faster.

Dinner was spaghetti and meat sauce from the Leshes' pantry. We had already gone through the milk for coffee so now we drank it black.

Nothing on television was worth watching. Even the news on Fox was all bad. They were rioting again in California. They didn't like free speech.

The rain had let up to a misty fog that reduced visibility to a couple hundred yards. The street-lights glowed in it. This was like something out of a horror flick. The monster in the fog. They'll come tonight, I thought.

"There's a car driving slowly up and down," Doc said. He was in the living room with the lights out, watching the street. I was in the dining room watching the backyard. It was three in the morning. "He's been by three times now. Same car, a dark sedan."

I called Travis. "We think we may have someone driving by looking us over."

"Dark sedan? We had one that went by four times at about midnight. Then he left."

"Maybe he's over here now."

I hung up and checked the pistol with the sound suppressor. It was a Beretta nine. All I had to do was flick the safety off and squeeze the trigger.

I trotted upstairs and woke Armanti. He came downstairs with his favorite weapon, a sawed-off pump shotgun loaded with Number 4 buckshot. It was noisy, so we didn't want to use it unless we had to. We would try to make do with silenced pistols.

If these were the guys, I wondered how they would come into the house. Pick the lock like they did with Rosa Caputo's door? Or hammer out a window? If I were breaking in with the family at home at this time of night, I would be as quiet as a bad dream. Too many people had shotguns and deer rifles in closets, not to mention a pistol in the dresser drawer by the bed.

We had doused all the lights before midnight except for a night light in the hallway and one on the stairs. Those glow-worms cast a good bit of light when your eyes were accustomed to the gloom. Curtains and drapes on the windows kept people outside from seeing in, except in little places.

"It's just one car, and it's stopping. Two guys getting out."

That was a load off. If we had a crew to deal with, silenced pistols weren't going to do the trick. With two guys, they might.

"Back of the house is clear," Armanti whispered on his way to the living room, which was to the right of the door. I knew he was going to hunker down behind a stuffed chair, which should help stop any subsonic bullets flying his way. If he had to let go with the shotgun, Doc and I were well out of the line of fire.

Doc was at the top of the stairs with a good view of the door, and I was in the kitchen, ready to step around the jam and open fire.

After all the waiting, the climax wasn't much. We heard the scratching at the door lock. It wasn't very loud, but I have good ears. Apparently they decided to pick it, which was tactically wise.

After a couple of minutes the door opened. They shouldn't have had that much trouble with the lock. They stepped inside and closed the door behind them, then one of them turned on a flashlight and waved the beam around.

I stuck both hands around the jamb and let loose on the guy holding the light. Little *pops*. After two the light fell and broke.

More *spluts*, little *pops*, and a terrible groan. The sound of a pistol hitting the floor. I emptied the magazine, all thirteen, aiming low, then popped it out and reloaded.

Absolute silence. I reached for the light switch

with my left hand and turned it on. Both men were lying sprawled in the hallway. Blood was visible. They didn't even twitch. Doc came down the stairs, carefully, and fired a bullet into each head.

Armanti turned on a living room light.

We had filled them full of holes. I had fired thirteen and Doc fired eighteen, he said.

With the light on in the hallway we looked them over. "They look young," Armanti said.

"Young guys making their bones," Doc reflected.

The burglars had been armed with silenced pistols.

"Think these were the ElectTech guys?"

"Maybe. If we had access to the bullets from the victims we could find out if the guns are guilty, but no such luck."

Armanti put on gloves, then backed their car, a light green Chevy sedan with New Jersey plates, into Lesh's garage and we looked it over. More weapons, a GPS, a directional listening device, and some other paraphernalia that all good assassins are equipped with for a night's work. They also had a radio receiver/direction finder for locating radio beacons. We helped ourselves to the stuff they didn't need anymore and emptied their pockets, then loaded their bodies in the trunk.

I examined the stuff in their wallets. Both

guys lived in the same zip code in Newark. One twenty-two years old, the other twenty-one. The usual tattoos, as far as I could see without undressing them.

I wondered how many people these two had killed.

"Do you think these are the jail shooters?" Armanti Hall asked.

"I'm trying to picture them walking into that jail," I acknowledged.

"Too young," Doc Gordon said. "Gonads still too small."

I called Travis at the Shepherd's and told him about our encounter.

"Everything's quiet here," he said.

We agreed that he and his guys should wait at least another twenty-four hours on the off-chance that some more hitters would arrive to do the Shepherds, but with every passing hour that seemed more and more unlikely. Two were plenty, and we had done them.

The entryway where our two went to their reward was a little messy with spent cartridges and blood. I took the time to pick up the shell casings and mop everything up. No sense upsetting Mrs. Lesh when she came home, if she ever did.

There were a couple of bullet holes in the front door a few inches above the floor. The subsonic bullets hadn't gone through, so I laid down on my side and used my pocket knife to dig them out. I doubted if anyone would ever notice the holes.

At six the next evening I parked their car, now sporting the beacon from my old Mercedes, in the CEO's assigned parking space in the Red Truck Investments garage in Fort Lee, New Jersey. Walked down to the street and climbed in beside Armanti Hall, who had followed me there. We rolled.

Jake Grafton was summoned to the White House to meet with the new president's chief of staff, Reem Kiddus.

Kiddus was not much for small talk. "Tell me why the president shouldn't ask for your resignation?"

"Perhaps he should. That's for him to decide. But instead of talking about that, why don't you level with me about why you don't want any investigation of possible fraud in last November's election."

Kiddus's lips tightened. Not much, but Grafton saw it. He continued, "Let me guess. For some reason you think, or suspect, that an investigation might uncover evidence that the tally machines in some key counties in swing states were rigged to favor Mr. Conyer. You don't want anyone mucking around and letting stories like that leak because they might start a firestorm that casts a pall on Conyer's presidency."

Kiddus's gaze wandered, then came back to Grafton's face. "I don't know you."

"What don't you know? If I'm honest? If I'll stick a knife in Conyer's back?"

Kiddus looked at his hands.

"Tell you what," said Jake Grafton. "I think you need to talk to some people who *do* know me. That shouldn't be difficult, since this town is full of them. If you decide that you don't or can't trust me, call me and I'll have my resignation on your desk that afternoon. If you do trust me, I want to know who told you about rigged voting machines, and how you came to suspect they might be rigged for Conyer."

"I'll think about it," Reem Kiddus said.

"You might also think about how a few whispers in the right ears have put the fear in you, which means that no one is investigating possible fraud. If there was fraud, and apparently there was at least a little, the people who did it, here or abroad, are getting a free ride. And they can try it again. Elections come with surprising regularity."

Grafton stood up. "When you make your decision, let me know."

He didn't want to go back to Langley, so he had his driver and bodyguards take him to the university. He called Callie on her cell and rendezvoused with her for lunch at the faculty club.

"This is a pleasant surprise," she said, scrutinizing his face.

"It's a slow day for spies," he said and grinned. They went into the dining room holding hands.

On the way to New Jersey, I had bought a new battery for the beacon at a filling station when I stopped for gas and changed it out. I didn't think the car would move during the night, but we were taking turns watching it, just in case. We were watching from the street. The off-duty watchers were sacked out in a motel just off a freeway exit. The other three guys would be joining us in two days, when they wrapped up the stake-out at Shepherd's house.

I would have traded a meal at my favorite McDonald's to see the faces of whoever opened the Chevy's trunk and found the shooters' bodies. I kinda hoped it would be Nick Liszt or Heiki Schlemmer, but life rarely has that ironic symmetry that completes the loop. More than likely it was going to be someone from the towing company who hauled it off, unless someone at Red Truck Investments recognized the car. That was the card I was playing for.

Sarah Houston had been busy hacking and data mining, so we knew a good bit about both the Red Truck folks we had names for: ages, addresses, marital status, spouses' names and occupations, offspring, vehicles and so on.

I had to figure out our next move.

Going up the ladder as fast as possible before the principals had time to figure out a strategy or lawyer up seemed wise to me. Or before someone decided to sever the ties that bind with bullets. Fortunately we didn't have to worry about search warrants and all the other legal procedural steps because these people weren't going to be prosecuted. Jake Grafton wanted to know who the brain was behind the operation and if a foreign government was involved. Everything would be fine unless our extracurricular activities became public knowledge; then Jake Grafton would be caught in a shitstorm. Illegal wiretaps, B&Es, computer hacking, all that would get the lawyers and privacy advocates really fired up. Of course, he knew that.

My cell phone rang and I checked the caller ID. Sarah.

"Why are you still up?" I asked.

"Because I'm working. Are you in a bar someplace watching television and soaking up suds?"

"Uh, no. I'm sitting in a car with a weather eye on a parking garage."

"That sounds exciting."

"Like watching paint dry."

"Those two guys you called about"—these were our dead shooters—"have rap sheets that started when they were thirteen. Burglary, shoplifting, that kind of thing until they were sixteen, then the drug possession arrests began. Always probation. It looks as if they were street corner dealers and the prosecutors bargained the charges down to simple possession in return for a guilty plea. No arrests in the last two years."

"Sounds like they got mobbed up."

"It does. Do you want to know more about the crime syndicates in New Jersey?"

"Maybe later. I can't see a godfather setting out to fix an election. Having some punks do some hits for a friend, perhaps."

"Red Truck is indeed an investment vehicle for one of Anton Hunt's hedge funds."

"Who or what is the Red Truck?"

"The founder was Edward "Red" Truck, but he died filthy rich ten years ago of acute old age."

"Lucky dog."

"I have a list of names of the people who work there and how they relate to the hedge fund, but it's non-public information and hard to pin down. Most important is Nick Liszt. He's been with Hunt for twenty years and was one of the brains who masterminded the big short of the pound that almost broke the Bank of England. He's a player."

"If Hunt is involved, do you really think the object of the ElectTech shenanigans were to get Vaughn Conyer elected?"

"Lord, no. Hunt is way out there on the left

wing. He believes in a world without borders, world government and all the rest of it. He gives big bucks to organizations that promote that stuff and his foundation gives a lot more. He is a close friend of Cynthia Hinton and gave millions to the Hinton Foundation. I can't imagine him doing Vaughn Conyer any favors."

"Doesn't make sense, does it?"

"On the other hand, using his organization would be a perfect cover for a foreign intelligence agency that *did* want Conyer to win. For example, the Israelis. They hated the previous administration, which used American taxpayer dollars to try to sway the Israeli electorate in the last election there, made a deal with Iran, sold out Israel in the UN, all that stuff. Hinton was promising more of the same. Putin also hated Hinton. So if the election fixes were uncovered, everyone would say, *Anton Hunt, the left-wing crackpot?* The investigation would founder right there and everyone would suspect Vaughn Conyer. So it is possible. Heck, anything is possible."

"Why would Anton Hunt cooperate with Israeli intelligence or the Russians?"

"My guess would be money. If he is."

We talked a bit more before we hung up. She was on her way back to her apartment to get some sleep. Just thinking about sleep made me yawn.

I checked the beacon on the hitter's car. It was still where I parked it. Terrific.

The car sat in the Red Truck parking garage all of the next morning. Finally, at twelve minutes after two in the afternoon, a tow truck turned into the garage and disappeared up the ramp. Doc Gordon was on duty, and he called me.

I was there when the tow truck pulled the puke-green Chevy out of the garage and went off down the street. It wasn't much of a tow truck, an old rusty Ford F-350 that had once been bright red, with dual rear tires and a hook. The faded sign on the side said, "Pete's Towing, Hoboken."

The beacon was still working, so we stayed well back, out of sight, Doc in one car and me in another.

First it went to Pete's Towing, on a dingy industrial street in the wilderness of Hoboken. A ten-foot, chain-link fence topped with three strands of concertina wire surrounded the half-acre, which was full of cars, presumably towed. The green sedan went into a garage.

I wondered how this would go down. Would Pete call the cops? Would he call some funeral home to come get the Newark heroes for a Christian burial? Or . . .

While we waited for the verdict, I called Sarah and asked her to see what she could find on Pete's Towing. She called back an hour later.

"New Jersey DMV says Pete is Pietro Vitalle. He was convicted of chopping cars in 2009 and sentenced to two years, but was released on probation after serving nine months. His brother, however, Bordeno, has had a few more run-ins with the law. He was convicted of bribing two city councilmen in 2007 and served two years. The Feds prosecuted him under RICO in 2013 but the jury refused to convict. That thing was about union pension funds. The witnesses couldn't remember."

So Pete knew people and people knew him. We chatted for a few more minutes, and I told her I missed her. She said she missed me too.

Two hours and ten minutes after we arrived, the same tow truck backed up to the garage and came out with the green sedan on the hook. Away it went, past us, the beacon still chirping away. I noticed the license plate was missing from the sedan. Well, stolen plates that weren't radiating heat were valuable commodities.

We ended up at a landfill a half-hour away from Hoboken. The thing was huge, covering several hundred acres. The mountain of buried garbage on one side of the place had to be a couple hundred feet tall, which made it one of the natural wonders of the Jersey landscape. Heck, maybe it was the highest mountain in New Jersey, for all I know.

We sat outside the fence and watched through

binoculars as the tow truck took the killers' car into a pit out of sight. Doc turned his car off and walked back to sit in the passenger seat of mine. The beeper was still going. Garbage trucks coming and going roared past us spewing diesel exhaust and lots of decibels. The gate to the landfill had some kind of automatic thing that counted them, we thought.

As we watched through binoculars a big Caterpillar bulldozer came clanking around a pile of garbage and went into the pit. In a few minutes the tow truck reappeared with an empty hook, negotiated its way past an endless stream of garbage trucks going in and out, and disappeared in the direction of the Jersey 'urbs and 'burbs. The driver ignored us as he drove by. He had a cigarette dangling from his lips.

Doc and I watched the gulls, about a million of them by my count, soar and swoop over the garbage uplands, and the trucks and dozers roaring and snorting diesel exhaust into the spring evening. The sun had set on our way here and now the evening was fading to twilight. Lights on poles illuminated the endless stream of garbage trucks.

It didn't take long. Twelve minutes after the tow truck departed the beacon went off the air. Silence.

CHAPTER SEVEN

Doc Gordon went to the county to see what he could learn from the public records about the suicide of Harry Tanaka. Sarah was checking online newspaper files and called me first. "The seventh of December. Tanaka lived in East Orange. According to the papers, he hanged himself in his two-car garage while his wife was Christmas shopping. She found the body when she came home and opened the garage door with her remote. She had to be sedated. Two days later she told reporters she was stunned, but admitted he had been depressed. She was pretty broken up. Hadn't thought he was suicidal."

An hour later Doc called. "No police investigation, apparently. The autopsy came in death by strangling. The body was released to the family and cremated. His ashes are in a family crypt."

Wonderful. Did he or didn't he?

I drove over to Heiki Schlemmer's house in South Orange. It was an older, ten-room, brick mansion on a street without sidewalks lined with mature maples and sycamores. Sarah said that according to the county assessor, the house was 8,300 square feet, sat on a lot that was 1.23 acres in size, and was worth about $4.5 million. Heiki had never married.

My next stop was Nick Liszt's estate, and that was what it was. It sat on ten acres just to the west of Maplewood. The house was partially obscured due to the mature trees, all at least three feet in diameter. Sarah said Liszt had owned it for eleven years, and the county assessor thought the fair market value for the whole shebang—house, garage, caretaker's house, and horse barn—was $11 million. Anton Hunt's associates were well paid.

Liszt was on his third wife, Sarah had told me. He had two daughters from his first marriage, and only one was still in college. The other was married and living in Connecticut.

I merely scoped out Liszt's farm and kept going until I found a convenience store. I called Doc and told him to drop by the assessor's office and get plat maps that showed Schlemmer's and Liszt's estates. Then to check with the power company and see how the houses got power.

I suspected that things were tense at Red Truck. Both Schlemmer and Liszt had to have heard that the puke-green Chevy sedan contained bodies. The police hadn't been called, a fact that spoke volumes.

It seemed to me that the best move was to figure out how to learn what was going on at Red Truck and in Schlemmer's and Liszt's lives. I was hoping I didn't have to break and enter to actually plant bugs or tap phones. Sarah was mining the local internet provider's records. If each house had Wi-Fi installed and the computers and cell phones used it, which was probable, she could remotely load software onto the Wi-Fi that turned the computers and phones into listening devices, the signals of which she could monitor at CIA Headquarters in Langley. If by chance either of them had a home server, Sarah could hack into it.

Modern high-tech communications are wonderful and convenient, but they are less secure than an old party telephone line. Anyone with a devious nature interested in your emails, computer files, or cell phone calls can hire or rent some tech expert to figure out a way to read them or listen in. Apparently in this day and age there are a lot of devious people. The old adage is still true: if you want to keep a secret, don't tell anyone. Don't even whisper it aloud.

That thought brought me around to the cell phone in my hand. If this conspiracy did indeed involve a foreign intelligence service, such as the Russian SVR, the Israeli Mossad, or the Chinese Ministry of State Security, or some high-powered, well-financed American scumbag, listening in on cell phones would be in the cards. Perhaps we should go silent. Or at least switch to encrypted com gear.

That night at our motel we left the cell phones and computers in Armanti's room and over in my room we talked about com security. All six of us were there. Travis Clay, Joe Casillas and Ski Wisniewski had arrived in time to eat supper at the steak house across the street.

Joe had driven the van we used in Pennsylvania. He was our tech expert. "We have four encrypted telephones in the van," he said. "No reason not to use them."

"We've talked on unsecure cell phones today about this Schlemmer woman and Nick Liszt," I said. "If anyone was listening, they know we are here and who our targets are. And they know Sarah is going to parasite onto the targets' Wi-Fi systems."

"If they know, we won't get anything," Travis said with a frown.

"We may get dead," I said. "Those two clowns we popped in Kurt Lesh's house may not have been the ElectTech shooters. They were young street hoods trying to work their way into the Jersey mob. Maybe they were doing a favor for one of the big guys around here, who was doing a favor for a friend of a friend. You know how these things work."

"Tommy said the ElectTech guys were solidly professional," Armanti remarked. "Those guys yesterday both walked in the front door together, and they had their wallets and driver's licenses in their pockets, the getaway car sitting empty at the curb with the engine off in front of the house they were going into. The registration in the car matched the plate, and it was registered to the guy with the snake tattoos up his arms. Not even a stolen car or a stolen plate. The fool drove his own car to a murder. Now I ask you . . . ."

"They didn't expect to get caught," Wisniewski observed.

"No," Armanti said bluntly. "They didn't expect to have any problems. That ain't the way pros work, and you know it. You are one."

"Anyway," I said, summing up, "the ElectTech hitters are probably out there walking around, and they may still be on the payroll. We may have worked our way up their list to a position of prominence."

Travis Clay looked at me, disgusted. "You knew it all along. You set us up."

"Gotta bait the trap with something," I explained.

"Why don't we just snatch this Nick Liszt and sweat him?"

"Not yet," I said. "If he's as smart as Anton Hunt thinks he is, he won't tell us anything. And we don't have anything to threaten him with. When we go after him, we have to have something that will open him up like a ripe tomato."

Armanti Hall said, "Tommy, you're still my favorite asshole."

"I love you too," I told him.

After a few more housekeeping details, I told

them, "I'm going back to Washington tonight. Travis, you're in charge. I want you to find a motel that you can defend and move everyone there. Set up a perimeter. As of this moment, we are in a defensive mode. No cell phone calls. Secure phones only. Wrap your cells in aluminum foil. Don't use your computers. Stay off the internet. Let Sarah Houston know where you are, no one else. I'll be back in a day or two."

They all nodded. They had all served in the Middle East and knew exactly what I was talking about. If anyone wanted a piece of us, we had to be ready.

I walked out to the parking lot and after a careful look around climbed into my old Mercedes and set sail for Washington.

I was in Delaware when I realized that I had a tail. I had pulled off on an I-95 freeway exit to gas the car and was standing in front of the station drinking a cup of coffee when I realized that I was looking at a car I had passed fifty miles back up the road. It was a dark, new Chevy SUV with New York plates. The driver was gassing his car and paying no attention to me. He was middle-aged, fit, with short salt-and-pepper hair, wearing nice trousers and shoes and a dark jacket, even though the spring night was warm. I was wearing a windbreaker to cover my shoulder holster.

Another man came out of the store and without

glancing at me walked over and climbed into the Chevy's passenger seat. He too was wearing a windbreaker. The only problem was that I suspected that bulge under his shoulder was a gun.

I finished my coffee, fired up my ride, and pulled out of the filling station. When I was out of sight of my tail, who was still gassing up, I whipped into a drive-through McDonald's, parked, and shut off my lights. Less than a minute later, the SUV came ripping out of the filling station. It shot across the interstate overpass and turned left at the on-ramp to head south.

I shed my jacket, buckled my seat belt, turned on the engine and the lights, and followed them. Got a hundred feet behind them and stuck there.

I couldn't see if anyone in the vehicle was using his cell phone, but being paranoid, I suspected the passenger was. If so, there was more than one vehicle. That made sense. I had been watching for vehicles tailing me and had not seen any of them, if there were any. No one stayed behind me long enough for me to notice. They were in front or passing and racing ahead to come up behind later when the follower peeled off. A classic rolling surveillance, and difficult to spot, but if you paid attention to the cars you saw, eventually you would tumble to seeing them again and again, as I had.

I wanted to see what this dude would do. If he was a pro, he would soon exit the interstate and call for someone else to pick me up. Sure enough, he did. He got off at a Wilmington exit. I rolled on for a mile and pulled over on the edge of the highway. Turned on the emergency flashers and killed the engine. The Beretta with the suppressor was under the seat, so I grabbed it and climbed out of the car. Went down the embankment and moved fifty feet or so behind the Mercedes and hunkered down.

Up on the road, the Mercedes flashed its distress signals forlornly.

I wished I hadn't shed the jacket. If a state trooper came by, I was going to have trouble explaining the pistols.

The night was comfortable and frogs croaked agreeably as traffic rolled by at the speed of heat, which hereabouts was eighty miles per hour. The concussion waves from eighteen-wheelers were palpable. The noise was awesome. The area where I was hunkered was littered with trash, beer cans, fast food wrappers, diapers . . .

I hoped that no drunk or soccer mom on her cell phone would slam into my car, which would ruin both of our evenings.

I watched the traffic, waiting for that SUV. Of course, in the darkness I wouldn't recognize it until it passed or stopped. Then it passed. Went by the Benz and I recognized it as the flashers did their thing. It went on down the highway.

They would be back, I thought. Down to the

next exit, back north to the exit I had just left, then south again to stop. Maybe eight minutes.

I couldn't see my watch, but I removed the Kimber from its holster and made sure the safety was on. It felt heavy in my hand. The suppressed Beretta I stuck in my belt.

I was at a disadvantage here, and I knew it. If these guys were merely Good Samaritans, it would be bad PR to gun them. On the other hand, if they were professional assassins, they would shoot first and accurately. They wouldn't lose any sleep over accidental victims. I decided to give them the first shot. That wasn't as dangerous as it sounds, since this ditch was dark and I was nearly invisible from the road.

Of course, they would be suspicious and suspect an ambush. Still, forty-year-old sports cars aren't recommended by *Consumer Reports* for reliability.

Maybe I should get another car. One younger than I was. Much younger. Or a pickup. The problem with pickups was they used so much gasoline. That darn stuff was getting expensive again.

Every minute that passed made this ambush idea more iffy. A state trooper would be along eventually, and he would probably stop, which would complicate this problem.

As I mulled, the traffic roared by, an endless stream. The lifeblood of the nation and all that.

Then I realized that an eighteen-wheeler was in the right lane, slowing as he approached. Uh-oh. I hoped he wouldn't stop. He didn't. He slowed to perhaps forty and smashed into the Mercedes and sent it careening off the road down the embankment. The only thing that saved me was the fact I was fifty feet north of the wreck. The truck slowed and came to a gradual stop perhaps a hundred yards farther on. Its flashers lit up.

And here came the SUV. It braked and came to a stop abeam the Mercedes. The interior light was illuminated, and I could see that there were only two men in the vehicle. They both got out with flashlights. The SUV had its engine and lights on.

They were taking no chances. A careful, professional job. I would have taken my hat off to them if I had been wearing one.

They walked down the embankment toward the wrecked car, their flashlights scanning about. One guy went around behind the car and moved up on the right side. The driver of the semi had stayed in his cab.

Miraculously the flashers on my old Mercedes were still blinking faithfully.

I moved closer, staying low, holding my Kimber in both hands.

One flashlight beam went into the interior of the smashed car. "He isn't in it," the man with the light on the interior said to the other. The other guy flashed his light into the car too, the first mistake they had made. In the glare of the flashlights I could see that the man on the right had a gun in his hands. The other one held a flashlight and what looked like a bottle.

Screw that first-shot crap.

I shot the man on the right first and his flashlight fell. The other flashlight turned my way. He had dropped the bottle and was fumbling in his coat. I shot him before he could get his pistol out of its holster. He lost his flashlight as he went down. No more than a second passed between my first and second shots.

I ran toward them and shot the man on the right in the head as he lay on the ground. Went around to the guy beside the driver's door. He was on the ground and the contents of the bottle were running out onto the ground. I smelled gasoline. The bastard was going to burn me. His eyes tracked toward me. He was hit in the stomach, and I could see blood.

I also saw a kitchen match on the ground by the flashlight. I picked it up, struck it on my trousers, and tossed it at the bottle. The gasoline ignited with a *whoosh* and went under him. In seconds his clothes were on fire.

I ran around to the other guy and took his wallet and cell phone. Stowed the Kimber and climbed the bank to the idling Chevy SUV while the man on fire screamed.

The truck driver was still in his cab.

I threw the captured phone and wallet on the right seat. Put the SUV in gear and got underway. As I approached the semi accelerating I got a break in traffic and merged.

The truck driver was staring at me as I went by standing on the gas. I was too busy reading the sign on his door to get a good look at him. The cab belonged to a New Jersey trucking firm.

Those assholes! Smashing my car! And I had just filled it with gas!

I glanced in the rear-view mirror. The truck's right headlight was out. I hoped a cop would stop him. The truck was still sitting there beside the highway when I last saw it.

I fastened my seat belt and tried to get my breathing back to normal. There was half a cup of coffee still in the cup holder, but it was too cold to drink. When I put the cup back in the holder I felt something slimy. Turned on the overhead light and saw that I had some blood on my hand. Oh well. It would wash off. I wiped my hand on my sock.

I called Jake Grafton to tell him about the incident, and he gave me the number of my county sheriff. I called his office to tell the duty dispatcher that my Benz had been stolen. She told me to stop by the office in the morning to fill out a police report.

"The SUV is stolen," Jake Grafton said. He gestured at the wallet. "Fake ID."

We were sitting in his office at ten the next morning. I had spent the night at Sarah's and drove the SUV into the Langley facility lot. I didn't bother going to the local sheriff's office. Filing false police reports is a felony. I had done enough felonies this past week to last me. Now Sarah had the cell phone and was wringing out its secrets.

"Anything from the Delaware police about the guns and bodies?"

"They're getting fingerprints from the corpses and turned the guns over to the FBI, which is test firing them, normal procedure. We'll hear in a day or two what they find."

"And my car?"

"Totaled. Someone will probably send you a towing bill."

"I'll put the tow bill on my expense account."

Grafton sighed and didn't say anything, probably thinking, as I was, that the bean counters were not going to be pleased. It would be nice if I could stick my insurance company with that bill, but the prospects of that were dismal. I called them last night from Sarah's place and reported the loss of my ride.

"Do you know the fair market value of your forty-three-year-old Benz?" the agent asked. "Make that forty-four model years, since the new models are out."

"No," I replied hopefully. "But it's a classic. Give me the good news."

"We'll stretch a point and value it at a thousand bucks, then subtract your deductible."

"That's five hundred dollars."

"Correct. So you get five hundred bucks."

"Hell, I paid more than a thousand for the insurance last year."

"Check your policy. It specifically states that we are insuring the car against theft and collision damage for fair market value, less your deductible—"

Screwed again.

"Just send us a copy of the police report of the theft."

"There wasn't one."

"Well!" he said heartily. "You certainly can't expect us to pay a claim without a police report! How do we know that it was really stolen? You would be amazed at the number of people who sell their cars to a junk yard and try to collect on the insurance." He sounded pleased that he was saving his company five hundred bucks.

"The least you could do is cancel the insurance and refund the unused portion of my last payment."

"Of course. That's a hundred thirty-two dollars. Should we send it to your address of record?"

"Yes."

"And, of course, we'll report the cancellation to the Virginia DMV," he said with malice in his voice. "Virginia requires all vehicles to be insured. You'll undoubtedly hear from them."

"Virginia is for lovers," I told the asshole.

This morning I said to Jake Grafton, "Maybe I should buy a pickup."

He didn't bother to reply.

When I had called Travis Clay to tell him about my adventure with the assassins and the fate of my Benz, he said, "Serves you right, Tommy, driving a flashy car like that. Everybody thought you were compensating. But I'm glad you came out of it okay."

This morning I said to Jake Grafton, "I'll need an agency car to get back to Jersey."

"See the people in the motor pool."

"I'm going to need some direction here. If we don't have some way to crack Schlemmer or Liszt, it would be a mistake to approach them."

"Let's see what Sarah can find out about the dead guy's cell phone. Maybe they were talking to him. Hang around for a day or two and I'll get back to you."

"There is also this Edwin Riddenhour dude from American Voting. We could check up on him."

"Talk to Sarah about him."

That was it. I got outta there. I went to my cubby-hole office to call Travis to tell him how it stood. "Be on your toes," I said. "Don't assume all their soldiers are deceased."

"I would never assume that. Don't hurry back."

I attacked the stack of read-and-initial crap in my in-basket and trimmed my fingernails.

At one o'clock I took Sarah to lunch in the cafeteria, and afterwards, back in her office, mentioned Edwin P. Riddenhour.

"American Voting," she said, nodding. "There is no such company."

I must have looked surprised.

"And no Edwin P. Riddenhour."

"But at that county clerk's office we went to . . ."

"Just someone using that name."

"But, who?"

"I don't know."

At nine that evening Jake Grafton was locking up his office so he could go home to dinner when he was informed he had a visitor, the president's chief of staff. When Kiddus was escorted into the director's office Grafton had a fresh pot of coffee waiting.

"Black," Kiddus said, when asked how he liked it.

They settled onto the couch. Kiddus sipped coffee and ran his eyes around the office. "Okay," he said. "I asked around. You have an enviable reputation. Everyone I talked to told me that they'd trust you with their lives and the nation's life."

Grafton was at a loss for words, and his facial expression showed it.

"They also said that you cut corners and occasionally don't play by the rules, but you get results," Kiddus continued. "They said you were ruthless, could stand the sight and smell of blood, were a great friend and a terrible enemy." He waved his hand. "Cut the bull in half and I am still impressed. So, what do you want to know about election fraud?"

"Why you don't want it investigated."

"The president changed his mind. He does want it investigated."

"Cynic that I am, I thought you were worried that rigged voting machines are two-edged swords. Your political enemies can pick and choose their numbers and charge that the rigged machines actually were intended to make sure Conyer was elected."

"Rigged machines?" Kiddus was good with his face, but he had been expecting something else. Grafton assumed it was dead voters on voting rolls and illegal aliens of whom the latest estimates said at least 800,000 had voted, presumably for Cynthia Hinton. *"Are there rigged machines?"*

"Were. Two of our folks found some that were rigged over in Virginia. It was only one county."

Grafton reached into his desk and came out with several spreadsheets. He brought them to the couch and sat down beside Kiddus so that he could see them. "I had our analysts do some work on the election results of the usual Democratic strongholds, which are the big cities. Here they are. You will notice that some of the cities didn't have the Democratic turnout for Hinton that they had for the Democrat in 2012. There are three ways to explain that. One, the cities didn't go as heavily Democratic as they did in past elections. Second, the machines were rigged against Hinton. Third, the machines were rigged against Conyer."

Kiddus scrutinized the sheets. He rubbed his chin thoughtfully. "Were the machines rigged?"

"I sent two analysts, armed with fake credentials saying they were with the Federal Election Commission, to Milwaukee to check on the machines and the service records. Before the election the county clerk was visited by Junior Sikes of ElectTech, now dead, and after the election by a man we only know as Edwin P. Riddenhour, which is a fake name. We have no idea who that is. Yet. They serviced the machines. The machines are clean now."

"So your investigation has hit a wall."

"No, it hasn't." Jake explained about the ElectTech killings, the assassins who broke into a house in Pennsylvania and were ambushed there by CIA officers. "The New Jersey mob disposed of the bodies in a landfill. Then last night one of my officers was ambushed on I-95 on his way back to Washington from New Jersey. He killed them both. One of them had fake IDs, which we have."

Jake went back to his desk and came back with a wallet, which he handed to Kiddus. As the chief of staff was examining the contents, Grafton removed another document from his desk drawer. When Kiddus returned the wallet, he gave him the document.

"This is a sworn affidavit by a man named Kurt Lesh, who works for Allegheny, which owns ElectTech. It's six pages. Take your time."

Kiddus read it quickly once, then settled back to read it again, slowly.

When he finished he tossed the affidavit on the desk. "Do you want to get the FBI involved?"

"Not yet. This agency doesn't enforce the law or prosecute people. As I told you when we discussed this previously, our interest is finding out if a foreign government is involved."

"Congress and the FBI are going to investigate voter fraud."

"They'll try to determine if foreigners voted," Grafton said, "if people voted more than once, if county clerks stuffed ballot boxes, voter intimidation, that kind of thing. That's well and good. I want to know if a foreign government, working through ElectTech and a non-existent outfit called American Voting Incorporated, rigged voting machines; who directed it, paid for it, and what they were trying to achieve. What we find will go to the White House only, or, if you wish, the DNI." The DNI was the Director of National Intelligence.

"Whom do you suspect?"

"Anton Hunt."

Kiddus's eyebrows rose. "But he's extremely liberal and reportedly lost a billion dollars in the market after Conyer was elected."

"A perfect cover for a foreign intelligence operation," Grafton replied.

"You're saying this onion may have numerous layers."

"Most onions do."

Kiddus looked Grafton straight in the eyes. "Vaughn Conyer did not fix the election."

"I never thought he did. But someone was playing fast and loose with voting and tabulation machines last November, and we are fools if we don't find out who and why."

"Investigating foreign intelligence activities on U.S. soil is the FBI's bailiwick. It's more than a bailiwick issue: the CIA is essentially legally prohibited from intelligence activities in the United States."

"If you want to hand them this, Kiddus, be my guest."

"Call me Reem."

Grafton rolled on. "The FBI is going to have major problems getting anything from or on Anton Hunt, who will hide behind platoons of lawyers. When the story breaks, as it inevitably will, it will be a major stink bomb. The newspapers and news shows will be all over it—and all over the president. If the FBI can't uncover enough evidence to prosecute or get enough credible people to rat on Hunt under oath, the president is going to look like he is hounding a political enemy. Even if Justice thinks they have enough to prosecute, good luck getting Hunt on trial. If they get over that hurdle, good luck getting a conviction."

"You aren't going after admissible evidence."

"No. Our goal is to determine if a foreign government is involved, and if so, to stop it. There's always another election. The last one is history."

Reem Kiddus could make a decision without sleeping on it. He made one now. "You do it for a while. But if Hunt starts squawking, we have to get the FBI involved." He stood. "I'd like a copy of that affidavit and those spreadsheets to show the president. He'll want to know about this."

"You still haven't told me why you didn't want this investigated."

"The president didn't want—"

"Not good enough. Someone led you to believe that some voting machines were rigged to favor Conyer. Who was it?"

Kiddus took a deep breath through his nose. "You can't know that."

Grafton just sat, waiting.

Kiddus made his decision. "I'm going to reserve that."

"As you wish. But it's not a guess. It had to have happened that way. Nothing else fits."

"Report to me, no one else," Kiddus said. After Jake gave him the documents he asked for, the chief of staff shook hands and was on his way.

When I got to work the next day, Grafton summoned Sarah and me to his office. "The White House gave me a green light last evening on this election fraud investigation," he said.

I have known Jake Grafton for years and knew how he operated—man, I could write a book about this dude but I confess I was flabbergasted. "You mean you didn't have one?"

"No."

Talk about hanging it out for somebody to chop off.

Sarah didn't say a word. Maybe she knew he had been flying solo. Of course, being the closed-mouth op that she was, she'd never share that tidbit with me. Maybe she figured I already knew. Or she figured that Jake Grafton could dive head-first into a cesspool and come out smelling like Chanel Number Five. Man, I gotta get in another line of work.

What I said was, "You know how politicians' memories are. I hope you got it in writing."

He ignored me, which was par for the course.

"If this goes bad," I added, "they'll forget they even know your name."

"Make sure it doesn't go bad," he said flatly, then got down to giving orders, which is the thing Jake Grafton does best. Cast off and hoist the mainsail.

Aye aye, sir, three bags full.

To be a good combat leader, and Grafton was, you must be aggressive yet prudent, know what your troops can do and what they can't, and be willing to take risks. No one ever won a battle without taking risks and pushing to the limit of his luck. A leader must know when to hit, when to wait, and when to pull back to await another opening. No one wins all the battles—the trick is to win the war. Since I was just a grunt, I hoped this wasn't a battle Grafton was destined to lose.

When we left his office a half hour later I didn't salute, but I felt like it. Charge that machine-gun nest. You betcha, sir. Why didn't I think of that?

In the outer office Sarah must have read my mood. "Relax, Tommy, we can do this."

I glowered at her. "I've already shot four men over this pile of shit. You think they're done? This is war. They'll pull out all the stops, and if they're losing, they'll go nuclear."

Four hours later Sarah came to my office with news. Red Truck Investments in Fort Lee and

Anton Hunt's hedge fund headquarters in New York didn't have Wi-Fi. "They have private servers that are seriously encrypted. I can't hack in."

We discussed it. It looked as if I was going to have to go into both places to find a way to let Sarah in electronically. We discussed possible methods.

"I'm sorry, Tommy," she said, and meant it.

After she left I made a list of stuff I had to have and stuff I might need. I was going to need a truck to haul it. When I finished, I went down to the director's office and told Robin the receptionist that I needed to see Grafton. "He's in a meeting."

I wrote a note at the top of the list, signed it, stuck it in a classified folder, and asked her to give it to Grafton when he came up for air.

In the midafternoon Robin called me back. "Your document is signed, Tommy. You can pick it up." I did so and examined it. Grafton had stapled my list to the back of a requisition, which he had signed. He initialed the list. Then I trekked down to the equipment department to visit with my good buddy, Jasper Cerullo.

He looked at the list and whistled. "You going to bug the Russian embassy?"

"Ask me no questions and I'll tell you no lies."

Jasper nodded knowingly. "The company motto," he said.

· · ·

Sarah was in a good mood when I got back to her place that evening, so I figured things were going well at the office. She was smiling, cheerful, and had a good bottle of wine open. Since we never talk shop while at home, I didn't ask a single question. We drank wine, made a simple meal, and watched a silly chick flick on television. Got to bed early, and somewhat later, actually went to sleep.

At the office I followed her to her cubbyhole, curious as a cat. She gave me a list of cell phone numbers for the folks at Red Truck Investments and some for the staff at Hunt's hedge fund.

"Do any of the numbers on the cell phone I picked up in Delaware match any of the ones you have identified?"

"No."

It would be wonderful if we could listen in on these numbers, but that would take a warrant, which meant the FBI. Getting NSA involved would take a court order showing that we wanted to listen to Hunt talk to some foreigners that we thought were nasty. We weren't there yet. Without the FBI we would never get there.

So I wasn't as cheerful as Sarah was last night, but then I didn't have the triumph of hacking all those cell phone numbers. Celebrate the little victories when they come.

In the short run, I began fretting about Sarah

and Grafton. If these bastards indeed knew who was about to put the pressure on, they might decide to take them out.

I went to see Jake Grafton and was fortunate enough to catch him between meetings. He let me talk. I finished with the opinion, "You need more bodyguards, at least until we find the security dude. Sarah does too."

"I'll take care of it."

I told him I would leave for New Jersey tomorrow with my truck full of goodies. "I'm going to have to go into Red Truck and Hunt's office spaces."

"Don't get caught."

Sangfroid. Wish I had more of that. The problem was that he didn't know all the things that could go wrong, and I did.

"I hope we don't go to prison over this," I said.

"If we do, we'll make a lot of new friends."

I'm a big believer in paranoia. Keeps you alive occasionally, so why not have some on a regular basis?

That night when I got back to Sarah's I took a really good look at her apartment. It was on the fourth floor and didn't have a balcony. Two bedrooms, a living room, kitchen, and nook den, plus the usual bathroom with shower and facilities. I tried to recall just how I had left it that morning. Looked fine to me.

Sarah was working late and wouldn't be home for a while. I took off my jacket and shoulder holster, dumped them on the bed, and got busy searching. Found the first bug in the bedroom eight minutes later. It was a miniature audio receiver, not as small or compact as the state-of-the-art bugs the company uses, but adequate. It was pinned inside a lamp shade and had to transmit its signal. I left it there and kept looking.

Fifteen minutes later I had two more, one in the kitchen and one in the nook Sarah used for her home computer. So where was the booster that captured these signals and rebroadcasted them? It had to be relatively close, within fifty feet or so depending on how many walls the signal had to penetrate before it got there.

Twenty minutes later I was fairly well convinced the booster wasn't in the apartment. The obvious places were in a closet or at the back of a desk drawer or under a piece of furniture. No such luck.

Outside on a wall or in a treetop or on that power pole on the edge of the parking lot?

It was still light outside so I went out with binoculars and started looking. Examined the side of the building, everything I could see. Didn't see anything suspicious.

Well, it had to be somewhere. And if there was an eye on this place and on me, he or she knew I was looking.

I began looking at cars in the lot parked close to the building. Spaces weren't assigned, so the tenants merely took the first empty spot they found. Without opening and searching the four cars that I thought were probably in range, there was no way I could determine if they were clean. I did make a mental note of license numbers and wrote them down when I got back inside the apartment.

The elevator shaft seemed too remote. Of course, the booster could be in an adjacent apartment, on one side or the other, or above or below. I went to see the building manager, a buxom woman in her sixties.

We schmoozed a while, then I said, "I'm thinking about renting my own apartment. What do you have that's empty?"

She pulled out her chart. The one beside Sarah on the east side was empty.

"How much rent do you want for that one?" I asked and pointed.

She told me. I checked the apartments above and below and on the west side. Asked about how long people stayed, when apartments might become vacant, told her how much Sarah liked living here. We became fast friends. The apartments above and below Sarah had been lived in by the same couples for several years. Those apartments were the same floor plan that Sarah had. The one to the west was a little different, and the tenant, a single woman, had been in there for six months on a one-year lease.

"We ask for a one-year lease," she said, "and then let it go to month-to-month if the tenant is willing to take the chance the owners might raise the rent to match the market. If they want another one-year lease, we are delighted to do that."

"Only a year?"

"The owners won't let us go beyond that," she said apologetically. "They have to be able to raise the rent if the market requires it."

"I understand. How long has that one been unoccupied?" I pointed to the one to the east of Sarah. "Isn't that a two-bedroom?"

"Two bedrooms, yes, but on a slightly different floor-plan. That one was vacated about a month ago when the owner was transferred to Illinois. Can you believe it? Illinois?" She said it as if Illinois were Hicksville.

"I'm kinda thinking about two bedrooms. In truth, I just have too much stuff. You know how that is."

"Of course. Stuff attracts stuff."

"Maybe tomorrow or the next day you can show it to me."

"Anytime. I'm going off duty in thirty minutes, and I come in at ten during the week."

"Do you live here?"

"Oh yes." She told me her apartment number and how much she loved the location and the building. "We're so close to shopping here, and the people are usually professionals, quiet, nice to talk to. I wouldn't live any place else."

"Wonderful. I'll talk it over with Sarah and let you know." I winked at her. "Maybe I'll propose and we'll both move in."

I went back upstairs and knocked loudly on the door to the vacant apartment. Rang the bell repeatedly. Finally satisfied that no one was there, I used my pick and set on the lock. Took about two minutes. Then I opened the door and stepped inside.

Clean, neat and empty, without a stick of furniture. I got busy looking, and immediately found the booster in a closet. It was battery operated and had an on-off switch. It was set up to record what the system collected, then sent the data in a burst transmission when queried by a radio signal with the proper code, a feature that didn't require the listener to sit outside the building day and night. I didn't touch it. When I left a minute later I locked the door behind me.

Back at Langley I went to see Jasper Cerullo.

Sarah was home and fixing dinner when I returned. Holding my finger to my lips, I installed a wall listening device in our bedroom, which was the closest place to the booster. I listened for thirty minutes, until dinner was ready. Sure that the neighboring apartment was still empty, I unlocked

145

the door, went straight to the booster, and turned it off. I was back outside in fifteen seconds.

We ate a nice baked chicken with a salad and white wine. Then I took up my station with the earphones to listen to what might happen in the empty apartment.

It was a long evening. Sarah went to bed and I catnapped in the chair with the earphones on. Finally I heard something. A key turning in the lock. Then footsteps.

Eleven minutes after three.

I slipped out of the chair and out the door into the hallway.

Whoever was in there—I was praying it was only one person—must be having a disquieting moment. The booster/recorder had been turned off. That meant someone knew it was there, and the someone who turned it off might be Sarah or me. Not good.

Would this person or persons decide to play it safe and call for backup? Or would they merely turn the unit back on and vacate the place as soon as possible? I suspected he or she was thinking it over.

Decision time.

Flattened against the wall so I wouldn't be visible through the security peephole, I looked up and down the hallway. I was hoping that no one came staggering home at this hour. The manager lady had said the tenants were mostly professional people, a phrase that suggested regular habits, and quiet, which implied they didn't carouse until the wee hours. At least on a weeknight. Of course, some guy could be sneaking out of a lady's apartment . . . or some lady could be sneaking out of a guy's bed. It's the brave new world we live in.

I heard the doorknob turn and was ready when the person came out. It was a guy. I slammed him on the head with the Kimber and he collapsed.

The door was closing, so I jammed it open with my shoe and dragged him back into the apartment. He hadn't seen me before the roof fell in, and if he stayed out he wouldn't.

He was wearing a security company shirt with his name, Bob, above his left shirt pocket. He hadn't swallowed his tongue. I was worried that I had hit him too hard. Pulse strong and steady. Maybe just a little concussion.

Don't die on me, fella.

Bob had a wallet and cell phone, plus some hand tools in a hip pocket of his jeans. No gun. A key to the apartment. Car keys to a Toyota. I pocketed the loot and left him there.

I exited the building on the side away from the main parking lot and, using the bushes for cover, searched for his Toyota. Found it. It was a little truck with a security company logo on the door that matched the one on his shirt, and a cover for the bed, which was full of tools, burglar alarms, wire, and miscellaneous stuff. A receiver and computer to record the burst transmissions from the booster were on the front passenger seat.

I could see no one in any of the cars that were parked around. There could have been someone watching from another vantage point, but in light of the fact that the booster was a burst-transmission type, I doubted it. How many people and how much money do you spend on one little bug monitoring system, one that hasn't yielded a darn thing and might never?

What did trouble me was the question of who ordered audio surveillance of Sarah Houston. Or perhaps it was me they wanted to listen to? I hoped it was me. If anything happened to Sarah . . .

Maybe this guy's cell phone would yield some answers. I went upstairs and returned his car keys to his pocket so he could get home when he woke up. Checked his pulse again and looked into his eyes. A concussion, but he was resting easy, with a steady pulse and normal breathing. I helped myself to the booster/transmitter.

I locked up and went into Sarah's pad. Sat down in the chair with the earphones on. I was sleeping when a noise next door woke me. It sounded like the guy was vomiting. At least he was up and about. Two minutes after six in the morning.

I heard him using the commode and running water in the bathroom sink. No doubt he had a hell of a headache. I had been pistol-whipped before, and I sure did when I came around.

Sarah was awake a few minutes later, and I held another finger to my lips. She saw the security guy's cell phone on the bed and played with it a bit.

She fixed coffee in the kitchen, and she turned on the television.

The guy left the apartment next door at a quarter to seven. Sarah was in the shower by then.

I pocketed the three bugs in Sarah's place and showed them to her. "This is why we don't talk business at home."

She merely nodded. What a woman!

"After you mine his cell phone and wallet, how about wiping off all the fingerprints, putting them in a box and mailing them to him? He's just a guy trying to make a little money on an illegal bugging operation. I doubt that he'll do it again."

"You hope."

"Every sinner has a future."

"Who said that?"

"I dunno. Someone smarter than me."

"You can use that as my epitaph," she said.

At ten the next morning Sarah gave me the news. "Your guy last night, Bob Ash, had at least six telephone conversations with Heiki Schlemmer."

"How about that," I said.

CHAPTER EIGHT

I had a command decision to make, and I wasn't ready to make it. With a bit of luck, we could get enough from Anton Hunt's headquarters in Manhattan to skip Red Truck Investments in Fort Lee all together. However, I was having deep thoughts about Ms. Schlemmer.

Cynic that I am, I suspected Hunt's troops would be expecting us. Four fatalities to date were certainly signs that they had a problem. "What I want to do," I explained to my troops whom I gathered in another motel room in New Jersey, "is get them looking the wrong way."

We discussed it, what was possible, what we could do without someone calling out a SWAT team, and the timing.

"I don't think we have to do anything spectacular," Travis Clay said while rubbing his chin.

Armanti Hall and Doc Gordon weren't so sure. "Tommy will need hours in the hedge fund office."

What we decided was that we didn't know enough about our target, how it was situated, who was guarding it, any of that. So we began watching.

"You're not in a hurry are you?" Ski Wisniewski asked me.

"Only to keep on living."

"They'll shoot, you know."

"Yeah," I replied, as dryly as possible. Ski was one of my slower students.

"Why not the old fire alarm trick?" Doc Gordon asked.

"You mean pull a fire alarm and let everyone evacuate?"

"No. I mean start a real fire and let the fire department put it out. Tommy goes in during the fire."

"Jesus, that's a felony," Joe Casillas objected.

"So is murder and rigging elections. Get a grip, fella."

"Fight fire with fire, huh?"

"Why not?"

"Why not a demonstration, complete with people waving signs and shouting obscenities? Plus some TV crews filming?"

I let them argue a while before sending them to bed for the night, those that weren't on duty. Then I got into one of the agency cars, a heap that had once belonged to a rental car company and wore Maryland plates, and went off to reconnoiter the buildings personally.

Hunt had his offices in the three top floors of a huge building on the Avenue of the Americas, just a few blocks down from the Trump Tower. He actually lived in an old brownstone on West 54th Street, two blocks east of Madison. One of the guys said he owned the brownstone. Why not if you're a billionaire? There were two guys standing out front on his Manhattan crash pad, with a car that looked as if it were armored standing at the curb.

It was two in the morning, so I found a parking place in a public garage and walked back, avoiding the garbage bags that were set out on the sidewalk for New York's finest to pick up. Yep, the guards were packing heat and wearing little earphones with wires that went down into their chests. They looked me over and ignored me as I walked by. No eye contact. After all, this was New York, America's friendliest city.

I walked on to the tower where the offices were. We could get the floor plans from the city or the manager of the building. I went into the foyer, where the tenants were listed on a board. A uniformed guard watched me as if she thought I was Ahmad the Awful, but didn't say a word. She looked Latina, maybe Puerto Rican or Cuban, and wasn't wearing a weapon. Since I obviously wasn't a street person wearing filthy clothes, she didn't try to run me out. Security cameras were recording my image, which was unavoidable. I suspected—make that hoped—that the security officer of Hunt's hedge fund didn't spend his or her mornings watching the lobby camera footage. What the three top floors cost Anton in rent I couldn't even guess. Heck, it wouldn't surprise me to hear that Hunt owned the whole building.

I turned and glanced at the security officer's desk. Yep, she had a log that all visitors had to sign, then the officer on duty called upstairs to see if the visitor was expected before he or she was granted access to the elevators, a typical New York setup. She was staring at me as if she were memorizing my handsome visage. I flashed a smile at her, she didn't smile back, and I went out the way I had come in.

The next morning at seven, while I was still half asleep, the encrypted telephone on the dresser buzzed. I staggered over to it. Sarah.

"You're up early."

"Sleeping in again, eh?"

"Yeah. I love these mini-vacations. Whatcha got?"

"The bullets from the I-95 guys don't match the ElectTech bullets or anything else in the FBI's archives. Guns are clean."

Wonderful. This meant there were shooters out there we hadn't yet seen. Am I lucky or what?

"And this suicide, Harry Tanaka. He had a PhD in political science. Wrote scholarly articles about voting statistics. Married. One kid who is apparently developmentally disabled. Lives in a facility."

"Uh-huh."

"Got his doctorate from the University of Chicago."

"Why was he working for Red Truck?"

"They obviously made him an offer he couldn't refuse. Probably money. Some people like to have some. Maybe he found he couldn't swing the private facility for his daughter on a college professor's salary."

I couldn't imagine why anyone would want a poli-sci PhD around except to teach. "Did he ever teach?"

"Yep." She named two colleges. One of them was in Indiana, and the other was Morehead State in eastern Kentucky, where my hero Phil Simms played football.

"Tell me about some of his articles."

She did so, for several minutes. She had actually read them online. You never know what people will find interesting.

"Got an address for the widow?"

At ten that morning I was parked outside the Tanaka house on a quiet, tree-lined street in East Orange. Tanaka obviously didn't make the money that Schlemmer and Liszt knocked down at Red Truck, or if he did, he wasn't squandering it on a mortgage. The house was a middle-class one-story with three bedrooms, two-and-a-half baths, a basement, and a two-car garage where Dr. Tanaka had hanged himself. No one seemed to be watching the place. A car was in the driveway, so maybe the widow was home.

I adjusted my sports coat and tie and walked

up the sidewalk to the stoop carrying my government-issue attaché case. The doorbell chimed four times before I heard footsteps.

Mrs. April Tanaka was petite, pretty, and of Japanese ancestry.

"Yes."

"Mrs. Tanaka?"

"Yes."

"I'm James Wilson with the Federal Election Commission." I passed my card through the crack in the door and she looked at it. "We're interested in some of your late husband's work. I wonder if I might have a moment of your time?"

She pulled the door open. "Come in."

We sat in the living room. "Your husband wrote a very insightful article for *The Atlantic* last year. Do his notes for that piece still exist?"

She frowned. "Yes, I suppose, but he foot-noted thoroughly."

"Indeed he did. Still, my boss asked me to drop by to see if he had any more statistics and possibly spreadsheets that he didn't use in his article. We'd like to look at them and if they are what we want, copy them for our use—with your permission, of course, and with attribution, and you would be paid for providing the material."

She looked drawn. I felt like a jerk. "He had so much research material," she said. "All he wanted to do in life was try to discover patterns of voting that would help him understand the

155

social and economic factors that caused people to vote the way they do."

I nodded encouragingly.

"He found politics fascinating."

"Did you share his interest?"

"No. I think politics is a blood sport played for money and power. I think it vile."

"Well . . ." I said.

"But he would have wanted you to see his research. He thought it important." She rose. "His office is this way."

Actually the office was the third bedroom with a desk, a couple of chairs, and a big filing cabinet. A desktop computer, printer, and lamp sat on the desk. The window looked into a little side-yard where the garbage cans rested. The view was of the wall of the house next door, which had its bedroom window shade drawn. I suspected it was never raised.

I decided to get personal. "Did you have any inkling he was so depressed that he might take his own life?"

"I knew he was depressed about the election results. I never dreamed that he was suicidal."

"So he was surprised that Cynthia Hinton lost?"

"Let's just say it was not the result he expected. He didn't like either of the candidates."

"You have my sympathy, Mrs. Tanaka. His death must have been a shock."

She swallowed several times and made a

gesture with her hand that took in the room. "Look at anything you wish." She left, leaving the door open.

The computer was tempting, yet undoubtedly password protected. If it were online Sarah could probably hack in. I lacked her skills and patience. I tackled the filing cabinets.

The second drawer turned out to be a treasure trove. Spreadsheets on every county in the nation, voting statistics for the last four presidential elections, charts of how the vote swayed between the parties, and a series of spreadsheets on the most volatile counties in swing states. What it all meant I didn't know.

The bottom drawer had more nuggets, including spreadsheets that calculated how much of a vote swing in the key volatile counties would be required to swing the state. As I sat at the desk studying this stuff, I was impressed with how small the percentages of change had to be. Miniscule, I thought. And that had been Harry Tanaka's essential insight too. In a society as divided as our own, elections are determined by a few uncommitted souls.

The printouts were stapled together. On the top of the first one in the upper corner was one word: Armageddon. The final battle between good and evil—was that really Hinton versus Conyer? Maybe he thought so, if he committed suicide over it. The big question was: had Harry Tanaka sold his research to Red Truck? Had it percolated down to Junior Sikes at ElectTech?

I decided I didn't need the printouts. What I needed, if it existed, was the master computer program that incorporated all this data to show which counties had to swing how far to win an election. That wouldn't necessarily prove anything, but it was something.

I suspected that if the program existed, it wasn't here; it was on a computer at Red Truck, or more likely on a computer at the bottom of the Hudson River. But just to cover all the bases, I flipped on Tanaka's computer. If it was on, Sarah could make it do amazing things.

I opened the desk drawers, starting with the top one under the computer. Pencils, pens, paper clips, a half-empty box of staples, some thumb drives still in their packaging, a fingernail clipper, an eraser. I went on to the others and found household files about checking accounts; their daughter—her name was Ruth—had a half-dozen files.

After a glance at the door and a careful listen to see if Mrs. Tanaka was coming back or lurking in the hallway, I dug into the daughter's files. Dozens of evaluations by development experts, psychologists, even two psychiatrists. She had seen one psychiatrist eight times throughout the years.

There had to be a thumb drive, but where was it?

The desktop was sitting there, waiting. What was his access code?

On a hunch I typed in RuthTanaka and hit enter. Nothing.

There was a telephone, a landline, there on the desk. Checking the letters under the numbers, I typed in 2762433366, the numbers for Armageddon. Hit enter. Nope.

I tried the numbers for RuthTanaka, 7884826252. Hit enter.

Bingo. I was in.

Now I needed a file. Typed in Ruth Tanaka. I got a file, all right, but it was a correspondence about money. He still owed the facility where she was housed more than fifty grand.

I got out of that and sat there thinking. Well, why not? I typed in Armageddon.

And there it was. The file was so big it took about fifteen seconds to load. It was a spreadsheet containing counties with plus or minus numbers after each entry, which I knew were voting totals from the 2008 and 2012 elections.

I got a blank thumb drive from the drawer, stripped off the packaging, plugged it into a USB port, and copied the file.

If Harry Tanaka made a copy of the file on a thumb drive that still existed, I suspected it was in the office where he worked for Red Truck.

As the computer did its thing, I wondered what the weasels at the top of the chain were worried about. Certainly not hard evidence because there probably wasn't any. No prosecutor could get over the hurdle of proving a crime had been committed without proof of rigged voting machines. People who did the dirty work ratting them out? No. That wouldn't be enough to get guilty verdicts in any court in the land. Even with the computer program that set out the votes they wanted and presumably got, without proof that the voting machines had been rigged, no prosecutor would have a case. And if the machines were wiped, as most of them already were, it was case closed.

They had to be afraid of a scandal. Of suspicion.

I ejected the thumb drive, left the computer on, and made sure I had everything put back together. Mrs. Tanaka was seated in the living room with her knees together and her back straight as a rod.

I sat down to visit. "I found what I wanted, Mrs. Tanaka."

She merely nodded.

I looked around again at the room that she and her husband Harry had shared. It was a nice room, a comfortable room, where they helped each other with the tragedy of their daughter. The furniture wasn't new; it had undoubtedly come with them from Kentucky. I broke the silence by saying, "Your daughter . . . Ruth . . . she was the reason your husband resigned his professorship at Morehead State and went to work for Anton Hunt."

It wasn't a question, but she swallowed several times then said, "Ruth's care . . . he paid our moving expenses and the cost of transferring Ruth to her new home. Doubled Harry's salary."

"Why did Hunt need a political science scholar?"

"He told Harry that there was a lot of money to be made if he knew for certain ahead of time how elections would turn out. He wanted Harry to make predictions."

"But when I arrived a while ago you said the result was a surprise to Harry."

"It wasn't the result he predicted."

"He wasn't the only one," I said, a comment that I instantly realized wasn't very tactful. After all, Harry Tanaka had been an expert employed to predict results.

She merely blinked.

"Did you watch the election returns here?"

"Of course."

"What did he say as the states turned red?"

He had his laptop open and was constantly checking the results county by county. He couldn't believe what he was seeing."

"Did he explain?"

"No. He was just stunned. I was frightened and wondered if the results would affect his job with Mr. Hunt."

"But he worked for Red Truck."

"Same thing."

"Did he say anything about his job being in jeopardy in the weeks that followed?"

She merely shook her head. If he had commented, she wasn't going to share it.

I stood, thanked Mrs. Tanaka, and told her that if my boss wanted copies of anything I found, I would be in touch. I didn't tell her I had copied a file from his computer and stolen a thumb drive. So I am a liar and a thief—no news there. On the other hand, if Grafton thought the thumb drive had information that pointed to Anton Hunt, he was going to pay for it.

I walked out scanning the neighborhood for watchers. In my car I used the encrypted phone to call Sarah. If April Tanaka had called someone on a cell phone, I hadn't heard her; but that didn't mean she hadn't done it. I told Sarah about the thumb drive and that Harry Tanaka's computer was on. I gave her his password and the file name.

"You figured that out all by yourself?"

"I have hidden talents."

"You're just damned lucky."

"In my line of work it is better to be lucky than good," I said. "You'll live longer."

As I drove away with the Armageddon thumb drive in my pocket I would have bet every cent I had that Harry Tanaka's death wasn't suicide. The man had too much to live for.

Reem Kiddus had an office just down the hall from the Oval Office. He had three telephones on his desk and lights blinked on all of them. He shook Jake Grafton's hand, showed him a chair, and then closed the door.

"Thanks for coming over. You wanted a name."

Jake nodded.

"Bill Farnem."

"Who is he?"

"The Number Three man at the FBI. He's still there."

"What did he tell you?"

"That the FBI had learned that some of the voting machines in key counties were rigged to favor Conyer."

"When?"

"Two weeks before the election."

"Why did he tell you this?"

"He and I went to school together. We were fraternity brothers. We talk from time to time, and I was up to my armpits in the election. Sometimes the pressure is so intense you need to hear from real friends—you know, the ones who will be friends regardless of politics or elections. During the campaign I got some Sundays off to recharge my batteries. I would call friends and we'd catch up on wives and kids and careers and hobbies. I needed contacts in the real world occasionally. Still do."

"And Farnem is one of those people you called?"

"Yeah. A career FBI guy."

"Looking back, do you think he wanted to score points with you in case Conyer won and needed a new FBI director?"

Kiddus glared.

"A simple yes or no will do," Grafton said softly.

"How the fuck can I answer that? He said what he said. I don't know why he said it."

"So what did you do with that information?"

"Not a goddamn thing. What the hell could I do?"

"I haven't the faintest," Grafton replied, his voice so low that Kiddus almost missed the remark.

"Our private polls said Conyer was doing well," Kiddus continued, "had unexpected strength. The networks and newspapers had polls they published every night that showed Hinton three or four points ahead. Vaughn Conyer didn't believe them, and I didn't either. We thought the liberal media was flat-out lying. We were confident. He was attracting huge crowds to his rallies. Hinton was having trouble filling little venues; her staff and the networks were photo-shopping her crowds to make them look bigger. Her VP candidate had to cancel appearances because no one was coming to hear his shit. We thought the jobs and immigration issues were resonating with the voters. Hinton was damaged goods, with enough baggage to fill a Boeing. We thought the politicians underestimated how fed up the voters were with the Hintons, what a shrew they thought she was. She had the charisma of a snake. We were confident. We were in the race with a good chance."

"Uh-huh. What was the context of Farnem's comment?"

"You mean, why did he say that? Fuck, I can't remember. It was a couple weeks before the election, maybe three or four. We were just schmoozing."

Kiddus slapped his hand upon his desk. "Look, I knew we hadn't rigged those machines. And we were hearing bad things from all over. Not about rigged machines, but about illegals voting and Democrats planning to vote the graveyards and prison rolls. California, New York, and the big cities were going to go heavily Democratic—they always do. We knew that. We had to get the rest of the country. That was it in a nutshell. If I let myself get distracted . . . anyway, you asked and deserve an answer. So there it is. Bill Farnem. Number three at the FBI."

"Okay."

Jake stood and shook down his trousers. He stuck out his hand. "Thanks."

"Don't tell Bill I gave you his name."

"I won't. Probably won't ever talk to him. But at this point, who can say?"

Reem Kiddus shook hands and Jake left.

When he arrived back at the CIA's Langley facility, Jake Grafton went straight to Sarah Houston's office. He knocked and was admitted. He carefully closed the door behind him and sat down across the desk from her in the only extra chair, which was sited at a spot that allowed him to see her through her bank of monitors.

"Did you ever hear of an FBI senior officer named Bill Farnem? A career guy."

"No."

"I hear he's number three in line over there. Using just these computers, not the NSA capabilities, what could you find out about him?"

"Does he have Wi-Fi at home?"

Jake shrugged.

"If he does and does his banking online, I can find out everything about him worth knowing, except how often he showers. If his spouse or live-in significant other uses the same Wi-Fi, maybe even that."

"I want to know if there is a link between Farnem and Anton Hunt. Money, cousins, investment advice, same club, mutual friends, telephone calls, whatever you can find."

"You've put a lot on my plate these last few

weeks, admiral, and Tommy keeps calling wanting more than I can give him. There are only so many hours in a day. I could use some help."

Jake hesitated, then moved his head about an inch from side to side.

"Our people are trustworthy," Sarah said, inclining her head toward him as her eyebrows moved a quarter-inch closer together.

"If someone even whispers that the CIA is investigating the FBI, a volcano will go off under this building," he said. "The risk is too great. Some people will see it as salacious gossip, not classified information. People are people. Do what you can and we'll live with that."

"Aren't you worried about me?"

"I trust you and Tommy with my life. You two would go to your graves without telling anyone anything. There aren't many people I can say that about."

The admiral stood, opened the door, and started out.

"As you can see, I could use a slightly larger space," Sarah fired at his back.

He turned, grinning, moved his head from side to side, scanning the small room and crowded desk as if they were a soundstage. The grin stayed in place. "I'll see what I can do."

The next time she talked to Tommy on an

encrypted telephone, she told him, "The admiral is trying to get me a bigger office."

Tommy said, "The hell with the office. You should have hit him up for a raise."

"Don't you ever think about anything but money?"

"Yeah. Sex."

Spring had arrived in New York and so had rain. It fell steadily from a gloomy sky. The weatherman on television said it was going to last for several days. Flood warnings were issued for New England.

We used the rainy days to make a plan and worry over what-if scenarios.

Sarah was sending me data on Hunt and his investment empire via encrypted emails, a veritable torrent of information. I had to read all of it to see if there were nuggets in there that my team needed to be aware of. And found some. There were breakouts of all the top people, how long they had been there, their responsibilities, salaries and bonuses, families, etc. The hedge fund business was a wonderful way to corral jack. If the spook business went south, maybe I could start one of my own.

We had obtained aerial photographs of Hunt's buildings and had blown them up so we could tape them to a wall for examination and study. The top of his aerie, a penthouse floor with a balcony, contained a small garden full of evergreens and perennials. Joe Casillas was something of a gardener and studied the blow-up with a magnifying glass. He identified most of the plants. I wasn't sure that info would help, but thanked him anyway.

More to the point, on top of the penthouse was a helicopter pad with a windsock on one corner. There, I thought, was a way in. Maybe.

We used the magnifying glass to see if we could see any evidence of surveillance equipment or alarms. The cameras were tiny, but they were definitely there.

"Can we wipe out the cameras with lasers?"

"Probably, if we can find a suitable place for the lasers." That led us to examine surrounding buildings, several of which were actually taller than Hunt's.

"What about an e-grenade to knock out their electronics?" An e-grenade was an EMP device. The explosive force was converted into one strong electro-magnetic pulse that would overload any adjacent wires with energy and blow circuit breakers and fuses, knocking out the circuits and the equipment that they powered.

"Only as a last resort. I would like to get in and out without them knowing I was there."

We examined photos of the loading dock in the basement under the building. We had gone in there with a federal police car and filmed everything we could see, then left. Police cars can go anywhere. The security cameras were there all right, four of them.

"Does the building have a back-up generator?"

Three generators, it turned out. So a power surge or failure in the neighborhood would trip the relays to turn them on.

"Can we get into the building from the sewers or storm drains?"

That question sent two of our guys into the sewers for several days as the rain fell. They came back with plans of the building. "A subway runs under the street in front. The tunnel that contains the utilities can be reached from an access door in the side of the subway tunnel. We might have to enlarge the entrance somewhat, but it looks like a way in."

So I put on my jeans and ratty tennis shoes and went to see for myself. Whatever stories you've heard about the rats in the tunnels under the city are all true. "This is like the *Tunnels of Cu Chi*," Travis said, swearing. "Man, those guys had balls."

Wearing miner's headlamps, Travis, Armanti, and I made the journey to the utilities entrance. It was merely boarded up with two-by-fours and plywood around massive pipes, power cables, and telephone cables. Yes, this was my way in. I figured that I could climb an elevator shaft to the top of the building, spend the night inside doing my nasty little thing, then exit the same way.

At least it was a plan.

Hunt was a man who carefully guarded his secrets. "Maybe they just have armed guards in the offices at night," someone mused.

"Has anyone seen uniformed, armed guards entering the building at night and leaving in the morning?"

No one had. But my watchers had some plain-clothes candidates. I looked at the photos and began to fret. Several of these guys were fit and trim and wore sports coats that looked as if they might cover weapons. Short, military-type haircuts.

Plainly, we needed to do more watching. "These guys or any others like them. When they enter, when they leave."

I suspected the hedge fund offices were rigged with state-of-the-art cameras. If people were in there day and night there wouldn't be lasers or motion detectors. "Where is the office security system monitored? Where are the wires?"

"They are undoubtedly fiber-optic," someone said.

"They needed a permit from the city when they were installed."

While we were researching the answers to those questions I made another call to the equipment department in Langley; we took delivery via FedEx.

If the city had issued a permit for a private

security system, it wasn't in their files. My guys looked at every building permit issued on that building from Day One. It wasn't there. So if there was a private security system it was monitored on the premises. They should have gotten a permit, but if they kept the whole installation in-house, they could have gotten away without one.

We went back to watching the people going in and out of the building. We ended up with eight possible security candidates, who entered the building within minutes of each other and stayed for eight hours. Two were on from eight to four, and two were on from four to midnight, and then two were on from midnight to eight. The other two rotated shifts, we thought.

I was there one evening in front of the building to watch the changing of the guard at midnight. Two guys went in within three minutes of each other, signed in at the desk before midnight, and were lifted. At a quarter past, two guys came down in the elevator, signed out, and walked out of the building together, then went their separate ways.

"They could be the night shift at another office," Travis Clay mused. I looked at the photos again. Ex-military or police was my guess.

"I'm assuming they are in the suite on top," I told him.

"When that elevator starts up, they'll be ready for you to pop out of it."

"Maybe I can fix that."

"We may be looking at the ElectTech shooters," Armanti Hall objected. "Trying to sneak in there is nuts, Tommy. It ain't worth it, dude."

I made a call to Langley and caught a plane to Washington the next morning. First I went to pick up a black box that Sarah and her tech wizards had set aside for me—something that would help her tap into Anton Hunt's server, if I could make my way into the building. Then I went to see the head tech guy, an engineer with a PhD in physics who was wasting his talents in the CIA. He should have been building Eiffel Towers or Mars spaceships. His name was Jerry Graham.

"I need a colorless, odorless gas," I said, "that will put people to sleep for at least four hours and naturally dissipate so it can't be detected six or seven hours later."

"How big a space are you going to fumigate?"

"The plans say two floors of ninety-five hundred square feet, and one of three thousand."

Jerry pursed his lips and stared into my handsome brown eyes. "We have just the thing. Classified, of course. Dissipates within thirty minutes. If anyone gets a good whiff they're going to sleep for a while. How do you intend to induce it?"

"I thought maybe the HVAC system. The top three floors of an office building are a suite that has its own HVAC system. The units are on the roof."

"Okay . . . and how are you going to get the magic stuff into the HVAC system?"

"Use a helicopter to carry in a new one with the sleeping gas installed and haul the old one out."

"And the technicians?"

"Go in and out on the chopper."

Graham's brow wrinkled all the way up to where his hairline used to be. "You can get authorization for all of this?"

"Jerry, Jerry, Jerry. Do you really think I want to get you mixed up in my private burglary business? You'd demand a cut, yet there's barely enough profit to fund my Caribbean island, yacht, and girlfriends. Today's request is for a nefarious secret company project."

"Is there any other kind?"

"You write it up, and I'll go get the admiral to scribble his name on it."

"Okay."

"Oh, and I'll need some uniformed HVAC technicians to twist wrenches and all of that. Plus, of course, a helicopter with pilots."

"Where is this building? Moscow?"

"Pyongyang."

He sighed. "You know, when you tell out-rageous lies, not a muscle in your face twitches."

"If you'll invite me over to your house for

another evening of poker, I'll give you another lesson."

"I lost a hundred twenty-seven bucks during my first lesson. I don't need another."

"Actually, it's Manhattan."

He sighed again.

"Start writing. I'm in a hurry. They're moving the diamonds in two days."

By three o'clock we had the details ironed out, and at a quarter to four Jake Grafton signed the authorization and assigned a project number to keep the bean counters happy.

"Do you really need to install a new HVAC unit?" the admiral asked before he scrawled his name.

"If building maintenance or Hunt's people check up on us, there had better be a new unit on the roof to mollify them while they hunt for paperwork. By then we'll have squeezed 'em dry."

Grafton sighed too, just like Jerry Graham, and signed the thing.

"Maybe we can use the old unit here at Langley," I suggested. That's how frugal I am. Waste not, want not.

I caught the five o'clock plane back to New York at Reagan National with five minutes to spare.

CHAPTER NINE

The HVAC guys were ready on Friday afternoon. We loaded the helicopter at "an undisclosed secret location" and slung the new HVAC unit under the helo. There wasn't room for the whirly bird on the roof, so the guys would have to rappel down. They were going to arrive a bit after five o'clock.

"Relax, Tommy," the head HVAC pro said. "All these units are delivered by air. It's normal operating procedure."

"Right. But do the technicians usually arrive like SWAT team guys?"

"Ah, no," he admitted. "We're usually waiting on the roof, elevated by Otis."

"Oh, well."

I watched them chopper off into the New York haze then walked around chewing gum and fretting. I wanted to get in, open Hunt's system to Sarah with no one the wiser. If I failed I would have to answer to Grafton, and Sarah. I didn't want to be caught in Hunt's aerie, or for him to even suspect I had been in his headquarters where he plotted chaos to make serious bucks shorting currency, commodities, stocks, or bonds. Millions. Hundreds of millions. Billions. If ever there was a man who wanted to mine the silver

176

lining in every black cloud, Anton Hunt was his name. If a black cloud wasn't looming on the horizon, he worked hard to create one. A man for our times.

On the other hand, what if I were caught up there? They would probably initially think that I was a finance spy, out to learn where Hunt was putting his money. Actually, one suspected that was Hunt's biggest fear. Moneymen think life is all about the bucks. He probably had security in there since he moved into that office nine years ago. On the other hand, after they figured out what the black box was for, I was going to be in big trouble. Nine dead so far. Hunt wouldn't hesitate to make me Number Ten. If I got cornered up there, I was going to have to shoot my way out.

It was getting dark when the helicopter came back with an HVAC unit swinging under it. The pilot deposited his load on their trailer with me guiding him, then set down beside it. As the rotors wound down, the technicians exited the machine and came over to me. One of them lit a cigarette.

"No problem, Tommy. No one paid the least bit of attention to us."

"Great."

"Anytime, fella. Anytime."

Ten minutes later they had their tools and gear stowed in their van, the HVAC unit tied down, and were on their way back to Washington. The helo was long gone.

I went back to our hotel and arrived in time to accompany the guys to dinner at an Italian restaurant. Say what you will, if you want real Italian, there is no place like New York. Forget Roma, Napoli, Milano, or Palermo. All the real Italian chefs are in New York.

On Sunday we were as ready as we would ever be. We had discussed every contingency we could think of and had plans. Armanti Hall and I made our way through the tunnel to the utilities entrance and attacked the two-by-fours and plywood with crowbars. We made enough noise to wake the nearly dead, but no one showed up to investigate. Took three minutes, and then I was into the basement of the building, under the parking garage. Conduits carrying fiber-optic and telephone wires lined the walls.

I found the elevator shaft and used my picks on the padlock. Once inside, I stood looking up. There was a ladder between the shafts, and I was going to have to climb it unless I could hitch a ride on an elevator upward bound. I climbed the ladder to the second floor and waited. I had all day and all evening to get there, and fifty stories was a heck of a climb.

Just when I had about given up hope, I heard doors closing on the second elevator in the shaft.

I monkeyed over and got on the roof. They stopped at the tenth floor.

Well, yeah, Tommy. You're in the wrong damn shaft.

Not a good start to my adventure.

I waited and rode the same elevator down ten minutes later and changed shafts.

Eventually I got to the thirty-fifth floor, I think, and moved over to the shaft that went to the penthouse and started climbing. I was tired of waiting for the Sunday afternoon crowd. The shaft was lit with dim safety lights every few stories, and I was wearing a miner's headlamp, so I could easily see where I was and where to go next, yet the empty shafts loomed beside me. It was a long way down from here and a good long way to the top.

There was, of course, a stairwell to allow emergency egress of the building right beside the elevator shafts, but I wanted nothing to do with the stairwell. It was probably festooned with sensors that would betray the presence of anyone in there. And the doors to the penthouse floors were one-way, to prevent guys like me from gaining entry. Even if I could have defeated the sensors, I would have needed a blowtorch to open one of the doors.

I wore a backpack. I hoped I wouldn't need most of this stuff, but since I didn't want to come back again—couldn't unless we changed out another HVAC unit—I had to be ready for whatever might happen.

The door openings all had the floor number painted above them, so it was no mystery where I was. I was near the top of the proper shaft when I saw the number "54" above the door. I climbed up one more story and sat down to rest. The top of the shaft, filled with machinery, was only five feet or so above me. I leaned over the edge and looked down. The little safety lights let me see all the way down, all the way . . . down . . . It made me kinda dizzy looking down, so I gave that up and sat back to wait. It was only six in the evening. The gas bottle inside the HVAC unit was on a timer and would be released into the air circulation system at one in the morning.

Last night as I lay in bed trying to get to sleep, I tried to recall how many embassies I had broken into without being discovered. Eight, as I recalled. And fifteen foreign government offices. And I had only been caught once, which is an adventure I will save for my autobiography, if I ever write one.

As the evening progressed I thought about April Tanaka and Harry. About their daughter Ruth. And about Heiki Schlemmer. Where did Heiki come into the picture? Did she help Harry figure out how to ensure Cynthia Hinton won? And if so, why did Hinton lose? Two ways to figure that:

Harry screwed up, or someone doubled-crossed him.

I liked the double-cross idea. Treachery can be very profitable if you can pull it off. I recalled that Anton Hunt lost a billion dollars in the aftermath of the election. Even for a big cheese like Anton Hunt, a billion bucks is a billion bucks, and its loss must have stung him. Did he order Harry Tanaka killed?

I strongly suspected that he might have. This was a guy who joined Hitler's SS as a teenager. Not just anyone could get into the SS, the *Schutzstaffel*, or in English, Protection Squadron. To get in you had to be a fanatic. Led by Heinrich Himmler, they were the Nazis' personal bodyguards, ran the death camps, and even had their own parallel army, complete with tanks, artillery, and all the rest of it.

Which led me to contemplating the similarities between the so-called progressive Left of today and the World War II fascists. Both hated free speech for anyone except themselves and believed that democratic elections were the tool of fools. Any opinion that they didn't agree with was labeled *verboten*, prohibited, and must be silenced by social stricture, intimidation, or, if necessary, force. I decided a leap from the SS to the progressive Left wouldn't be difficult for a fanatic like Hunt. More like a baby step.

I checked my watch for the hundredth time and

turned off my headlamp to save the battery. The two shafts here at the top of the building were lit by tiny night lights that led off like a string of pearls into the gloom below. This being Sunday evening, the elevators only moved occasionally.

My mind wandered back to Heiki Schlemmer. And who the hell was Edwin P. Riddenhour? He was a man who didn't exist who worked for American Voting Incorporated, which didn't exist, yet kept popping into and out of county clerks' offices. How many offices? Where?

Man, we would need an army of investigators to answer all these questions. Or the FBI. We had neither.

Thinking about the FBI got me onto the subject of who put the beacon in my car in Pennsylvania when I was there with the Election Fraud Task Force, after the ElectTech folks were popped. I drove there from Washington, spent less than forty-eight hours in town, and came home with a beacon. Who was it that wanted to keep tabs on me? Why me?

The only possible answer was that I was with the CIA, and only the members of the task force would have known that. Had someone put beacons on the FBI cars? No way to know that without asking . . . maybe I should ask Maggie Jewel Miller, the special agent in charge. She would know. Or she wouldn't. The agents were all driving government sedans from a motor pool. I was the only one there driving my own ride. But why me? Of all the people there from the task force, I was the only one with another master. I sat noodling that revelation as the hands of my watch crawled toward midnight.

Finally nature called. I stood up, unzipped, took it out, and let my golden stream flow into the abyss. I hoped Anton Hunt owned this building.

The elevator going down the shaft alerted me. The elevators weren't particularly noisy, but the wire ropes hummed and the huge counterweights disturbed the air. The big box fell into the gloom, causing the shaft safety lights to blink as it passed on its journey down.

Finally it reached bottom, and then it was rising and the counterweight fell away. The journey upward seemed quick. I didn't time it, but it couldn't have taken more than a minute for the elevator to reach the penthouse, slow, then coast to a stop without a jolt on the top floor. I heard the door open then close. Two minutes later it started down again.

At twelve-fifteen, the elevator started down with its last load. This would be the off-going security dudes, I hoped. The elevator stayed at the bottom of the shaft.

I settled back to wait.

One o'clock came and went. The gas should be released by now. Fifteen minutes should be enough. I rooted in my backpack and got the gas mask out, checked it, and put it on. Made sure I had a good air seal. Rearranged my miner's light upon my brow. Sat there in the gloom breathing softly and waiting. I must have looked like the creature from the black lagoon. Put on latex gloves so that I'd leave no fingerprints.

At twenty after one, I worked my way around the shaft to the ladder beside the door to the floor. I reached up and tried to trip the switch that the elevator activated when it arrived, enabling the doors to open. The arm of the thing seemed frozen.

I got out my Kimber and pushed hard on it. No luck. Finally I hauled off and smacked it as hard as I could. The arm moved to the up position.

The door opened slowly and the interior lights of the floor filled the shaft.

There was no way to tell if anyone was waiting on me.

No guts, no glory.

I swung myself over and stepped through the opening while the empty shaft yawned below me. The floor looked empty. I found that I had the Kimber in my hand. Sure enough, I saw a security camera looking at the elevator door.

I went exploring. Found the guards in an office with a computer and five monitors mounted on the wall. The men were asleep. A black guy and a white guy, short haircuts, obviously fit, in their thirties. I recognized both of them from the photos I had studied. The monitors displayed video from various security cameras throughout the complex, cycling between cameras.

I patted them down. Yep, they were armed. I thought about taking the weapons in case they woke up with me in the penthouse but decided against it.

The only way to ensure they didn't find me on a computer video tomorrow morning was to disable the equipment. I got busy on that. Playing with the computer, I went back to 1:00 a.m. and erased everything after that. Then I shut the computer down so it would cease recording.

I kept looking. The place reeked of serious jack, with original art on the walls, plush wall-to-wall carpet, some sort of textured treatment on the walls, and subdued lighting from suspended lights. The chairs looked comfy and opulent.

Just for kicks and grins I went into the executive suite and took a look around. Hunt's office was undoubtedly the corner office. I looked the place over carefully. He didn't have conventional doors on his office. They were open and looked like wood, but beyond them I could just see slots that looked as if they housed elevator doors. I knew what they were: steel doors that would close automatically if an intruder was detected. That meant there were sensors, and I used my eyes. No doubt he had heat-sensitive and motion sensors in that office.

I turned my goggles to infrared then blue light. I could see laser beams wandering around. I watched. They were moving randomly. So going into Hunt's office for a quick search was out of the question tonight. I left it and went back down the corridors.

The computers in various offices I ducked into were on but password protected. They were all hard-wired into a server. I found the server in a closet that was also used to store office supplies.

Okay.

I took a small box out of my backpack and placed it beside the server. Plugged the power cord into a nearby jack. Connected the two with a USB cable. Then I unplugged the server. After about a minute, I plugged it in again. It would reboot and work through its program, and the black box would capture its secrets, or so Sarah and the wizards assured me. All I had to do was return the black box to them.

I waited eight minutes. That was three more than the wizards said was necessary, but I didn't want to come back to do this again.

Just as I was packing the box back in my backpack, I heard a helicopter. I glanced at my watch. The gas was released forty-two minutes ago, so I should be safe. I whipped off the gas mask, took a sniff anyway to see if I was going to pass out. Thankfully I didn't, and added the mask and filter to the backpack.

I ran back to the little security office and tried on a sports coat that was hanging on the rack. Too small. The second one was even smaller. Oh well. Left the backpack there on the floor.

Stripping my gloves and stuffing them into my pocket, I hotfooted it up to the top floor and was just in time to see the chopper lifting off and the door opening. A woman stood there.

"ID please," I said curtly.

She produced a laminated Red Truck ID, complete with her photo. Heiki Schlemmer.

So this was the woman herself! She was in her late thirties or early forties, of medium height with short dark hair and black eyes. Her mouth didn't seem to have any lips. Her clothes didn't come from Wal-Mart and looked rather trendy, especially for this early on a Monday morning.

She was eyeing the Kimber in my shoulder holster as I handed the ID back. "Thank you, Ms. Schlemmer." I moved aside and ensured the exterior door was firmly closed and latched. "Good morning."

"Umpf," she said, and marched away along the hallway. I stood there with bated breath, hoping she wouldn't head for the hallway that led to the open door to the elevator shaft. She didn't. She disappeared down the interior stairwell.

I tiptoed along behind her. This was the woman

who had arranged for Bob the security guy to bug Sarah Houston's apartment, probably because of me. Did she know what I looked like? I hadn't seen a glimmer of recognition when she laid eyes on me, but . . .

What was she here for at—I looked at my watch—one forty-three on Monday morning? What was so hot she couldn't wait until business hours? I stood at the top of the circular interior staircase mulling it. Was she on the phone with one of her thugs right now?

I went down the staircase and walked along the hall, listening for her voice. The deep carpet muffled my footsteps. Halfway down the right-hand hallway I heard a clicking. She was pounding a keyboard. The next office down. The door was open.

Should I get while the getting was good or should I wait to see if she left in a little while? She wouldn't take the helo that had delivered her—it was gone. She would depart in an elevator, probably the one on this floor.

I was torn. This broad was in this mess to the roots of her black hair, which had looked dyed. Probably to hide some premature graying. I would have loved to sweat her, but that would have blown the op and probably get me arrested. Perhaps wait until she left, if she did, then turn her office inside out.

No.

Let Sarah do her thing on Heiki's computer. Maybe Sarah would find the Armageddon file. Or something equally interesting.

I went back upstairs to the security office, made sure the boys were sound asleep, put on my gloves and backpack, and ran up to the top floor to scrub the door handle to the helo pad with my shirt tail. I didn't think I had touched anything else barehanded. Except Schlemmer's ID card. Well, she would overlay them with her own prints or life would scrub them off soon. Nothing I could do about it anyway.

I hotfooted it to the open elevator door. Carefully I grasped the ladder around the corner and eased my way out onto it. After I triggered the exterior latch, the door eased closed silently. Luxuriously. After all, this was Hunt's aerie.

It was a long way down that ladder, so I started down quickly, making sure I didn't fall. If Heiki Schlemmer found the security guards asleep and didn't find me, she might call the gal at the lobby desk, who might have someone waiting at the bottom of this shaft. Unless I leaped off the building, this was the only way down.

So I got after it. All in all, I felt pretty good about my night's work. The guards would wake up before sunrise and would be groggy and confused. Would they give an alarm? I doubted it. Would they look at the computer video to see who had been in the penthouse? Probably, but the thing would be off.

Human nature being what it is, I would bet money that the powers that be would never hear a peep from the guards, who would lose their jobs if they opened their mouths. Maybe they would decide they just fell asleep.

Down, down, down that ladder. The latex gloves wore out so I took the shards off and pocketed them. My hands got filthy and sweaty from the dirty ladder rungs. James Bond never had to work this hard.

I was pretty tired by the time I hit bottom. With my feet once more on concrete I opened the door to the shafts a crack and surveyed the dark premises. Very little light in that basement. Stepped out and glimpsed a man waiting just around the corner with a pistol in his hand.

As I went for my piece I saw that it was Armanti Hall. He lowered his pistol and said, "It took you long enough."

"Yeah. Good morning to you too. Let's get the hell outta here."

I caught the 6:00 a.m. Acela Express train to Washington from Penn Station. Flying would have taken less travel time and puffed up my ego, but I didn't want anyone x-raying my box. I rode with the backpack containing it on the floor at my feet. Drifted off to sleep a couple of times, only to wake up at Philadelphia and Wilmington, then drifted back off.

I arrived at Union Station before nine, took a cab to Langley and went straight to Sarah's office. She gave me a quick grin and took the box. Plugged it into a power source, connected the box to her computer via a USB wire, and settled in. I went to sleep in her chair.

I awoke a couple hours later and found Sarah was still there staring at a monitor and manipulating a mouse. It was a few minutes after noon. I let myself out, found a restroom, and went to the cafeteria level for coffee and a sub. I also bought a coffee for Sarah.

"Are you ready for some information?" she asked, staring at me between her monitors.

"Always."

"The reported election results in key counties in swing states have no correlation to Harry Tanaka's Armageddon file."

I stared at her.

"I compared his numbers to actual results yesterday, and there is no correlation."

"You mean the election wasn't fixed?"

"No. I am stating that there is no statistically significant correlation between the Armageddon file and the actual reported results."

I leaned back in my chair to think about that.

Finally I said, "So they didn't use Tanaka's numbers."

"They didn't. I think his numbers were altered to make Conyer win the election."

"Proof?"

"I have none." She gestured to the monitor. "The Armageddon file as Harry Tanaka wrote it is on Heiki Schlemmer's computer at the hedge fund. She had an office there too, as you know. The file matches the file on the thumb drive you gave me, and on Tanaka's computer at home. But actual results don't correlate."

I couldn't stay in the chair. I stood and stretched my arms. Finally I did the smart thing: I asked Sarah what she thought.

"Someone rigged the tally machines with new numbers." She handed me a legal pad. "These are the numbers we found on the rigged machines in Virginia. They don't match Tanaka's numbers. They are lower. Those machines were rigged to suppress the vote in that county for Hinton. That's the only possible conclusion. The machines there *were* rigged."

"So they screwed up."

"I doubt it," she said. "Whoever rigged those machine got exactly the results they wanted. The rigged numbers correlate exactly with the final election totals."

I sat down again and finished the sub as I exercised the little gray cells. When I finished my meal I wadded up the paper that it came in and tossed it in the classified burn basket, then wiped my fingers on my trousers.

"Don't do that," she said. "It's gross. You'll ruin those trousers."

"So who wanted Vaughn Conyers to win?"

"I don't know. Finding that out is your job."

Someday she is going to be running the CIA.

"So what the hell was Heiki Schlemmer typing last night? This morning?"

"An email to her Swiss banker."

I confess, I hadn't expected that.

Sarah handed me a copy. It was not encrypted but was in code. Four words in English. Presumably the officer at the bank in Zurich was also in on the code. Safe, neat, and practical. There was no way to crack the code.

"Those Swiss bankers," I said and handed it back. I wondered if Anton Hunt knew Schlemmer had a Swiss bank account. Or accounts.

What did it all mean?

At five that afternoon I rendezvoused with Sarah in Grafton's reception area. We had been there three minutes, talking over dinner plans, when Robin the receptionist waved us in.

Grafton was behind his desk and didn't get up. He gestured toward chairs and said, "Talk to me."

Sarah told him what she had learned about the Armageddon file, about Heiki Schlemmer's Swiss bank accounts, and about the investment decisions that Anton Hunt's hedge fund was making. He sat and listened without questions. He was the best listener I had ever run across.

"You asked about the FBI agent, Bill Farnem," Sarah told the admiral. "Heiki Schlemmer and Farnem communicate via encrypted email."

That was certainly news to me, and I suppose Grafton. He asked point-blank, "Can you crack the code?"

"I'm working on it. If I could get the NSA involved . . ."

"No. You figure it out."

"I wish I had the faith in you that you seem to have in me."

Jake Grafton smiled. Then he grinned, showing teeth. "Tommy has his gifts, you have yours. Use them."

She took a deep breath and said, "Nora and Fred Shepherd have stopped using their credit cards. The last transaction was two days ago in Cancun."

"They're dead," I whispered, knowing it. So the hitters had caught up with them. That was inevitable, I suppose. "So where are Kurt and Rosamery Lesh?" I asked Grafton.

"At the McLean safe house. Why don't you check up on them tomorrow, Tommy?"

We talked about housekeeping details for a few more minutes, then Grafton stood, a signal that our interview was over. He looked at me and said, "Stay for a moment, Tommy."

When the door had closed behind Sarah, he asked, "Where do we go from here?"

"That was the first I've heard of an FBI connection," I said, trying to marshal my thoughts. "Someone put a beacon on my old Mercedes up in Pennsylvania when I was there with the FBI Election Fraud Task Force. Now I'm kinda wondering if perhaps some FBI agent did it."

"And you found the beacon when you returned to Langley?"

"Yes, sir."

"Why did you even get suspicious enough to look?"

I shrugged. "Seven dead people after the snitch had his lawyer call the FBI. Someone got there fast and did some good trigger work. The possibility that it was the FBI crossed my mind, I guess. I get uncomfortable knowing that assassins are running around loose."

"What are your thoughts on the disparity between actual election results and the Armageddon file?"

"There's another file around someplace on a hard or thumb drive, or was, and I suspect that if we ever find it we'll see real correlation between it and the actual results."

Grafton scratched his head with the eraser of his pencil. "Where could it be?" he asked.

I squirmed a little. This was like being asked what part of the haystack the needle is in. "If such a file still exists, Schlemmer might have an inkling or two."

Grafton tapped his pencil point on his desk. "It's beginning to look as if Mr. Hunt got double-crossed."

"That's a possibility."

"He'd be unhappy if he gets that idea too."

Boy, I thought, he sure would. At least a billion dollars worth of unhappy.

Grafton continued, "Ms. Schlemmer might get concerned if the possibility entered Hunt's head somehow."

"Or she thought it had," I said thoughtfully. "Perhaps a bit more than concerned."

He nodded. "Think about it. But don't do anything until Sarah cracks the encryption code Schlemmer and Bill Farnem are using for their love notes."

"Riding, walking, or sitting on my ass, I get paid just the same," I said flippantly. Perhaps I was a bit out of sorts over the Shepherds, whose fate apparently hadn't dented Grafton's armor.

The admiral frowned and said, "Use the down time to exercise your brain," then shooed me out.

In the broom closet the company euphemistically calls my office, I did some thinking. One of these days Anton Hunt might ask to see the Armageddon file, and if he did Heiki Schlemmer would have to produce it. The numbers had to match reported election results, and she had to sell it to Hunt as Tanaka's work. That would be a trick, since Hunt was nobody's fool.

Perhaps Hunt had already asked and gone over it with Heiki before he sent Harry Tanaka to his garage gallows. But what if he asked to see it again? That was always a possibility, and so the odds were she still had the doctored file.

She had to be able to get to it reasonably quickly.

Where was it? On a thumb drive in her purse? A safe deposit box? Maybe her car, but that was a long shot. Not in her office nor her house. Hell, she might have had it on her last night.

All my surmises were based on the premise that Heiki had altered Harry's original file for her own purposes, and I had no proof of that.

I needed to wait until Sarah cracked the encryption code. If we could read her emails and files, we would know one way or the other.

I was showered, shaved, and wearing my best Hugh Hefner lounge-lizard robe with nothing on underneath when Sarah got back to the apartment. I was already two drinks ahead, so was feeling no pain.

She gave me The Look and poured herself a glass of white wine from the bottle in the refrigerator. She took one sip, then held the glass in front of her face and stared over the rim at me. I knew she was uptight from work, but the rule was to never talk about the office at home, and we didn't. After a bit she shook her head and went into the bedroom and bath for a bit of privacy.

Thirty minutes later when Sarah came out in slacks and a cool top that displayed her cleavage, I had the television on. I turned the volume way up and motioned her over. "Talk to me," I whispered into her ear.

She whispered into mine, "I'll never crack Hunt's encryption code. It's a progressive code, changing with every stroke on the keyboard and with every message. I don't even know if it's possible to crack it, but if it is, the mathematicians at NSA are the people to do it. I don't have their algorithms or computer capacity. Grafton doesn't under—" I held a finger to her lips.

"We know that Bill Farnem has a copy on one of his computers."

"Don't even think that, Tommy. It's probably on one in the Hoover Building. You are not going into the Hoover Building under any—" I stopped her again with a finger.

"If I do, it will be with Grafton's permission."

That seemed to calm her down. I used the remote to reduce the television audio to more pleasant levels, then kissed her. She kissed back. I discovered that she wasn't wearing anything under the top or slacks. We made love on the couch while Tucker Carlson watched.

CHAPTER TEN

I asked Sarah, "If you had Farnem's computer and he had erased the hard drive, could you still recover his files?"

"If he uses a commercial acid bath, no. If he just deleted the files or tried to scrub the hard drive, yes. All the files are still there but can be written over."

"Show me the encrypted emails that he and Schlemmer exchanged." She had hard copies and handed them to me. "They're short," I said. No more than a paragraph each.

"Can you tell what kind of machine they were typed on?"

"No."

"Could this encryption file go on an iPad?"

"I suppose," she said. "But one would suspect a laptop of some kind or a desktop; iPads are notoriously difficult to type on, not something you use for serious communication." Since I didn't own an iPad, I accepted that as gospel. After all, Sarah was my expert.

I visited Robin, Grafton's doorkeeper, and begged for some face time with The Man. "He has a full schedule . . ." she said, flipping though his classified appointment calendar.

"I gotta tell him what the guy beside me in the

bar at the Willard said last night. He works for the State Department but I think he's a Russian spy. He was drinking vodka neat and had a trace of an accent—"

"I'll see what I can do," she said primly. Actually Robin of the big hair was a warrior, a former Marine. Her office demeanor was just an act.

At ten after eleven I got the call and hotfooted it up to the director's office. Robin waved me in.

"Yeah," Jake Grafton said.

Mr. Personality. For Christmas I decided to give him a copy of *Seven Habits of Highly Effective People.* "Sarah says she has a snowball's chance of cracking that encryption code. She wants you to authorize her to give the problem to NSA."

"No."

"Any reason, or do you just feel negative today?"

He took a deep breath and let it out. "The director of the NSA and the new FBI director, Robert Levy, are old friends. The wizards at NSA will see that the messages are to and from Bill Farnem, big weenie at the FBI. That news will get to Levy, then to Farnem. So the answer is no."

Bureaucratic politics. I wasn't surprised. "I've been thinking about Farnem. He's got a computer somewhere with that damned encryption code on it. I doubt if it's in the Hoover Building. If the IT people there suspect him of having a private encryption code on his office computer, his ass is toast. I think it's on an iPad or laptop he carries around or keeps at home. I want to steal it."

His eyebrows went up. "You could do that?"

"If Sarah had Farnem's computer, she could hack in. There's no password she couldn't figure out—it has to be something he can remember. That's the weakness of passwords. Once she's in, the encryption code will vomit its secrets into her lap."

"Not a good analogy, but tell me what you're thinking."

I did. Ten minutes later he told me to do it. I told the admiral any guy trading encrypted emails with Heiki Schlemmer deserved to be screwed. He didn't dispute that point.

I called my guys in New Jersey and told them to come back to Washington. I had a job for them.

By definition, safe houses were places the company could stash people for short periods with no one the wiser. The neighbors couldn't know that the houses or apartments were owned by the government or the company, and there had to be some explanation for strangers coming and going. These parameters narrowed the choices drastically. The best ones were out-of-the-way places where people couldn't see who came and went, and no one would notice if the amount of trash increased or decreased, or if there were extra people around. The company had a small staff that did nothing but maintain them, shut them down periodically (especially if a high priority person had been there for more than a few days), and acquired others.

The one the Leshes were in was an old B&B, now closed. The lady who lived there, a retired CIA officer, told the neighbors she only took in old friends.

Kurt and Rosamery did not look happy when I sat down in the Victorian parlor to talk with them. The drapes were pulled, and the room was gloomy. "When are we going to get out of here?" Rosamery demanded. "Our lives are on hold. My practice is going to hell. We're hiding here like felons."

"You remember Kurt's former Allegheny colleague, Nora Shepherd? Did you ever meet her or her husband, Fred?"

A nod that I took as yes.

"They boogied off to Cancun, Mexico, the night before you came to Washington. They stopped using their credit cards several days ago. We think they are dead."

That shut her up.

"We're checking up on them, carefully, of course. Perhaps they are still ensconced in their hotel, hale and hearty, getting nice tans and reading bestsellers, but have switched to strictly cash. That's a possibility. More probable, assassins found them and they have landed in a Mexican morgue or are sleeping with the fishes."

Rosamery stared at me. Apparently she had seen the *Godfather* movies too. When she found her tongue, she said, "Can't you just call them and see if they are there?"

"If they are still alive and being hunted, that inquiry might help the assassins find them. As you probably know, Mexico is notoriously corrupt. We sent a person to look. We'll hear in another day or two."

"But what about us?"

"You are safe here. No one outside a small circle of company employees knows that you are here. The man who lives upstairs and looks like a permanent boarder is your bodyguard. He's armed, alert, and competent."

"How long do we have to stay?" Kurt demanded.

"If you want to make a run for it, you can leave anytime. Mrs. Gascon"—that was their host— "can call you a taxi or Uber anytime you wish."

"Anton Hunt can find us any place on Earth," Kurt said, more subdued.

"He can't find you here," I said positively. I even hoped that was true. "We'll let you know when we think it's safe for you to leave. If I were you, I'd try to make the best of a bad situation."

"I gave you a sworn deposition. We cooperated. We're not going to be prosecuted, are we?"

"The company is not a law enforcement agency.

That's the best I can do, but as it stands, I doubt if there will be any prosecutions. As my colleagues told you when you gave your deposition, our job is collecting intelligence. How are you getting along with Mrs. Gascon?"

"She's very kind and never asks questions," Rosamery acknowledged.

"Is the food okay?"

They both nodded their heads.

We visited a while longer, and I had a chat with Mrs. Gascon and the bodyguard, who was sitting with Mrs. Gascon in the kitchen drinking coffee. Then I went back to the parlor, shook the Leshes' hands and said goodbye.

"Your target is Bill Farnem, the Number three honcho at the FBI," I told my little gang of badasses. "I want a rolling surveillance on him. From the time he leaves the Hoover Building in the evening until he walks into it in the morning. Does he carry an attaché or computer case? Does he go straight home to the little wife, or does he have a mistress or girlfriend? Does he play cards with his buddies? Shoot pool? Whatever.

"And watch his house. If he doesn't carry a laptop or iPad back and forth to work, there's one in the house. What are the wife's habits? Any kids at home? A sister-in-law? An elderly mother? How can I burglarize the place, if necessary? You know what I need. Chop chop, do it."

When his wife left for her afternoon bridge club, we tapped his home land-line without entering the house. Joe Casillas set up the van a block from his house and by the second evening had both Bill Farnem's and his wife's cell phone numbers and was recording their conversations.

Meanwhile we found that the Shepherds couldn't be found in Cancun. They hadn't checked out of their hotel, but they weren't there either. The hotel had put their bags in storage and rented the room to someone else.

So they were dead. I knew it and Jake Grafton knew it, but . . . Rest in Peace, Nora and Fred.

The third evening of our surveillance of the Farnems we learned that Bill had a secret life. I know this will shock you, gentle reader, as it did us. The third ranking agent in the FBI? Yes, the sad truth was that he liked hookers and spent at least four hours one evening a week in their company. The flavor of the week was Angel, an illegal Mexican about twenty years of age with an awesome bosom. After I saw a photo of Mrs. Farnem, who had gained at least a hundred pounds since she and Bill committed matrimony and now looked like a walking sausage, I understood why Bill was violating the Sixth Commandment.

I asked Armanti, "Do you think Angel's tits are home-grown?"

"Doesn't matter," he said. "They all taste the same."

But Farnem's hobbies were dross. Where was his damned computer? He did have an attaché case, and some days he carried it and some days he didn't.

The question was answered on the Monday of the second week of our surveillance when Heiki Schlemmer sent him an encrypted email that evening while he was at home, and he answered it fourteen minutes later.

The computer was in his house.

We waited until Bill was at work the next day and Mrs. Farnem was off to bridge club, and I broke and entered, technically. They didn't have a home security system. Go figure. They did have a cat, which rubbed against my leg, so I scratched its ears. I searched carefully. The kitchen cabinets were packed with potato chips and popcorn. Apparently Mrs. Farnem shopped at Costco and bought lots of the big bags. Down in the basement I found a gun safe with a combination lock. It was apparently bolted into the concrete. It would take a blowtorch to move it. On the off chance it was unlocked, I tried the handle. Nope. Locked tight.

There might be a computer in that thing. Well, if the one on his desk upstairs didn't have the codes, I could come back with the proper equipment and open the lock and look.

After a careful search, I concluded the Farnems had just one computer in the house, a laptop on a desk that apparently they both used, so I stole it, making the crime burglary.

I had entered by picking the lock on the front door, but I wanted to make the place look like it had been hit by an amateur. I left the front door unlocked and broke out the window in the door with the butt of my pistol. The glass showered the foyer. As far as I could see, no one in the neighborhood paid the slightest attention, probably because they were all at work or inside watching Oprah. Not a kid in sight.

Back at Langley that afternoon, Sarah attacked the Farnems' laptop. It took her four minutes to get the password, which was the Farnems's anniversary. The encryption code was one of the files.

I was sitting in her new office, which was at least twenty square feet larger than her old one and had a window, drinking a cup of Starbucks' best from the shop beside the Langley cafeteria, when she turned to the printer. She handed me the sheet that came out. I looked it over.

Heiki wrote, "Apparently someone broke into Hunt's offices in Manhattan. It might have been Carmellini. If so, the CIA is still after us. Can you do something about them?"

The answer was short and to the point. "I'll try."

Sarah was watching me and said, "Well! What do you know?"

I took another sip of coffee, which was getting cold, and said, "Two ships passing in the night."

It took Sarah another five minutes to print out all the Schlemmer/Farnem correspondences. She checked to ensure she had all the emails, correlated them, and handed me the pile. I started in, oldest one first.

Ten minutes later I asked for a classified envelope, put the pile in it, and set sail for the director's office. Grafton was out; he'd be back in a couple of days.

"Where is he?" I asked Robin.

She regarded me with cold, fish eyes and kept her mouth firmly shut. I'd have to hold her down and tickle her to get the information, which might cause a scandal.

I went back to my office, spread the emails on my desk, and studied them carefully, reading what was said and trying to read between the lines. Finally I looked at my watch. 5:30 p.m. I called Mrs. Grafton.

"Hello."

"Good evening, Mrs. Grafton. This is Tommy Carmellini. I'm trying to find the admiral. Is he home?"

"No, Tommy. He left for Switzerland this morning."

"Thank you. I'll catch him at the office when he gets back."

Darn that Robin. The company travel office certainly knew where the boss had boogied off to, and so did Robin. Why not tell me, his confidential, top-secret executive assistant and favorite burglar? I should have tickled her.

Special Agent Bill Farnem arrived home at six to find a police cruiser parked in front of his house. He parked in the garage and walked into the kitchen, where his wife, Kathy, was waiting with two uniformed officers.

"I didn't want to call you at work, Bill," she said, "but when I got home at four I found that someone had broken into the house."

"They came in through the front door, Mr. Farnem, after they smashed out the window glass and reached around to the knob," the senior officer said. He had three stripes on each sleeve.

"What did they take?" Farnem asked.

"Your wife has been checking, yet the only thing—"

"They stole the computer off the desk, Bill," Kathy blurted.

"Nothing else?"

"That is all your wife can find that is missing—"

"I checked my jewelry box and the gun safe first," Kathy said positively. "You know that good diamond my mother left me? It's still there. That was the best thing in the house. The most expensive. I can't understand—"

He walked through the house with the officers while Kathy talked non-stop. They inspected the gun safe. Intact and apparently untouched. Nope, the only thing missing was the computer.

"Probably stole it to sell for drug money," Kathy opined. "A used computer like that, four years old . . . why, they couldn't get fifty bucks for it at a pawn shop. They must be having DTs or something."

Farnem tried to pay attention to the police as they filled out a report. Forty-five minutes after he arrived home, they left. He shut the front door behind them and stood looking at the glass, which had yet to be cleaned up.

He went to the liquor cabinet in the dining room and poured himself a drink of vodka on the rocks while Kathy chattered on. "I was so thrilled that Snookums is okay. You are okay, aren't you, Snookums?" She picked up the cat and cradled it as she walked from the room.

Bill Farnem went to his den and sat in his favorite chair, a recliner he sat in for Sunday football games. He sipped at the vodka and tried to put his thoughts in order. Someone stole his laptop. The only thing of value on the machine was the program that he and Schlemmer used to encrypt their emails.

Kids? Dopers? Not hardly. It was that damned CIA asshole, Carmellini. He was a thief. Farnem had checked the file on him when Carmellini was assigned to the Election Fraud Task Force. A thief for the CIA. A techie who broke and entered to install bugs.

Farnem instantly understood that this house might be bugged. That didn't matter. He always operated as if it were anyway. If the spooks wanted to listen to Kathy prattle, so be it.

But that wasn't it, he suspected. Carmellini wanted that encryption code. That meant they would read the emails. Damn, he was in trouble.

He swabbed at his forehead and took another drink.

That night when his wife was asleep in the bedroom, Farnem went to the basement to his gun safe. He took a gym bag along. As Kathy said, the safe was intact, apparently untouched.

That douchebag Carmellini could have opened this thing if he had taken the time. Farnem worked the combination and swung the door open. The money was there, so he put that in the bag. The pistol was on the top shelf, along with the suppressor. He added them to the bag. Also put in his false passport and driver's license. He would need those too. Then he closed the safe and locked it again.

Keeping the pistol had been a calculated risk. Maybe he should have gotten rid of it, but he might need it again. Looked like life was breaking that way.

• • •

The Swiss Federal Intelligence Service (FIS) is responsible for the security of the state, which in our violent age meant it was concerned with Islamic terrorism. The FIS worked with other European intelligence agencies and the CIA on acquiring and sharing information about terrorist threats. The director was a man in his fifties, a career intelligence officer who was fluent in the major Swiss languages—German, French, and Italian—and also in English and Arabic, and he knew enough Farsi to get along.

Nattily dressed in a gray suit and subdued tie, the director escorted Jake Grafton to a conference room separated from an operations center filled with screens so that the duty staff could monitor news, emails, and telex traffic in real time. Beyond the operations center were large windows, through which could be seen several large old trees that were leafing out in the twilight. The scene reminded Jake that all intelligence agencies weren't huddled in windowless bunkers. Natural light lowered the stress levels of the staff.

Jake had worked with and liked the FIS director. While every intelligence agency jealously guarded its own secrets, the fight against terrorism was world-wide. The more information you passed along to your international colleagues, the more they passed along to you.

The American passed a paper copy of Heiki Schlemmer's email to her banker to the Swiss spy master. "I'd like to know about this account and any others this woman might have in Switzerland. Balances, deposits, withdrawals, and where the money originated."

He knew that under the new Swiss banking laws, recently passed due to excruciating political pressure from American and European tax authorities, foreigners had to present passports and declare their nationality when opening an account.

The Swiss said, "If she opened the account in her own name . . ."

"That is her email address as the sender, so she doesn't seem to have used a false identity."

"I assume this is an intelligence inquiry, not law enforcement?" If it were a law enforcement matter, it would have to go through other bureaucracies. Having a Swiss bank account to avoid taxes elsewhere was not a crime in Switzerland.

"Yes, it is," Jake Grafton said.

"Help yourself to some coffee, admiral, and I'll be back with you in a moment. This will obviously take some time, probably until tomorrow when the banks reopen. Perhaps we might eat dinner in our private dining room and talk shop."

On Thursday evening I was sitting in Jake Grafton's living room chatting with his wife,

Callie, and drinking beer when the admiral came through the door.

Callie kissed him and asked, "Are you hungry?"

"I ate on the plane, hon. I could use a drink though."

He poured some bourbon over ice and I followed him into his study, where he closed the door and dropped onto the couch. I pulled the classified envelope from my attaché case and handed it to him.

He opened it and began reading. When he finished he handed the pages back to me and sipped at the booze. "So Bill Farnem is in it to the roots of his hair."

"The ElectTech hitters were former FBI agents."

He didn't say anything.

"Are you ready for more?" I asked.

"What?"

"Senator Westland, the senior minority senator on the Senate Intelligence Committee, wants you to drop by his office at nine tomorrow morning. I don't think the appointment is optional." The Senate Intelligence Committee provided oversight for the CIA, among other intelligence agencies. The United States had sixteen, last I heard.

"I wondered how long Anton Hunt was going to wait before he began pulling strings," Grafton said.

"He was pulling them yesterday and the puppets began dancing. The senator was unhappy to hear that you were out of the country. Maybe you should have asked for asylum. I hear the skiing is great in Switzerland and the summers are delightful."

"Does Reem Kiddus know about this?"

"Yep. He was on the telephone too. I talked to him. Westland is screaming at Kiddus that Hunt is being illegally investigated by the CIA. I think it's safe to assume that is the subject that he wants to grill you on."

"Umph," he said. He stretched his legs out and slouched down on the couch.

"Kiddus wants to know what you are going to say. He thinks that Westland will demand that any investigation of Hunt, in fact any investigation by the CIA of anybody within the borders of the United States, be turned over to the FBI. That is, Kiddus reminded me, what federal law requires."

"So it does."

The scrambled telephone on the desk rang, and Grafton elevated himself to answer it. He plopped down in his desk chair, leaned back and put his feet up on an open drawer that he pulled out. "Grafton."

In a few seconds he said, "Yes, Reem. One of my aides is here at the house and has been briefing me."

He listened to Kiddus while he played with

the instrument cord, which was knotted. "I understand. Why don't you join us for the inquisition? I can brief them and you at the same time."

He listened a while longer, grunted a few times, and said, "I can't control the senator's leakers."

After a few more grunts and a curt goodbye, he hung up. "Kiddus will be there tomorrow," he told me. "I want you along too."

"If they ask me questions, what do I say?"

"I'll do all the talking."

"Roger, closed mouth. I hear Westland is a jerk."

"He's a politician who has been playing the game a long time. No doubt he is a personal friend of Anton Hunt, who has contributed big-time to his campaign, and wants to know who is holding what cards before he takes a stand."

"How are our cards?" I really wanted to know what, if anything, he had learned in Switzerland.

"We need a few more, but we have enough to open."

I left the email intercepts with Grafton, said good night to Callie and went home to Sarah. No one appeared to pay any attention to me. I was driving an agency sedan. As I drove I wondered what Bill Farnem had on his mind tonight. Nothing good, I thought gloomily. If Grafton whipped out those emails between Farnem and Heiki Schlemmer tomorrow, Farnem was toast.

He would spend tomorrow night in a federal jail.

That thought warmed the cockles of my hard, little heart. I hoped it would come to pass.

As I approached Sarah's apartment building, the passenger side window exploded. I stood on the gas and the squirrels under the hood gave it their all.

Three blocks farther along I saw a Burger King and whipped in. Abandoned the car and took cover behind a pickup with the Kimber in my hand. I was breathing hard.

Minutes went by. I wondered if Sarah was all right. Sure she was. If they had broken into the apartment and killed her or tied her up, they would have waited for me there. That's the way I figured it.

I examined my watch. Watched the minute hand march on toward tomorrow. A few cars entered the lot and people went into the restaurant. Two cars went through the drive-through. A mixed-race gay couple came out holding hands and climbed into their ride. Two male-female couples came out, got into their cars and left.

When fifteen minutes had passed and no car had careened into the parking area to disgorge armed men, I went back to the agency heap, staying low, moving erratically, and inspected it through the missing window. Glass pebbles were all over the interior. There was a bullet hole in the driver side door. Inspection showed that the bullet had gone through the door and continued on bound for Ohio or Indiana. It had missed me by inches, went under my arms and above my lap before it punched through the door. Probably a rifle. Talk about luck!

It was doubtful if the sniper was still out there waiting for another shot, and I had no desire to brush the glass pebbles off the car seat to sit in it. I walked home, taking my time, staying in the shadows, looking at everything.

Sarah was drinking wine and watching a period British drama on television. She kissed me, looked me over, and said, "You have some cuts on your cheek and forehead, and glass in your hair."

I fingered my face. A scab on my right cheek. I went to the bathroom sink and used my fingers to get the glass bits out of my hair. There were at least eight tiny cuts in my skin. A shard of safety glass came out of my cheek as I swabbed the scab off with a paper towel. Why a glass pebble missed my eye I'll never know.

"Want to tell me about it?" Sarah said as she watched.

"Someone took a shot at me. Got the car. It isn't dead, just wounded. Thank God it wasn't mine."

"Who?"

"Damned if I know." If it wasn't Bill Farnem, I would have bet serious money it was one of his pals.

Truth was, I was pissed. And in a way, pleased. Someone was very worried, probably Farnem. As a rule, scared people don't think very well. Killing me wouldn't solve his problems. The bastard had panicked.

I tried to calm down so I could keep thinking. I had been around enough to know that my brain was the only thing that was going to keep me alive. That and luck. I had used up a lot of luck tonight. I hoped I still had some good juice left.

CHAPTER ELEVEN

Having survived the political wars for almost three decades, Senator Orville Westland had a corner office suite in the Russell Senate Office Building. The senator's personal office was actually on the building's corner, so he had windows on two walls. The great man's remaining wall space was covered with framed prints of him with the famous and powerful. Memorabilia junked up most of the flat places. One wondered how much paperwork, if any, the senator actually did here—I tried to envision the senator at his desk reading some important bill and pondering its merits, but couldn't. The room did provide a nice place for photos when the home folks came to Washington to visit their champion.

A staffer pointed Jake Grafton and me toward a couch against a wall. I took my seat as Grafton shook hands with Robert Levy and Reem Kiddus, who got comfortable leather chairs. Grafton hadn't managed to park his bottom when Senator Westland and a male and female colleague, both Democrats from the Intelligence Committee, came breezing in. There were no introductions since presumably all these people knew each other. They pumped hands and murmured hellos and found seats in the comfy chairs.

Westland sat down behind his desk, the surface of which was large enough for a model train layout.

Westland jumped in with both feet. "Admiral Grafton, I understand your agency is investigating Anton Hunt."

That wasn't a question, so Grafton didn't have to provide an answer. He asked a question of his own. "Where did your information come from, senator?"

Orville Westland wasn't going to let this meeting get away from him. "I don't think that's germane to the issue. Is or is not the CIA investigating Anton Hunt?"

"We are looking into the possibility that a foreign person or government agency conspired to commit election fraud in the 2016 presidential election. I am not prepared to discuss our lines of inquiry or sources but can confirm that we have discussed this matter with several Americans."

The female senator, Hilda Rutherford, jumped right in. "Let's cut the crap, Mr. Grafton. Is the CIA conducting an investigation on American soil?"

"We are attempting to learn if a foreign power conspired with Americans to fix the 2016 election."

Senator Westland interjected, "It is a violation of federal law for the CIA to conduct investigations within the United States. You know that, admiral."

So he was back to observing the proprieties, such as titles. A former federal prosecutor, Westland knew to be polite to defendants even as he was cutting their nuts off.

He directed the next question at Robert Levy. "Is your agency investigating election fraud?"

"No, sir. We have no reason to suspect anyone committed a federal crime during the voting in 2016."

"Bullshit," said the other senator, Joe McCormick. He had a magnificent head of wiry black hair, undoubtedly dyed, and an enviable physique for a man of seventy. He was easily the best looking man in the room, not counting me. "The press has been full of accusations of voter fraud in half a dozen major cities, and Russian hacking of Cynthia Hinton's staff emails. There's a lot of smoke, yet you aren't looking for a fire or two?"

"Misconduct in precincts and counties are under the jurisdiction of the states involved," Levy said. "If they find there was possible criminal violation of federal election laws, they will report it to the U.S. prosecutors involved. The Justice Department has not asked for FBI assistance."

"A cop-out," McCormick snarled. I had to suppress a smile. Although I knew little about election law, I was old enough to know that blanket statements about the law were usually gross over-simplifications. Levy didn't want to investigate anything and McCormick knew it.

Westland fired a statement at Grafton. "I understand you are investigating Anton Hunt, a prominent progressive who is a bitter political enemy of President Conyer. That smacks of a witch hunt."

Senator Rutherford stood. "Turn your little inquisition over to the FBI, Grafton. Or drop it." She started to leave.

"Aren't you even curious about what we've learned?" Grafton asked Rutherford's back. That froze the senator in her tracks and drew every eye in the room.

As Rutherford lowered herself back into her padded leather chair, the admiral said smoothly, "I can't discuss methods or sources, yet we have made some progress. I should state categorically that we are not gathering evidence for a criminal or civil proceeding. We are gathering intelligence that I believe may point to foreign involvement in the past presidential election. We aren't there yet, but we have pointers. Which leads right back to my initial question to Senator Westland: where did your information about our activities come from?"

Westland looked as if he were sucking a dill pickle. Since there was no real reason to deny it, he said, "Anton Hunt is a personal and political friend. We discussed the matter."

"Thank you."

Grafton reached for his attaché case on the floor, popped the catches, and pulled out a file.

Damn, it looks as if he is going to dump the load right here, which will blow the lid off.

I wondered if any of our political masters were recording this for *The Washington Post*.

"Our interest in this affair grew out of the arrest of an employee of ElectTech, a company that sells and services voting machines, tally machines, and election paraphernalia of all kinds. The company has sold machines to counties in over half the American states. His name was Junior Sikes, and he was arrested for having child pornography on his computer at work.

"While in jail, he asked his attorney to call the FBI because he wanted to tell them about a conspiracy to fix ElectTech tally machines to deliver a certain result in various counties. His attorney did call the FBI, which notified the Election Fraud Task Force, which was investigating election fraud, regardless of Mr. Levy's protestations. When the Task Force got to Pennsylvania to interview Mr. Sikes, he was dead. Murdered in his jail cell. Three jail officers were also killed. Two other employees of ElectTech were murdered that night and one person who was in an apartment with an employee. Seven people total. All were killed by single bullets fired into their heads. They were assassinated."

No one said a word. I have never seen a more attentive audience.

He took a document from his file and handed it to Westland. "This is a sworn deposition from an employee of the company that owned ElectTech, Kurt Lesh." As Westland scanned it, Grafton continued. "Lesh stated under oath that ElectTech employees set up tally machines in key counties in various states to deliver certain results. The results ElectTech wanted favored Mrs. Hinton."

I thought Rutherford was going to stroke out right there. Her face turned red and she opened and closed her mouth three times, but held her tongue. Westland stopped reading and stared at Grafton. McCormick lowered his eyes to the floor. Robert Levy glared at Grafton, who had obviously made an enemy.

"Two company officers checked the tally machines in two counties in Virginia. One county still had the ElectTech program on the five tally machines that were checked. The other county had been visited by Junior Sikes after the election and the machines were benign."

"So you are saying ElectTech tried to fix the election, at least in one lousy county, maybe two, to assist Secretary Hinton?"

Grafton shook his head. "It isn't that simple."

"What has this got to do with Anton Hunt?" Rutherford demanded. Apparently she too was a personal and political friend of the progressive financier.

"His hedge fund controls Red Truck Investments, which controls Allegheny Corporation, which owns ElectTech. It's a corporate hairball."

"So you have no proof Hunt's fund or funds had anything to do with this wannabe snitch, Junior Sikes?"

"I wouldn't go that far. You are welcome to read the deposition Senator Westland has in his hand. The deponent, Mr. Lesh, admitted his and his colleague Nora Shepherd's role in the conspiracy and implicated his bosses at Red Truck. One of them is a woman named Heiki Schlemmer, who is one of Hunt's long-time employees. Another is a man who has been with Hunt on some of his financial coups for twenty years.

"But moving along, Nora Shepherd and her husband fled the country and we believe they were murdered in Cancun last week. One of my officers, Mr. Carmellini, who is sitting beside me, was in Lesh's house when two armed men broke in, presumably to kill Kurt Lesh and his wife.

"A few days later Mr. Carmellini was attacked by two armed men on I-95 in Delaware. He killed them both. At least one of the men had fake ID on him."

He continued, telling them about the man who didn't exist, Ridenhour, and finally got around to my gal Heiki. "We have learned that Ms. Schlemmer has a Swiss bank account containing over a half million U.S. dollars. The Swiss are investigating, but they believe that the original source of the money was a Chinese consortium in Shanghai."

"Are you implying that the Chinese tried to buy the election for Cynthia Hinton?"

"No. I believe there were two plots here, one by someone in Hunt's organization to aid Mrs. Hinton, and one by Heiki Schlemmer to aid President Conyer. Schlemmer was in a position to ensure the ElectTech efforts would not bear fruit, and hers might."

Reem Kiddus snarled, "Grafton, you son—"

"Before anyone goes off half-cocked," Grafton said, ignoring Kiddus, "I want to say we have found no evidence that would be admissible in court that either effort succeeded."

Levy said, "Schlemmer double-crossed Hunt?"

"Apparently she double-crossed someone, I have no idea who. I don't know if Hunt knew what was going on. We have seen no evidence that he did."

"Maybe there was a legitimate reason for that payment," Rutherford suggested.

"You think?" Levy said acidly.

Westland tossed Lesh's deposition on his desk and said, "Jesus H. Christ!"

Grafton continued, "We have seen no indication

whatsoever that either the Hinton or Conyer campaign, nor the RNC or DNC, had anything to do with these efforts, or even knew about them. We have seen no indication that any political figure in either party had the slightest inkling these conspiracies were occurring."

What he didn't say was that we hadn't questioned anyone under oath, except Kurt Lesh, and indeed there might be evidence of a political conspiracy if this mess were properly investigated, with search warrants and subpoenas and all the rest of the FBI's arsenal. Or there might not. We hadn't turned over enough rocks to rule anything out.

Westland and the other senators sat digesting and cogitating for a long minute. "So the only evidence," Westland said, "of Chinese involvement is financial shenanigans in Switzerland?"

"So far. The Swiss Foreign Intelligence Service is investigating. If the Chinese thought they were paying for a certain election result, we'll never get evidence that we could get a court to accept."

Westland looked at his colleagues. "Do you have any thoughts?"

They didn't. That was probably the first time in her political career that Senator Rutherford was at a loss for words.

"The bottom line is this—" Grafton said, smooth as old bourbon, "—we are investigating a national security matter. I suspect the president and secretary of state will carefully consider our relationship with China before they decide on any course of action, if we do in fact find credible evidence that the Chinese had a hand in one of these conspiracies. What I can tell you is that we are not obtaining evidence admissible in court."

"You lie, cheat, steal, blackmail people, and cultivate traitors," Joe McCormick muttered. The thought crossed my mind that he had just written my job description.

Grafton captured his eyes. "Our investigation methods are designed to ferret out facts in order to inform government decision-makers of what is happening beyond our shores, not find criminals for the justice system's digestive tract. That is the FBI's job."

Levy nodded and didn't say a word. He didn't want any part of this stinking manure pile, and I didn't blame him.

"This isn't the forum to discuss agency intelligence gathering practices," Westland said flatly. "We live in a dangerous world. Our enemies don't play by rules. We'd be fools to handcuff ourselves."

The other two senators read the Lesh deposition, kicked the can around a while, then wandered out. Grafton stowed the deposition in his attaché case. Kiddus said to Grafton, "Call me this afternoon." The admiral nodded. Kiddus left. Grafton and Levy shook hands with Senator Westland, who looked preoccupied.

Right then I was trying to decide which of our three elected savants would be the first to spill the beans to the press. My guess was Rutherford. The only woman I knew who could keep a secret was Sarah Houston. This secret was molten.

Levy and Grafton walked out side-by-side with me in trail. In the hallway outside Westland's suite, Grafton said, "Tommy, I'll see you back at Langley." Then to Levy, "We need to talk."

"Lunch?"

"Your place or mine?"

"Mine," said Robert Levy. He was not naïve. He knew that Grafton had only scratched the surface in Westland's office and was undoubtedly nearly bursting with questions that couldn't be asked or answered where anyone might overhear.

I looked at my watch. It was a few minutes after eleven. I felt as if I had watched The Great Blondin walk a wire across Niagara Falls without a safety net or harness, holding my breath for his whole trip. Maybe I was also still a little wound up from last night's adventure. Getting shot at is hard on the nerves.

I thought a drink would do me good—it was five o'clock someplace—so I walked to Union Station to take care of my thirst and get a sandwich. I didn't see anyone following me or watching from a car. Believe me, I looked.

• • •

When his office was empty, Senator Westland picked up his telephone and told the receptionist to hold his calls. Then he leaned back in his chair and did some serious thinking.

He owed Anton Hunt for his contributions to his campaign and PAC. Hunt had also donated $200,000 to his daughter's tax-free education charity. So he was going to have to call Anton Hunt and tell him how the morning meeting went. There was no way out. The fact that the CIA was wire-tapping Hunt, or doing "electronic surveillance," was on his mind as he picked up the instrument for his private line and punched in the numbers, which he had on a contact sheet.

"Senator Westland for Mr. Hunt," he told the person who answered.

The line went dead. Not even Bach or elevator music.

In about thirty seconds Hunt came on. "Hello, Orv." Only Senator Westland's friends called him "Orv," so the elected one winced at the thought that this familiarity might be on a transcript of this call and might embarrass him somewhere down the road.

"Senators Rutherford, McCormick and I just finished a meeting with Admiral Grafton and Robert Levy in my office. Grafton has learned some things that trouble us, Mr. Hunt." He wasn't going to call the bastard Anton. "So far, there are eleven bodies associated with the CIA's inquiries into election fraud, and perhaps thirteen. These killings are being investigated by the appropriate law enforcement agencies."

"Stop right there, Orv. The CIA is busy violating American law on American soil. That agency has no right to investigate anything within the United States. You know that."

Westland took a deep breath. "The FBI didn't choose to investigate the allegations of election fraud, and the CIA did because Grafton was concerned about foreign powers interfering with our elections. Illegal? Yes. But eleven bodies cannot be ignored . . . and Grafton has found at least one county in Virginia where the election results were fixed by ElectTech, which is one of your subsidiaries."

"We have subsidiaries I don't even know about."

"I wish you didn't have this one. I hope it makes you lots of money because it's going to cause you major headaches. Why in the hell do you own anything that has to do with elections?"

"Presumably because it makes money. For Christ's sake, we are a hedge fund. Making money is what we do."

"Pizza and beer make money. Toothpaste and diapers. Cell phones and Cialis. Election equipment?"

"What is your point?"

"The point is that Grafton and Levy left here arm in arm. If Grafton has been flying solo, he's got a partner now. The FBI is going to dive head first into this mess."

Silence. Then, "What about foreign involvement, which is Grafton's excuse to violate Americans' constitutional rights?"

Remembering that this conversation was probably being recorded, Westland said, "Grafton has evidence that one of your staffers received a half million dollars from the Chinese."

"People betray their employers on a regular basis," Hunt said contemptuously. "That isn't news."

Westland sucked it up and said, "Hunt, let me give you some advice. If you and your organization had nothing to do with election fraud and the eleven corpses spread across Pennsylvania and Delaware, call in the FBI, answer all their questions under oath, and let the chips fall where they may. Guilty subordinates can take the fall. Get this behind you."

"I wish you would make some noise about illegal activities of the CIA."

"I am not going to commit political suicide to protect traitors in your organization who took money to fix an election. Get naked and clean, *then* I'll lead the crusade against Grafton. I'll crucify the son of a bitch."

Hunt hung up on Westland.

The senator sat holding the phone in his hand and finally cradled it.

Anton Hunt was nearly ninety, with paper-thin skin, baggy eyes, and wispy hair. Disgusted, he reflected on the fact that you can buy friends, but they don't stay bought without constant infusions of cash. The question is not, what did you do for me yesterday? It is, what are you going to do for me tomorrow?

Westland was a fellow progressive, but he would abandon his friend and patron Anton to swing in the wind at the first change in the weather. Hunt was used to little people. He had been around them all his life. They were there to be used, for a greater end.

There were moments when he felt like God, as if he were looking down from heaven on all the little people grubbing for dollars, food, shelter, and warmth. He knew what they needed, even if they didn't. He could get it for them. Making money was his talent, but using it to change the world for the better was his destiny.

He wanted to change the world, to make it better by empowering a progressive state that would sweep away reactionary impediments. Hitler had tried, Marx had tried, as had Lenin and Stalin, but by God Anton Hunt would find a way to get it done. He knew how to erase human misery from the Earth. It was going to take a revolution, a collapse of this rotten civilization, then progressives could rebuild a better world from the ashes.

Cynthia Hinton was flawed clay, yet he could have worked with her if she had gotten into the White House. She was greedy and could be bought. He had the money to do the buying. It would have worked . . .

But she lost. And he was old. How many years did he have left? Not enough. Not enough.

Barry Soetoro had sowed the seeds of discord. Hinton could have harvested the fruit. This obsolete American Constitution could have been jettisoned and progressives could have taken power. *Taken power!* Wrestled it away from the stupid little people who could only see to the end of their noses, who gave not a damn for the human race or the problems that mankind faced.

But obsessing over what might have been was time wasted, and at ninety he didn't have a lot of that commodity left.

He sat in his corner office with the view of the skyscrapers of Manhattan out the windows and tried to prioritize. Stopping the investigation into his attempt to get Hinton elected was Job One. Perhaps the investigation was unstoppable. If he were prosecuted, they would never convict him. There simply wasn't enough admissible evidence. Still, he would try to derail his enemies. He had to. The worms always win in the end, yet the worms had to be fought. And even they couldn't stop the progressive revolution.

There were other problems, and in the long run, they were perhaps more important. He always thought about problems in the long run. Keep your eye firmly on the ball. The world wasn't made in a day. Keep working toward your goal. Keep working toward a better world for all mankind. God in His heaven understood that.

He thought about those problems now and considered his options.

This Conyer, this boob, this fool! He couldn't be allowed to succeed. He might undo much of the work Soetoro had accomplished. If only he had realized years ago that Conyer had this political potential, that he was a dangerous enemy, he could have ruined him. He had dismissed him as a stupid dilettante, a fop. But the past was water over the dam. Yesterday was gone.

There needed to be more demonstrations, more protests, more violence, more riots, more blood in the streets. Anything to prove that Conyer was incompetent, anything that would drive people to reject him. Only then . . . only then . . .

The bartender in Union Station had CNBC on a television above the bottles. As I munched a ham and swiss on toasted rye I kept my eye on the screen to see if the talking heads broke away for a hot news conference with one of the morning senators. They didn't. One of the financial expert interviewees thought the stock market would go up, one thought it would sink. The whiskey slid down smoothly, like the pessimist thought the stock market would.

I wondered how many more hours or minutes Bill Farnem had before the roof fell in. That Jake Grafton was sealing Farnem's doom over soup and salad, I had no doubt. Would Levy be properly grateful that Grafton hadn't trotted out Farnem's sinful dalliance with Heiki Schlemmer before the elected ones?

I also wondered how many other FBI folks were involved. The ElectTech killings, bugging my car, whacking the Shepherds in Mexico . . . the villains who did those things weren't street hoods from Hoboken.

Ahh . . . Grafton had certainly stroked the pols. While it was true that we hadn't yet found any evidence of Anton Hunt's fingerprints, I knew in my bones that the former SS trooper was the spider in the center of the web.

When I finished the sandwich, the bartender removed the plate. I waggled my finger at my glass and he poured me another.

CHAPTER TWELVE

It was sheer coincidence that Bill Farnem was leaving for lunch when he saw Director of the FBI, Robert Levy, and Director of the CIA, Jake Grafton, step off an elevator together on the executive level as he was boarding one to descend. He got only a glimpse, but he had had the CIA very much on his mind since his computer was stolen from his house this past Tuesday, three days ago.

He knew when he saw those two men together that he was in big trouble. The only thing on the stolen computer of any value was the encryption code he used to communicate with Heiki Schlemmer. And the only people who would steal it were the assholes from Langley.

As the elevator descended Farnem tried to get calmed down. Still, this was it. The end. He dare not wait until Levy called him into the office. He was a dead duck if that happened.

He got off in the basement and walked down the corridor to the gymnasium. The attendant said, "Hey, Mr. Farnem."

"Hi, Jack."

He went into the locker room and opened the combination lock on his locker. His gym bag was on top, so he pulled that out and took the bag beneath it, the one with the money and his gun. Replaced the one that held his socks, jock, and tennis shoes. Relocked the locker and walked out with his gym bag, nodding at Jack.

In the parking garage he looked around to see if anyone was watching as he went to his car. No one was, apparently.

He unlocked the car, seated himself, and belted himself in. He couldn't wait around to give Levy time to hear the news from Grafton and give orders to find him.

Bill Farnem drove out of the garage for the last time, turned right on the street, and set about disappearing.

As I walked out of Union Station my cell phone rang. I dragged it from my pocket and looked at the caller ID. Joe Casillas.

"Yo."

"Subject is out and moving."

So the bastard was running. "Where is he?"

"Going north on Wisconsin Avenue."

"Stay with him. Well back. Have Travis pick me up in front of Union Station."

Silence, ten seconds, fifteen . . . then, "Ten minutes, he says."

I hung up. Took a deep breath. Maybe this was it. I wanted the bastard with the rifle. Maybe Bill Farnem would take us to him.

● ● ●

Tourism is the second biggest industry in Washington. As I stood in front of Union Station, hordes of citizens and foreign visitors lined up to board buses for transport to hotels, then on to the monuments, public buildings, museums, and visits with elected representatives. Men, women, children, laden with cameras and shepherding piles of luggage. Small boys ran around burning off energy. The kids were going to be bored silly by the Washington experience, I thought, but they say it is "broadening, educational, essential to their growth into responsible citizens." Or so went the come-on.

As I stood smelling the diesel exhaust and watching bus drivers load the plunder while the people trooped up the stairs to settle in their seats, I wondered if Bill Farnem had ever been educated and broadened on a tour. Maybe not.

Colorful open-top tourist buses had a stop just to the west of my position, and maybe a hundred people were climbing off and on the three that stood there. Thankfully it wasn't raining and the sun was shining through high broken clouds. The air was warm. Across the boulevard the trees were well leafed out. The cherry trees down by the river had blossomed, according to the press.

When Travis Clay pulled up in his pickup, I trotted over and climbed aboard. He had an encrypted radio transmitter/receiver in his hand and it was squawking away.

As Travis merged with traffic, he said, "He's up in Maryland. Doc and Armanti are closer. They were staying with your pal Willie Varner at the lock shop."

Trust Willie the Wire to make a grab for every government dollar he smelled going by.

I took off my tie and put it in my pocket.

"Has he made any cell phone calls?"

"No. We're just tracking his phone."

"Who is driving the van?"

"Ski."

Another transmission came in as Travis headed for New York Avenue and Route 50 East to the beltway. No doubt he figured that was the fastest way to the north side of the city at this time of day. Getting out of Washington is always a crapshoot.

"How come Farnem picked Friday afternoon to boogey?" Travis asked.

"Jake Grafton went over to the FBI building for a private conference with Levy at noon. He probably got wind of it somehow."

"Losing his computer on Tuesday probably lit a fire under him," Travis mused. "That and a guilty conscience. I bet he's had a hell of a bad week."

"Our good buddy Bill was cocked and ready," I admitted. "He only needed a nudge."

Just before we got to the beltway, the encrypted

radio came to life. It beeps as it syncs itself, then there is the transmission, and when the transmission ends, it beeps again. Same when you transmit. After a bit you get used to all the beeping.

I could hear Joe's voice. "He's getting a telephone call but isn't answering."

"Who is it?" I asked.

"No way of telling until he answers," Travis explained. "Only then can we capture the number and listen to the conversation."

Perhaps Mr. Levy was looking for his wayward lieutenant, I mused. Or his wife wanted him to pick up milk on the way home. Or his hooker had the hots. Or Heiki Schlemmer wanted to hear his soothing manly voice. Lots of possibilities.

"How do you like your truck?" I asked Travis. It had a four-door cab, a roomy back seat, and a short bed with a cover.

"Love it. Got it during a pre-Christmas sale. My Christmas present from me to me."

"How's the mileage?"

"About thirteen around town and seventeen on the highway."

"Gas is expensive," I noted.

"The company pays me mileage on government business. That covers it."

"Except when you aren't on government business."

"You're a cheap bastard, Tommy."

"Frugal."

"Someday you're going to be the richest man in the graveyard."

"Huh-uh. That'll be Anton Hunt."

Twenty minutes later we learned Bill Farnem's destination. It was a strip mall in Bethesda. When we coasted into the lot we saw his sedan and it was empty. Our van was parked in front of a hardware store. Armanti's ride was in front of a nail salon.

Armanti came over to the pickup. "Joe says he think's he's in that pool room over there."

"Has he ever seen you?"

"No."

"He's white, about five-ten, early fifties, small spare tire and a salt-and-pepper crew cut." I had seen photos of Bill and Kathy in their house. "He's probably still in trousers, leather shoes, and a sports coat. Maybe a suit. Go in and see if he's there meeting with someone."

Armanti went. He was back three minutes later. "They got a pay phone on the wall and he's on it. Wearing a suit. Three guys in jeans playing pool and no one in the two booths."

"Okay. Let's scatter and cover the exits to this lot. Someone will either join him or he'll drive off. Be ready."

The afternoon crawled on. The sky clouded up like it was thinking about raining.

My cell phone rang. Jake Grafton.

"Yes, sir."

"F has disappeared. Do you know where he is?"

"We're sitting on him."

"They're getting a warrant. L is hopping mad."

"I'll bet."

"Do you want me to notify L?"

"No. I want to see what he does. He'll meet someone or go somewhere."

"Okay." The call ended.

Grafton was often abrupt. The fact that he was letting me call the shots meant a lot to me. Fact is, I liked working for the guy.

"If you want to take a leak now is the time," I told Travis. "Try the hamburger joint on the corner." When he came back, I went, then bought a cup of coffee to wake me up. The two drinks at lunch had made me a bit sleepy; I figured I was going to need every wit I could muster before the day was over. Armanti and Doc saw us trooping that way and soon followed, one by one. I saw Joe go into the hardware store, and when he returned to the van Ski went in.

The coffee was bitter and hot.

An hour and ten minutes after we rolled in, at seventeen minutes after three, a car came into the lot and parked beside Farnem's. A man in his fifties wearing jeans, Nikes, and a golf shirt got out and walked into the pool room. I used Travis's binoculars to get his license plate number and called Sarah on my cell.

"Hello, beautiful. I need you to run a Maryland plate." I read her the number. "It's on a fairly new Honda Accord, four-door, gunmetal gray."

"Okay."

I also gave her Farnem's number, which was on a Washington plate marked with the phrase, "No Taxation without Representation." I thought he was driving a government sedan. It wouldn't hurt to make sure.

"Call me back when you get them."

"Okay." She hung up.

Eight minutes later she called back. "Farnem's plate is on a government sedan registered to the General Services Administration. Probably his company car. The plate on the Accord belongs to a guy named John Shipper. Car is three years old. Apparently he bought it new." She read me his address, which was in Silver Spring. I copied it on the back of a sheet of paper I had in my pocket.

"See what you can find out about Shipper."

"Right, general."

Five minutes later they came out together and scanned the parking lot. I was watching with binoculars from perhaps eighty yards away. If they noticed our vehicles, they didn't go on full alert. As Shipper fired up his chariot, Farnem unlocked his trunk and removed a gym bag that sagged a little. He put in inside Shipper's car and joined him on the passenger seat. The Accord

245

moved out of the lot and headed west on the street.

"Let's go," I said to Travis. "Stay behind Joe and let him do his thing following the cell phone."

"Aye aye, admiral."

Maybe I was giving too many orders.

Oh well.

I called Grafton and told him Farnem had apparently abandoned his car. I gave him the location and plate number. He said he would send someone to check it out.

We were on I-95 heading north when my phone rang again. Sarah said, "John Shipper was an FBI agent. Forced out, apparently, two years ago. They let him keep his pension."

"Know why they booted him?"

"Not a clue."

"Tell the boss we're headed north toward Baltimore."

"Roger."

It was beginning to rain, just a drizzle.

We rolled on, took the tunnel under the Chesapeake, and headed north toward Delaware. "When he stops for gas, our crowd should top off too when they can. Ask Joe about the gas situation in the van."

Joe said he had plenty. Armanti Hall was down to half a tank. Travis's truck had over three-quarters of a tank. "It's a forty-gallon tank. Got over thirty left. We're fat."

I told Armanti, "Hit a filling station now and catch back up."

Through Delaware past the scene of my Mercedes' last adventure, across the Delaware River Bridge, and into New Jersey. Travis punched up a CD and we listened to Meatloaf.

"Know where he's going?" Travis asked.

"I've got an idea," I admitted. I thought he might be going to pay Heiki Schlemmer a visit. I hoped so. We were due for some luck.

"Still hasn't used his phone," Travis remarked.

"He suspects we're listening," I replied. "He may be twisted but he's not stupid."

"That's what we say about you, Tommy."

I sat there wondering if Shipper had a rifle in the trunk of his car. After a while I mentioned that thought to Travis, who grunted.

"If you rear-ended him hard enough to pop the trunk, we could find out," I remarked.

That got a rise out of Travis. "This isn't a government vehicle. It's *my* truck. If I rear-end someone the insurance company will raise my rates. Forget it."

"Just a thought," I said.

"I thought you wanted to see where these guys were headed?"

"Yeah."

"Hold on to that thought, Carmellini, and stop thinking about my damn truck."

"I could drive if you get tired."

"Eat shit."

Night had fallen and the rain had stopped by the time we rolled into the Oranges. Yep, Farnem was going to Schlemmer's shack. I called Armanti and Joe.

"These two may be the ElectTech shooters," Travis said. "You considered that?"

"Yep."

"So what is your plan, admiral?"

"Take them when they come out of Schlemmer's place—before they get in the car. Alive, if possible. Then go in and get Heiki."

"Maybe she'll call 911."

"You think?"

"No."

Actually, I wondered if Heiki was still alive. The senators this morning had undoubtedly called their good buddy and patron, Anton Hunt. And no doubt they had filled his ear about Heiki. If she was still alive, one wondered if she would be home.

Well, we would soon find out.

"Pass the van and let's get there quick." I used the encrypted phone to call Armanti. "Follow us."

As we approached Heiki's place, I saw Shipper's car pull to a stop in the driveway in front of the garage doors.

"Let me out here," I told Travis. "When they go into the house, block the driveway and take cover behind the truck."

He slowed and I bailed. I vaulted over a little decorative three-rail fence—I was stiff from sitting so long—and hid behind a shrub. Farnem and Shipper were standing at the door. It opened. They went in.

I saw Armanti pass Travis's truck and stop on the other side of the driveway. Armanti and Doc bailed out and leaped the fence. I ran on a diagonal for the corner of the house.

The living room, if that was what it was, was lit up. Heck, there were lights in every window of the place. I got in her flower bed and sneaked to a corner of the living room window, then slowly raised my head just enough to see in through a gap in the thin curtains.

Heiki Schlemmer was suspended from a chandelier by ropes around her wrists. She was completely naked and had two bloody streaks that ran from her breasts to her hips. Apparently they had just started working on her with a knife. Two guys were standing there with guns in their hands frisking Farnem and Shipper.

They sure as hell weren't cops, not with Heiki hanging there like that. They hadn't yet got the information from her they wanted, so they hadn't killed her. All these thoughts went firing across the synapses.

The other thought that popped into my head was that they didn't have much use for Farnem and Shipper, so these guys weren't going to be long for this world.

I hoped there were only two of them.

I stepped back, aimed the Kimber .45 through the glass, and got a good sight-picture. The well-lit room and thin curtains made it easy. I settled the sights on the guy farthest away and squeezed the trigger.

He went down hard, and I shifted to the other guy. Squeezed it off as he was turning toward the window, and he went onto his back as if he were smacked by King Kong.

Farnem and Shipper were both flat on the floor by then, taking cover. For all they knew I was going to shoot them.

I used the Kimber to smash out the remaining window glass, cut my hand a little, then climbed through with the gun pointed. Farnem was trying to get to a gun on the floor. The first guy I shot had apparently dropped it.

Armanti Hall came through the door, which was still unlocked, apparently, with his shotgun in his hands. He jabbed it into Farnem's neck and that settled him down. Shipper hadn't twitched.

Doc Gordon came in behind Armanti. "Check the house," I said, and he went trotting away with his pistol in his hand.

I said to Armanti, "Check these two for car

keys." He did and held up a set. "Give them to Travis and tell him to find their ride."

I could hear Doc upstairs.

Heiki was dripping blood on the floor. I jerked my head at Armanti. He found the knife they used to carve on Heiki and cut her down. Left her hands tied together and went to the bathroom for towels to clean her up.

Blood was dripping from my right hand. I took a look. The cut was perhaps an inch long behind my thumb. Rich, red blood was welling out.

One of the guys I had shot was still alive. I squatted down and asked, "Who sent you?"

"Call an ambulance. I need a doctor."

"Whether I call or not depends on how honest you are. Who sent you?"

"Wouldn't you like to know."

He had been hit in the chest and was bleeding profusely. He wouldn't last long. I turned him over. The shot had gone clean through, leaving a messy exit hole, which was also bleeding. I checked his pulse. It was erratic and fading.

"You don't have long," I said. "Anyone you want us to notify?"

His eyes bulged and he collapsed. A few eye flickers and his heart stopped. His eyes were open, focused on infinity. I checked his pulse again. There was none.

Armanti put Farnem and Shipper seated against the wall with their hands in their laps. My cut was gushing and dripping all over. I went to the bathroom and found a towel to wrap my hand in.

I went outside and waited for Travis to return. A couple minutes passed before he came in a black SUV. He parked behind Shipper's Accord. "Get your truck, then search both vehicles."

"It was parked a block away."

He walked back to get his truck. When he arrived, I climbed in and used the encrypted phone to call Jake Grafton. He picked right up. As I was reporting what had happened, Travis opened the Accord's trunk. He pulled out a gun case, unzipped it, and showed me the weapon. It was a scoped rifle. Then he zipped the case back up and did the interior of the car.

Shipper had a small suitcase full of clothes and toiletries. The other bag, which Travis opened on the driver's seat of the truck, held wads of cash, a 9-MM pistol and a suppressor that screwed onto the barrel. I motor-mouthed, told the admiral all about it.

He didn't express any opinion when I told him about shooting the two guys who were cutting up Heiki Schlemmer. Didn't ask if it was really necessary, did I regret it, none of that bullshit. His attitude seemed to be, if you shot 'em it must have needed to be done.

"Sit tight," he told me. "I'll send a helicopter and a doctor for Heiki. We'll bring her back to Langley, clean her up and fix her up. After she's out of there, you call the FBI and tell them where you have Farnem and Shipper."

We put plastic ties around the wrists of the two FBI dudes, behind their backs, and sat them against a wall. We used a plastic tie on Schlemmer with her wrists in front of her.

Doc Gordon, who had once been a Navy corpsman with the Marines, retrieved the first aid kit from the van and set to work on Schlemmer. Put antiseptic on her wounds, taped them shut, and bandaged them. She was conscious and alert, and didn't say a word. Her eyes stayed on Doc and me.

When Doc had finished with her, he said to me, "Come over to the sink and let me see that cut."

I did so. He ran water on it to clean off the blood. The towel I had used was sodden with it.

He squeezed it, which made it bleed profusely and almost sent me through the roof. "You've got a piece of glass in there, Tommy, and it has to come out."

"How arc you going to do that?"

"Watch." Holding my hand under the water, he used both thumbs on the wound, and forced the glass up, like a splinter. Finally I could see it, a tiny, shiny piece sticking up above my tender, bleeding flesh. Using a piece of paper towel, he raked it until it came out and held it up for me to see. A shard about a half-inch long.

After applying an antiseptic, he bandaged the wound.

"You're good to go." He threw the towel in the garbage and mopped the blood from the counter with a paper towel. Then he scrubbed it.

While we were waiting for the chopper, we took all four of the wallets and cell phones and lined them up on Schlemmer's dining room table. I inspected every item.

I was especially interested in the cell phones of the guys who had come to do Heiki. They had called each other, and one of them had talked to a Maplewood number three times that evening. It might have been a pizza joint, but I was betting it was Nick Liszt. I put the number in my cell phone.

An hour passed before we heard the helicopter. A couple of the guys got in the backyard with flashlights, and before we knew it the thing was settling, with bright landing lights blinding everyone.

We hustled Heiki Schlemmer out and put her aboard.

After the helicopter departed in a cloud of last fall's leaves and grass clippings, I obeyed Grafton's orders and called the FBI.

I didn't plan on waiting around. "Come on, Travis. Let's you and me go calling."

When we were in the truck, he asked, "Where to?"

"Nick Liszt's place, west of Maplewood. Maybe we can ruin his evening."

CHAPTER THIRTEEN

All the lights were out in Liszt's three-story mansion. He had a wrought-iron gate across his driveway to keep out the riff-raff, and it was closed. Travis and I sat in the pickup with the lights out, looking.

"What do you think?" I asked, finally.

"Looks like the Addams family lives there. All we need are some lightning flashes."

"Maybe he turned out all the lights and died."

"Is he married?"

"Got a wife, his third. Two daughters, one married to a doctor and living in Connecticut, the other a senior at Vassar."

"How old is this guy?"

"Sarah says fifty-nine."

"Well . . ."

"Ain't it amazing how that gate sort of stands there with no fence on either side? As if no scumbag would drive around it."

I could tell Travis was less than enthusiastic, but driving on Liszt's lawn and leaving ruts did appeal to his baser nature. He left the lights off and did it.

"Around back," I said.

Behind the house we parked in front of the closed garage door and got out to survey the situation.

"Man this rich oughta have a caretaker," Travis remarked.

We used flashlights to examine the rear windows for an alarm system. Didn't see a thing.

"This guy has gotta have a burglary alarm system," Travis said, and swore softly. "We're just a few miles from the Jersey sewers."

I got out my cell phone and played with it a bit.

"I don't like this, Tommy. Let's get outta here."

I looked up Liszt's number and dialed it. It rang and rang but no one answered. Finally it rolled over to a voice mailbox. I turned the phone off and put it back in my pocket.

"Maybe he's dead," I said.

"If he is, we'll read about it in the paper."

That's when I spotted the camera lens behind us, high up on the wall of the barn, under the peak of the roof. A little red light was on.

"Camera," I said, leaping for the door of the truck. "Let's go!"

Travis whipped the truck around the house and set sail across the lawn toward the closed gate as a police car with lights flashing came roaring down the street, squealing to a stop in front of the closed gate. Two cops bailed out. Travis locked his brakes and slid to a stop in the grass.

Two more cop cars came blasting up with red lights flashing. The place was beginning to look like a major crime scene on a movie set.

"Get out of the vehicle with your hands up."

That came over a loudspeaker. Spotlights hit us.

"That sounds like good advice," Travis said. He turned off the truck and got out with his hands held straight up. I did the same. We were lit up like we were rock stars.

We were disarmed, cuffed, stuffed into the back seat of police cars and taken to a lock-up somewhere in the Jersey 'burbs. There we were read our rights, photographed, printed, and booked. They asked if I wanted to make a telephone call.

"What county is this?"

"Essex."

I used the phone on the desk and dialed Sarah's number. No doubt they were recording it, so I just told her I had been arrested and booked in Essex County, New Jersey.

"What for?" she asked.

I asked the cop, "What was I arrested for?"

He looked at the form in front of him. "Carrying a concealed weapon, possessing burglary tools, trespassing, and resisting arrest. We'll probably add to the list during the night."

"Did you get that?" I asked Sarah.

"Yes. How fortunate that you got popped on Friday night. You'll have a long, wonderful weekend."

"You have a great weekend too, babe."

I hung up and said to the cop, "I get arrested so often she doesn't think it's any big deal."

"Strip, clown, down to your shorts and get into that coverall and them flip-flops."

A plain-clothes officer wanted to converse, probably about my wicked ways, but I told him I wasn't saying anything without my lawyer at my side, so he motioned to the turnkey. That officer escorted me to the cell block and locked me in with an emaciated guy with only half his teeth and wisps of hair. Then he took my cuffs off.

"What you in for?" my cellmate asked.

"Kicked the shit outta a guy. How about you?"

He muttered something unintelligible and retreated to his bunk. I sat on mine. After looking him over carefully, I decided my friend was in the grips of a love affair with meth.

Ten minutes later they brought Travis in and locked him in the adjacent cell with two skinny, tattooed black guys. They were in for drugs, they said. Travis looked at me and I looked at him, then we both lay down on our bunks and closed our eyes. The cells were undoubtedly bugged. Even if they weren't, one or all of our cellmates were probably snitches that would love some dirt to sell to the prosecutor.

The place didn't smell too bad. The cut on my hand throbbed. I rubbed the bandage and shifted around, trying to get comfortable on the thin mattress pad.

That's when I realized I hadn't eaten since lunch at Union Station.

What a hell of a day this had been! From rubbing elbows with senators and a delicious lunch with good bourbon, to killing two thugs and "camping in" with street trash.

Life in America! Why would anyone want to live anywhere else?

After the lights were turned down to just the eternal illumination in the corridors between the cells, things settled down. Some drunk down the cellblock was retching and someone was moaning softly, just barely audible, not as if he were in pain, but as if he were whacked out of his mind. Some guys shouted for him to shut up, but he didn't.

Despite those distractions, conversations petered out, the coughing and hacking subsided, and the snoring started. I lay on my thin pad staring into the darkness, listening to the keening of the addict. Maybe the doper had used so many drugs over time that there was nothing left upstairs, if there had been something up there to begin with.

I thought about dying. If a jailer comes for Travis and me in the middle of the night what choice will we have? What can we do? Refuse to leave the cell? Wait to be dragged kicking and screaming to an interrogation room to receive a bullet in the brain? Or walk to the room hoping and praying there was a real FBI dude in there with his recorder and notepad and fancy credentials . . . and no gun?

Maybe Farnem and Shipper were the ElectTech shooters. The FBI would learn if bullets from their pistols matched the bullets recovered from the victims. Surely the shooters weren't so damn stupid that they kept the guns. Yet pistols and silencers that can't be traced are difficult to obtain. If there's a possibility you might need one again, would you toss it and try to obtain another?

Maybe we hadn't even seen the ElectTech shooters. Maybe they are out there somewhere in the great wide world living like normal people, but waiting for a call to go kill someone. That's what assassins do, I guess. Wait for that summons that will mean death to someone they don't know.

Time to stop thinking.

Control the fear, Tommy. Do it, dude!

I am in no hurry to die. It isn't so much death I fear as being murdered. Looking at the killer, seeing the gun come up, waiting for the muzzle flash . . . but I won't see the flash. By the time my eyes detect the muzzle flash and tell my brain about it, the bullet will be smashing through my skull.

I want to live. I want to feel Sarah Houston's warmth, her humanity, her femininity, savor the taste of food, the relief of cool water, the foaming frothiness of beer, the smooth warmth of whiskey, the delight of a hot shower, the caress of a breeze, the sight of growing things, friends' faces, a night sky, flowers in bloom. I want to feel the heat of summer and the crisp coolness of fall . . . I want to revel in the sheer exuberance of being alive. Life is a marvelous gift.

Damn, I am going to miss all that if the jailer comes down the hallway to get me. But he won't.

Will he?

I try not to, but I strain to hear the opening of the door to the cellblock.

"You still awake, Tommy?" A whisper.

"Yeah."

"Think Farnem was the guy in Pennsylvania?"

"I hope."

"I've never felt so goddamn helpless in my life."

"That's the word," I agreed. "Helpless."

Travis said no more. Even the moaning eventually stopped. I listened for the door, and footsteps . . . and finally fell asleep.

When they brought our breakfast in the morning, Travis and I were still alive to eat it.

In midmorning my cellmate ventured a comment. "I've only got nineteen days to go."

I gave him a cold stare. I was pretty sure I didn't want to hear the story of his miserable life.

"My wife drove me to this," he said anyway.

Yep, I didn't want to hear it.

At eleven they took us out to the exercise yard for a half hour. It was raining and we got soaked. As we were trooping back to our cells, Travis said to me, "This is all your fault, Carmellini."

When they brought our lunch, I asked the jailer, "When am I going to get to see a judge for a bail hearing?"

"Man, I get paid eleven dollars and forty-two and a half cents an hour. I just work here."

"Sorry I asked."

"Next time ask somebody who gives a shit."

"I'll keep that in mind."

"You're welcome."

Somewhere people were playing baseball, lovers were gazing into each other's eyes, flowers were growing, and the sun was shining bright. But not in the Essex County Jail.

Of course, I knew that somewhere wheels were turning. Jake Grafton and Robert Levy were making things happen. I figured the bad guys were having as bad a weekend as I was, probably worse. I dreamed up all kinds of things for the feds to do, from getting search warrants and sweating miscreants to talking to county clerks and examining voting machines.

I wondered what Heiki Schlemmer was saying, if she was talking at all. I wondered what Sarah Houston was doing. I wondered if our Friday morning senators had given news conferences.

I wondered if Jake Grafton was still running the CIA or if he had been summarily retired and told not to leave the jurisdiction.

I wondered what I was going to do with the rest of my life.

More people were added to the cells Saturday night. My meth head and I got a guy who was picked up for DUI. He was stinking drunk and decided to sing. He was not a trained operatic talent.

Saturday night was not as bad as Sunday night would prove to be. The Friday night drunk had stopped vomiting, the doper was silent, and our cellmate passed out on his bunk at ten o'clock. The cellblock never really quieted down, not with people being jugged almost every hour or so.

Sunday morning I finally got some sleep. Missed the watery scrambled eggs and burnt sausage for breakfast. The drunk ate his and mine too.

By Sunday afternoon I had decided to quit the CIA and go straight. I was never ever again going to spend a night in jail. Although this was the nicest jail I had yet been in, it was still a jail.

Late Sunday night the guys in Travis's cell got into a fight. A biker had been added to the mix, and he didn't like black dudes or freaks like Travis, he said. I had been listening to them talk trash all evening, and just before lights out it turned into a brawl. Travis whipped all three.

It was pretty to watch. He could really handle himself with no wasted motion, making every move count. He had all three of them stretched on the floor when the jailers arrived and hosed water on him to stop the violence. Some of the stream splashed on me, which I thought was unfair.

At ten on Monday morning Travis and I were taken to see a judge. An assistant United States attorney was there and she was blistering the air. The local prosecutor was swimming upstream.

"Both these gentlemen are employees of the Central Intelligence Agency," our lawyer said, "carrying ID cards which gave their names, photos, and employment status, and the fact they are authorized to carry weapons. So much for the weapons charge! Mr. Carmellini is also a part owner of a lock shop in suburban Maryland. He is often asked to open locks for householders who have locked themselves out. The *so-called* burglary tools are merely tools of his off-duty trade."

The judge looked at the prosecutor. "Do you want to address this trespassing charge?"

"Your honor, when the defendants were arrested they were in Mr. Clay's pickup truck on the lawn of a prominent citizen of this county. They had driven around his locked gate and were leaving ruts in his lawn."

"Ruts in his lawn . . ." the judge intoned. "And the police just happened by?"

"A private security service called the police, Your Honor, and due to the owner's position in the community, the police responded immediately. They found the defendants still on the lawn in Mr. Clay's truck, which was impounded."

For the first time the judge looked us over. He said to the U.S. lawyer, "I'll dismiss all the charges except for trespassing, and give them two days in jail, with credit for time served. No fine."

The lady lawyer looked at Travis and me, and we shrugged.

"So how do you plead?"

"Guilty," I said.

"Guilty," Travis said.

"Next time stay off the grass. Two days in jail, credit for time served." He whacked his gavel. "Next case."

So we got our clothes, guns, money and stuff back, and after we signed receipts, the lady lawyer, Sarah Jane Cohen, escorted us outside.

She looked at her watch. "Mr. Carmellini, an executive jet will pick you up at Newark airport in fifty-two minutes. Mr. Clay, you will want a ride to the police impoundment facility to rescue your vehicle. I suggest you both grab taxis."

"Thank you," I said, shook hands with Ms. Cohen, and hailed the first cab I saw rolling down the street.

Travis had some choice words for me as the

taxi was stopping to pick me up. "This is all your fault, Carmellini, and you are going to pay the fee to get my truck outta hock or I'll take every last dime out of your worthless hide, you worthless son of a—"

He might have said more, but I climbed into the rear seat of the cab and slammed the door to shut him off. I told the hackie, who was wearing a turban, "Newark Airport, the FBO."

"Gotcha," he said in perfect English, dropped the flag, and stepped on the gas.

CHAPTER FOURTEEN

The jet dropped me at the FBO at Dulles Airport, where a helicopter was waiting. And so was Sarah Houston. She gave me a bag packed with toiletries, underwear, and fresh clothes.

"Where am I going?" I asked.

"The safe house in West Virginia. Grafton and Levy are there. I missed you, Tommy."

"I missed you too. I'll try to stay out of jail in the future."

We kissed. I grabbed the bag and hotfooted it across the ramp to the helicopter, which had its rotors turning. We were airborne before I had time to buckle up.

Apparently the pilots called ahead on the radio because when we settled onto the grass runway at the safe house, actually a farm, an SUV was waiting. We rode up through the woods to the main building, which I had visited before. This facility was designed and used to debrief defectors and former spies. It had a large living room, bedrooms, a kitchen and food storage area, a small medical facility, and two interrogation rooms, which were set up to surreptitiously film and record the person being interviewed.

I went up the front stairs, across the porch and found Grafton and Levy in the living room with their heads together. "Ah, Tommy," Grafton said. "How was your weekend?"

That was a rare Grafton funny, so I smiled to show I appreciated the effort.

He introduced me to the FBI director, and in a few minutes I was reunited with Maggie Jewel Miller, the special agent in charge of the Election Fraud Task Force. She briefed me.

Heiki Schlemmer had been flown there, sedated, and a doctor was in attendance. Her cuts had been stitched up and they hoped she was ready to talk. I gathered that the FBI wanted to grill her yesterday, but Grafton had insisted they wait until I could be there. I looked at him with a new respect.

I didn't know what I could add to the interrogation, but I fully appreciated the fact that he wanted me there at the finish. If we were near the finish, which I doubted.

They soon brought Heiki to an interrogation room we called "the den." It had six large padded chairs arranged in a circle, a refrigerator full of bottled water, a coffee pot and cups, but lacked a table. The video cameras were not in sight. Actually there were four cameras, so the interviewee could pick any chair in the room.

"Do you want me in the room?" I asked Miller.

"No. You can watch in the theatre. The two directors will be there too."

"By the way, when we went up to Pennsylvania

to interview the ElectTech snitch, who was your boss at the agency?"

"Bill Farnem."

"So where is he these days?"

"In jail, I believe, along with John Shipper." She looked at her watch and said, "I'll go get Ms. Schlemmer."

I settled into a seat beside Grafton in the theatre to watch the live production. The video from all four cameras was displayed on small screens across the bottom of the projection screen, and the operator could pick which camera feed he wanted on the large screen. He could include both the subject and the interrogator in a split screen. He could also zoom in if he wished, but zoom was rarely used because one lost the body language. Hidden mikes in the ceiling picked up everything that was said in the den. This was reality television at its finest.

Heiki was wearing a simple dress and no make-up. The fact that she was bandaged was evident in the way the dress fitted. I scrutinized her closely as Maggie went through the preliminaries. "You understand you are not under arrest and are merely being detained for your own protection?"

Yes, she understood that.

"We want to question you as part of an FBI investigation into election fraud. I'm going to read you your rights," which she did. Then

Maggie said, "Do you understand your rights?"

"Yes."

"If at anytime you want to terminate this interview, all you have to do is say so."

"I'll answer your questions."

Maggie was a pro. She started with name and education and fleshed out Heiki's biography. It took twenty minutes for Maggie to get around to asking if Heiki had known a man named Harry Tanaka, and another six minutes before she mentioned the Armageddon file.

Yes, after Harry committed suicide, she was given the job of supervising the Allegheny people and, through them, ElectTech. She found out then, she said, that ElectTech had been tasked with fixing the 2016 election. Maggie questioned her about how that was supposed to be done.

Then she asked Heiki an apparently simple question. "Who was supposed to win?"

"Mrs. Hinton."

"Well, why didn't she?"

Heiki covered her face with her hands, composed herself, and looked straight at Maggie. "I don't know. The results in the various swing counties that the ElectTech people had targeted didn't match Tanaka's file. He was dead by then, so I couldn't ask him."

"Do you really think he committed suicide?"

"I did at the time."

They explored that subject for a while, then

Maggie went back to the mine to dig more ore. "Did Junior Sikes and his colleagues actually install Harry Tanaka's program on the tally machines in their assigned counties?"

"I was told that they said they did. I never asked them myself."

"Who told you that?"

"Nick Liszt."

"Your boss at Red Truck?"

"Right."

"How did he know?"

"He said he and Harry had gone to the ElectTech offices and questioned everyone."

"I'd like to come back to that in a bit," Maggie said, "but first I would like you to tell me who was responsible for ElectTech's efforts to fix the election, if you know."

"Oh, I know all right," Heiki said bitterly. "Anton Hunt. That was an Anton Hunt operation all the way."

"Those men who stripped you naked at your home on Friday, tied you to a chandelier and were cutting you when you were rescued, do you know who they were?"

"Not their names."

"Who do you think sent them to do that to you if, indeed, you think they were sent?"

"Oh, they didn't just happen to be driving through the neighborhood and decide to torture some woman. Oh yeah, for the thrill of it we'll do the bitch in that house there. Un-huh. *They were sent*. Nick Liszt sent them. He knows some Mafia trash, and that's who those two were, I think. Jersey accents."

"What does Liszt have against you?"

"Nothing, as far as I know. Hunt probably told him to find someone to kill me."

"Has he ever ordered people killed before?"

"For a fact, I don't know. But when the people at ElectTech were killed, I thought it was Hunt and Liszt who wanted them dead. Nora Shepherd called me to tell me that Junior Sikes had been arrested for porn. I told Liszt. He probably told Hunt. Two days later . . . well, somebody went in there and murdered Junior and the people in the jail and two more ElectTech employees. Plus someone who was in one of the houses. It had to be Nick Liszt who sent the killers. He was the only one I told. Maybe Nora told someone else, but only Nora, Kurt Lesh, me, and Nick knew that Junior had a big secret. And, of course, Hunt."

"A very tight circle."

"Hell, yes, it was tight. The ElectTech crowd had tried to fix the election for the *president of the United States*. I was a month late getting into the conspiracy, after the horse was out of the barn and long gone, but I was in. No one wanted to go to jail, including me. This wasn't cocktail party chatter. 'Oh, yes, dear, we helped fix the election. How do you like our new president?' "

"But they didn't fix it. Cynthia Hinton lost."

Heiki Schlemmer rubbed her forehead. Finally she lowered her hands and said, "I don't know what the hell happened. That's God's honest truth. ElectTech, Kurt Lesh, Nora Shepherd, Harry Tanaka, Nick Liszt, and Anton Hunt tried to fix the election and fucked it up."

Jake Grafton turned off the audio in the theatre room and looked at me. "Is she telling the truth?"

"I doubt it," I said. "She hasn't been asked yet about the encryption code she used to communicate with Bill Farnem. He was probably the ElectTech shooter, or one of them, and I think Schlemmer knows that. She asked him to do something about Carmellini, and he said he'd try. Someone shot at me with a rifle Thursday night, admiral, when I was driving home from your condo. They came within a few inches of getting the job done. And two guys from the hood went to kill Kurt Lesh. Two guys tried to assassinate me in Delaware. Someone is trying to close mouths."

I pointed at the screen. "She had Sarah's apartment bugged, talked to the guy who did it six times on her cell phone. She wouldn't have asked Farnem to do something about me if she didn't know he was the ElectTech shooter. I think she's lying through her teeth."

"She says she doesn't know why Hinton lost the election," Robert Levy said thoughtfully.

"Someone does. That's the key to this puzzle. Who is that someone who knows? Who is that someone who made sure that Hinton didn't win despite ElectTech's efforts?"

"Anton Hunt," I said sourly. I jerked my thumb at the screen, "Or that woman there, for a half million bucks from the Chinese."

Grafton weighed in. "Robert, you are assuming that Junior Sikes actually managed to rig the tally machines in key counties. How many, twenty-four, twenty-six, thirty, thirty-six? Did he? We don't know!"

"And we never will know," Robert Levy said heavily. "The actual results don't match the results Harry Tanaka set forth in the Armageddon file."

"Perhaps Junior Sikes only fixed one or two counties."

Levy was skeptical. "Maybe. Then why are all these people dead?"

"Because Junior didn't do what he was supposed to do," I suggested.

"That theory doesn't work," Levy said dismissively, not even bothering to look at me. "Junior was killed five months after the election. If Hunt wanted him dead because he was a scofflaw, he would have died in November. Or in early December, like Harry Tanaka."

"The only theory that works," Jake Grafton said, "is that Anton Hunt had a side operation that we know nothing about to fix the election so

274

that Vaughn Conyer won. Or, if you want to turn it over, so Cynthia lost."

"Edwin P. Riddenhour," I said softly. "American Voting."

Then I saw it, in all its magnificent simplicity. I stood and shouted, "Yes! Yes! Yes!" I lowered my voice and looked at the two big bananas. "Get us some transportation. Maggie and I need to go to New Jersey."

Ten minutes later I was on the phone with Travis Clay. "You got your truck outta jail yet?"

"Yeah. The bail was two hundred eighty-seven dollars and eighty-nine cents. You are gonna pay me back."

"Put it on your expense account."

"Like those asshole accountants will approve a police towing and impoundment fee! *You* are paying."

"I might. Where are you?"

"Jersey Turnpike ten miles north of the Delaware line."

"Turn around. I want you to go to this address in East Orange"—I gave it to him—"and keep an eye on the place. I'll be up there later tonight and I want the woman alive."

"You got it. See you there. Bring money."

Going back to New Jersey took some time. Maybe it would have been quicker to drive, but after I explained my theory to the directors, they decided Miller and I needed a plane. It took time for a helicopter to come from Dulles to pick us up, so Maggie went back to spend some more time with Heiki.

"Ms. Schlemmer, I wish to remind you of your rights. You may terminate this interview at anytime. Do you understand that?"

"Yes," she said. "But where am I going to go on this planet that Anton Hunt can't find me?"

"Let me cover two or three points, then we'll break for dinner. What can you tell me about your Swiss bank account?"

Heiki took a deep breath and exhaled slowly. I watched her eyes and body language. "I opened it five years ago as a savings account. It's in my own name and I filed the form every year with the IRS when I did my taxes that showed I had it."

"You see how far behind we are," Robert Levy said in the monitor room. "If that's true we should have known that. And she wouldn't say it if it weren't true because she knows we will check."

I had to agree. To my disgust, I thought she was telling the truth.

"Why did you open that account?" Maggie asked Schlemmer.

"Hunt plays fast and loose with a lot of people who don't like his methods. I thought at the time that the day might come when I would have to leave, and I wanted money outside the United States that I could get to if that day ever came."

"We'll come back to that point later. How much money is in the account?"

"I opened it with twenty grand. Made other deposits through the years . . . Last I looked, the balance was about a hundred and ten thousand U.S. dollars."

"What would you say if I told you the balance was in excess of six hundred thousand dollars?"

Heiki Schlemmer gaped. "There's been some mistake," she managed. "I never put that money in there."

"The last deposit was a half million dollars, and according to the Swiss, it came from a Chinese consortium. In October."

"Which one?" Her disbelief was evident. If she was lying, she was damn good, I thought.

"GK Products."

"That's one of the companies Hunt does business with."

"Do you think he told them to deposit the money into your account?"

The life went out of Heiki as if it were air leaving a balloon. "My God! I thought no one knew I had that account except the IRS. He must have found out about it."

"So you didn't do anything to earn the money?"

"No."

"Tell me about the encryption software on your computer."

"I don't have any encryption software on my computer. I use the computers at Red Truck or the Hunt hedge fund. They are very secure."

"Do you know a man named Bill Farnem?"

"No."

"You met him Friday night. He was one of the men who came to your house, after the two men stripped you and tied you up."

"Oh. No one said his name. Or if they did I didn't hear it or it didn't register."

"But you never met him before?"

"Not that I can recall."

"Ever emailed him?"

"The name doesn't ring a bell."

"Perhaps he was using an internet alias."

She shook her head. "If he did, I didn't know it was Bill Farnem."

"Let's go back to the Armageddon file, if we may. According to you, it was used to give a program to ElectTech to rig voting tabulation machines. Was it on a thumb drive?"

"Yes."

"Was that thumb drive the one Liszt used?"

"I don't know."

"Where is that thumb drive now?"

"Anton Hunt has it."

I almost fell out of my chair when I heard that. "Why?"

"He put the file on his computer and made some changes. He thought Tanaka was too optimistic. He improved some of the numbers."

"Okay. Let's call it an evening and get some dinner."

"That would be nice."

"Anyone at Red Truck or the hedge fund could have traded encrypted messages with Farnem," Grafton said.

"Schlemmer may have been set up," Levy acknowledged. "The deposit to her Swiss account could have been a setup too."

I had my doubts, but on the other hand, Heiki looked to me like she was telling the truth. I have told a million or so lies and listened to at least that many, so I know lies and liars. As a fall guy, Heiki Schlemmer would have been perfect. A competent, smart career woman with flexible ethics who liked money and was obviously worried about her future. It made sense.

If you are a scumbag out to do nasty things, you hope everything will go well and your cheating or stealing will go undiscovered. But if things don't go well, it helps to have someone handy to lay the dirt on. Always have a Plan B.

Anton Hunt impressed me as that kind of guy. If he was, Nick Liszt was living on borrowed time.

CHAPTER FIFTEEN

There was an FBI agent with a car waiting when our jet landed at Newark at eleven that night. I had slept a little on the plane, so I was somewhat refreshed.

I gave the agent the address and we rolled with him at the wheel. I told the guy to stop when I saw Travis Clay's truck parked a half block away, with him in the cab. I got out and he rolled down his window.

"How's everything?"

"She's there. Came in at seven. Hasn't gone out. No visitors."

"Hang loose a little while longer. We may need you."

"Okay."

I climbed back into the FBI sedan and the agent rolled up the driveway and parked in front of the door.

The house looked the same as I remembered it. With Maggie Miller beside me, I rang the bell. Several times.

"She's probably in bed," Maggie said.

"Let's hope," I said. I wanted to get to April Tanaka with my bright idea before it occurred to Anton Hunt.

Six minutes after we first rang the bell, the

280

door opened to the length of the security chain.

"Sorry to disturb you tonight, Mrs. Tanaka, but our business can't wait. You may remember me, James Wilson of the Federal Election Commission?"

"I remember you."

Maggie already had her credentials out of her purse and held them up so Mrs. Tanaka could see them. "I'm Special Agent Maggie Jewel Miller of the FBI. We'd like to talk to you."

She closed the door, removed the chain, and opened it. Maggie held the credentials so April Tanaka could read them.

"All right. Come on in." She stood aside and closed the door behind us. She was in a robe and slippers. We had gotten her out of bed.

She led us to the kitchen, turning on lights as she went, and said, "Would you like some coffee? I think I could drink some."

"Caffeinated?" Maggie asked.

"Decaf."

"Sure."

We sat around the kitchen table as the coffee pot dripped. "As I said, I'm Maggie Jewel Miller of the FBI. I'm the special agent in charge of the FBI Election Fraud Task Force. We'd like to ask you some questions about your late husband."

"I wondered when you were going to come," April Tanaka said.

"Why?"

"Don't you know?" she said, looking from face to face.

"We think we do, Mrs. Tanaka," I said. "But we want to hear it from you."

She took a deep breath and exhaled slowly. Then she got up and looked to see how much coffee had dripped through. She was getting out cups and milk and a sugar bowl when I said, "We want you to tell us about Edwin P. Riddenhour."

Her shoulders straightened. "So you do know."

"Why don't you tell us about him?"

It came out in spurts of words between long silences. After he was hired by Anton Hunt, Harry Tanaka quickly learned that Hunt didn't want predictions of how various counties would vote; he wanted Tanaka to create a plan to ensure his candidate won. He wanted to fix the race. And the winner was going to be Cynthia Hinton.

April was crying as she explained that the Tanakas needed the money to fund Ruth's care, yet Harry was tortured by the fact that his work for Hunt was helping to destroy democracy. Harry had studied politics; his life's work was figuring out why people voted the way they did. "And now . . ." April sobbed.

Harry had enlisted graduate students who shared his passion for understanding politics. He created a name, Edwin P. Riddenhour, had business cards printed, and held training sessions for his volunteers. He had learned at ElectTech how easily voting and tally machines could be rigged, and how to ensure they were honest. So he sent his Edwin P. Riddenhours on a mission with their laptops to ensure that the 2016 election was honest.

"How many Edwins were there?" I asked.

"Six Edwins and three Susans. Some of them took so much time off to check and purge machines that they got in trouble with their professors. Harry was so proud of them."

"Then the election came," I said to encourage her, "and Hinton lost."

We were drinking coffee then, and April had drained her cup. Before she could move Maggie was up and poured her another. She flashed Maggie a smile and wiped at her tears, almost as if they were embarrassing her.

"I don't think Harry had given much thought to what Hunt's reaction would be if Hinton lost. He was so determined that the election must be honest, or as honest as an election can be in America.

"'The American people must decide for themselves,' he said two dozen times. 'If we humans do not have the freedom to rule ourselves, to make choices for the future, we are just farm animals waiting to be fed and slaughtered when the master chooses.'"

"Who did he think would win?"

A grimace crossed April's features. "I think

he believed the polls. He knew better, but he placed his faith in them. He was a liberal—most academics are—and Conyer frightened him. One candidate was a shameless criminal, the other was a bombastic populist with no experience in government. For Harry it was a choice between two evils. Do you want to die in the gas chamber or the electric chair? He told me he voted for Hinton. I never told him, but I voted for Conyer.

"Harry used to walk around the house talking aloud, lecturing to the world, bemoaning the fact that his beloved political process had produced two such terrible candidates. He was a passionate man. That's what his students saw in him; that's what I saw in him; that's why many of his students went on to get advanced degrees in political science; that's why I married him.

"Some people think that political scientists want everyone to vote as they do, à la Anton Hunt. Harry thought the political process, the collective decision-making process, was one of life's great miracles. Voters aren't always right, but the democratic process is self-correcting. Kings and dictators make wrong decisions too and those decisions wreck nations and ruin lives.

"He would tell his students to forget ideology. Someone must decide how we are going to fix the potholes, keep clean water flowing through the pipes, pay the teachers, protect our citizens. Someone must decide, not some saint or fanatic or idiot son. Very human, flawed people must make those decisions. That's us! *We decide because we vote.* We are the decision-makers!

" 'Look at America!' he used to shout. 'We have schools, highways, bridges, airports, garbage dumps, sewage treatment plants, hospitals, animal shelters, safe food for sale, a power grid that works 99 percent of the time, and *the rule of law.* Is our society perfect? Of course not. Will we imperfect people ever achieve perfection? Of course not.'

"Harry thought democracy was the last, best chance for mankind to learn to live together on this crowded planet with finite resources. He studied it, lived it, breathed it. That was his tragedy. To support us he had to work for a man who wanted to subvert it, make it something foul and slimy, manipulate it, and rob people of their God-given right to choose, so that he could make more *money.*" A shiver of disgust passed through her and she took another sip of hot liquid.

In the silence I could hear raindrops gently pattering on the kitchen windows. It had started to rain again.

I couldn't sit any longer, so I went to the windows and looked out though the smeared glass into the night. I wished I could have known Harry Tanaka.

I thought that April Tanaka might be wrong about Hunt's motivation. He lost over a billion dollars in the markets when his candidate lost because the stock and bond markets went *up*. He had shorted a ton of positions and had to scramble to cover. That fact had been in the newspapers.

Did Hunt really think that if Hinton won the markets were going to *drop?* The financial elites, including Anton Hunt, the billionaire King of Chaos, *wanted* her to win!

Something had happened last fall that I didn't understand.

Maggie said it first. "Mrs. Tanaka, you can't stay here. If Anton Hunt suspects that you might talk to us, you might end up like Harry."

April ran her fingers through her hair.

"Someone must be here for Ruth," Maggie said gently.

That did it. April Tanaka nodded and stood. "I'll go pack," she said, and left us.

When we were alone in the kitchen, I said to Maggie, "It's a miracle that she's still alive."

"She will never be called to testify in a courtroom," Maggie said. "Everything she knows is inadmissible hearsay. Hunt knows that. Still . . ."

The FBI agent removed her cell phone from her purse and turned it on. She had calls to make.

I arrived back in Washington at five in the morning. Dawn was showing through the clouds. At least it wasn't raining. I took a cab home and saved the fare receipt for my expense account. Frugal.

A shower was called for to wash off the jail smell, and after I did that I crashed. When I awoke, Sarah was gone and it was past noon. I had shaved, scrubbed the fangs, dressed, and was walking toward the parking lot when I remembered that I didn't have a car. No ride.

Damn!

I called a taxi and rode to Langley in the back seat. When he heard the address of my destination, the cabbie, from Lebanon I think, was full of questions about me and the CIA. I made him promise not to tell anyone, then let it be known that I was defecting from Canada. He didn't believe me. My Canadian accent wasn't good enough, he said. He dropped me at the main gate. I gave him a two-dollar tip and pocketed the receipt.

I went to see Jake Grafton to bring him up to speed on last night's events in New Jersey. He had just returned from West Virginia and was eating lunch at his desk between telephone calls. When I went into his office he told Robin to hold his calls.

He was all ears as I told him about Harry Tanaka's scheme to ensure the election was honest. He nodded his head repeatedly. When I finished he said, "Levy told me he was going to put Mrs. Tanaka in the witness protection program."

So he had been briefed before I got to him. It figured.

"I stole Harry Tanaka's research from his computer at home. Sarah hacked in too. We should pay her for it. I was thinking fifty grand."

"Why fifty?"

"That's roughly how much the Tanakas owe the facilities that have housed their daughter."

"I'll think about it."

"The Armageddon file is the key to this whole thing," I said, gesturing widely. "It's the Tanakas' property. We stole it, admiral. I'll go as low as forty."

He gave me The Look, so I changed the subject. "What I can't figure out," I said, "is how Hunt thought he was going to make money if Hinton won. He told Harry Tanaka that there was a lot of money to be made if he knew for a certainty which candidate was going to win the presidential election. Yet his funds took a lot of short positions, betting on the financial markets swooning if Cynthia won, and, of course, she didn't and the market didn't. The day after Conyer won the election everyone and their brother was shoveling money into the market as fast as they could, so Hunt was caught with his pants down. What did he think was going to happen if Cynthia won?"

Jake Grafton handed me a sheet of paper. "Here is a list of his short positions on November 8, Election Day. Sarah got these from public records."

I scanned the list. What I saw was enormous positions against the shares of banks and financial Exchange Traded Funds. It looked as if he had put about ten billion on the table. I whistled.

Grafton kept chomping his burger. With his mouth full, he said, "Hunt thought he had inside information about what Cynthia Hinton was going to do after she won. I suspect he did know. She was going to announce that she wanted to nationalize the banks that were too big to fail. And raise taxes. The whole enchilada."

That seemed to me to make sense.

"She was pretty far left," he continued, "yet the Democrat party was moving even further left. You remember the problems our favorite socialist gave her in the primaries. That old hippie captured the youth vote with his promises of free everything. Then there was that other senator, Marybeth Sporran—she had built a career railing against evil capitalists, and Cynthia was worried about her too. Cynthia's base was trotting left about as fast as it could go, and as a politician, she had to get out in front of it or she was going to get run over."

He licked his fingers and helped himself to a french fry, which he dipped in ketchup.

"If she had won and made an announcement like that, the markets would have gone into free fall. The Wall Street elites certainly didn't expect that a Hinton victory would mean that socialism was just around the corner. Hunt knew she was going to win—he had stacked the deck. And he knew she agreed with his socialist, world government agenda. He must have believed a quick move against the banks was in Hinton's playbook, so he bet big on her. When she lost, he lost."

"Thanks to Harry Tanaka," I remarked.

Grafton bobbed his head. "Yes. Thanks to Harry Tanaka and all those Susan and Edwin P. Riddenhours. And, of course, the good sense of the American voters." He popped the last bite of burger into his mouth.

"So what is the government going to do about Anton Hunt?"

The most amazing transformation came over Jake Grafton's face. It wasn't a smile, it wasn't a grimace. There was strength in the look, and malice. Then it mostly disappeared, with only a hint of muscle memory to show it had been there. "Robert has one idea, I have another. We'll see what the president has to say."

CHAPTER SIXTEEN

The storm broke the next morning. Someone had leaked the juicy news to the press that the election might have been fixed. The Fourth Estate was all over it. Senator Rutherford gave an interview and deplored the fact that her good friend Anton Hunt, a patron saint of the progressive movement here and around the world, was being dragged through the mud. She suspected the Conyer administration.

The FBI admitted that it was conducting an investigation into possible election fraud on the express orders of the attorney general, who refused to comment. No one knew if there was any fraud—that was one of the facts the press didn't have. The press didn't even slow down for that obstacle. The theory seemed to be that if the FBI was conducting an investigation, there must be smoke, and where there's smoke, there's fire.

As Jake Grafton predicted, the liberals, not just Senator Rutherford, attacked the president, suggesting that he had probably been the beneficiary of fraud because sane people wouldn't have voted for him. Conservatives attacked Cynthia Hinton and the Hinton campaign staff who had covered themselves in glory the previous year ensuring that Herman

Bernardi, the socialist, was derailed before he got to the nominating convention. The only thing the pundits could implicitly agree on was that all these people were perfectly capable of election fraud. The smell of it was in the air.

The FBI hit the ground running. They interviewed everyone at ElectTech and Allegheny, some of whom knew more than Heiki Schlemmer thought they did. The agents also went to every county clerk's office on Harry Tanaka's list and examined the machines and the log books to get the names of those who had worked on them.

In the bowels of the CIA's Langley facility, we learned from the FBI that three counties still had software on election machines that delivered the results contained in the Armageddon file. The agents found the names of Edwin P. Riddenhour and Susan Riddenhour in county after county in the swing states. But they couldn't find Edwin or Susan, although they searched and searched hard. Apparently April Tanaka's revelations, now in a sworn affidavit, didn't cut any ice with the Justice Department prosecutors.

Investigators turned up six Edwin P. Riddenhours scattered across the landscape. One was a seventy-three year-old farmer in Iowa, another was a disabled vet of the Iraqi war, one was in prison for smuggling drugs, one was in the second grade, and the other two had alibis that seemed pretty tight.

One of the Susan Riddenhours they found in the age range given by the clerks who claimed to have at least a hazy recollection of what she looked like was a stripper at a gentleman's club in Las Vegas and did some hooking on the side. She had been watching the television news shows. When the agents found her, she admitted she was *the one*. She had fixed the election. After she gave her statement, she called the local television station, which rushed a reporter and cameraman over for a live interview.

By then Susan was having a serious internal debate. Would it be better if she fixed the election for Conyer, or would she get more mileage out of this free publicity if she claimed she had tried to fix it for Hinton? She had tried the Conyer angle on the FBI, but by the time the television cameras found her she had switched to Hinton. Liberals loved it. Susan got spots on several news and late-night talk shows. She even got offers to do two commercials. These she accepted as she did more newspaper and television interviews and waited for Hollywood to call. The FBI discovered that this particular Susan Riddenhour had been laid up last fall with complications from breast enhancement surgery. If the press ever discovered this fact, they kept as silent about it as Susan herself.

The FBI discovered other Susans, of course, but for various reasons rejected them all. If they were having any luck finding the grad students who pretended to be the Riddenhours, they weren't telling the company about it. I suspected any grad student they talked to would deny the whole thing. Having access to a voting machine under false pretenses and diddling with it, even to clean it up, was probably a felony. If I were one of those guys I would have lied like a dog. Getting enough probable cause to convince a magistrate to issue search warrants to access airline and credit card records would be difficult, if not impossible.

While this was playing out, I was spinning my wheels at Langley. Sarah was deep into Anton Hunt's finances, trying to sort through his foreign transactions to find a link to the election. But I figured this was a waste of time because who in their right mind would have paid Hunt in advance to fix the election—certainly no suspicious, cynical foreign intelligence service. Then there was the problem of causation. Had she won, Hunt could have done the Las Vegas Susan Riddenhour trick and taken credit for the win. I could think of several ways around that problem, and no doubt Hunt could too, but not payment in advance.

I learned plenty about Hunt's businesses. His hedge funds were not his only investment vehicle. Hedge funds that have more than a hundred and fifty million in assets must file reports with the government on their investment strategies so the government can assess systemic risk. The FBI had access to those reports, which they shared with the company. However, it seems that most billionaires these days, including Anton Hunt, have private offices for their fortunes, and those are completely unregulated. The government has no idea what these people are doing with their money, or even how much money they have, unless they do something like accumulate a serious position in a publicly traded company and have to tell the SEC.

"How much is Hunt worth?" I asked Sarah.

"I've seen estimates all over the map," she told me. "Investments in stock, bonds, closely held companies and debt instruments are fairly easy to assign a value to, if you know about them. Derivative instruments and swap agreements and so forth are very difficult to value. I've seen estimates that he is worth anywhere between twenty to forty billion dollars. I suspect Hunt himself doesn't know."

"Could he have lost more than a billion when the market boomed after Conyer won?"

"Of course. We have only the vaguest idea of what he did overseas."

"What's your vague idea?"

"I think he lost about five billion dollars."

An investigation of Cynthia Hinton's plans for the banks if she had won might have turned up something, but that potato was too hot for the attorney general and the FBI. As far as I knew, they didn't interview anybody who might have had an inkling. When I mentioned that idea on one of my visits to the Election Fraud Task Force in the Hoover Building, Maggie Jewel Miller didn't even bother to reply. Cynthia Hinton would never mention it, like she wouldn't talk about Benghazi or the Hinton Foundation or her husband's sexual adventures. Unless one of the true believers decided to rat out Hinton, I figured we would never know.

In his corner office at the hedge fund, Anton Hunt huddled with Nick Liszt. This was the safest place in his empire to conduct a conversation without the possibility of being overheard. The windows on both walls of his corner office were triple-paned. Piped-in music vibrated the center pane. That would foil anyone trying to use a laser beam to listen to conversations inside. The office was swept carefully every morning for listening devices. During the night the space was protected by cameras, heat-sensitive sensors, pressure pads under the carpets, and laser beams that swept the room randomly. If anyone entered, including the guards, alarms would sound and the steel doors would automatically close. The security was as close to that in the gold vault of the New York Federal Reserve as a man with unlimited money and a paranoid fear of being spied upon could make it. Hunt had remarked on numerous occasions that the Oval Office, which he had visited repeatedly during several administrations, was not as well protected.

With the soundproof wooden doors closed, Hunt and Liszt took stock. Two televisions were on in a corner. One had CNBC, the other had Fox News; both had the audio switched off.

If Liszt was worried, it didn't show. He knew better. Hunt had fired trusted, loyal staffers who appeared nervous. Liszt was a survivor. The magnificent salary and bonuses Hunt paid when he pulled off a coup had made Liszt wealthy. He was pulling down more jack than a senior partner at Goldman Sachs.

"Our position is invulnerable?" said Hunt.

"Of course," Liszt said. "The people who tried to fix the election are dead, and the survivors have little direct knowledge. The FBI will never be able to prove that there was a concerted effort to fix the election, much less trace it to us with admissible evidence. Our friends will denounce anything the investigators find as fabricated for political motives. Sooner or later, Conyer will realize this investigation is harming him more than it is us."

"Tanaka betrayed us," Hunt said heavily. He was eighty-nine years of age, and knew he didn't have many years left. Hunt's life's work was advancing the progressive revolution by destroying the capitalist system. Cynthia Hinton's election would have been a large step in that direction. Yet thanks to Tanaka's treachery, that chance was gone, like sand through one's fingers.

We were so close, he thought.

The next presidential election in the United States wouldn't occur until 2020, when he would be ninety-three.

"We need to reevaluate our strategy," Hunt said softly. He rarely spoke above a whisper these days—the effort was too much.

They discussed it. When they had agreed, Hunt told Liszt, "Go to Europe and meet with those people. They will be difficult, but you can handle them. They are even hungrier than we are. Their enemies are pressing them severely."

"Yes, sir."

"And send the nurse in. I think it's time for another injection."

"Yes, sir."

Nick Liszt rose from his chair and strode from the room to do the great man's bidding.

Jake Grafton called me in on Friday morning. He said, "Nick Liszt got on a plane at Kennedy Airport this morning on his way to Rome. I want you to go after him, find out what he's up to."

"What's in Rome?" I asked.

"Hunt has a hedge fund office there, and one

of his private family offices. The Italian office of the company will have people follow him. Take a plane tomorrow morning from Dulles. Go see the travel office."

I had plans to take Sarah to dinner that night and a ball game on Saturday. The baseball season was in full swing. So much for that!

At least the company was back in the game. The FBI owned the U.S., but we had the rest of the world. "Yes, sir," I said and went.

At the president's golf course in Florida, Vaughn Conyer and Reem Kiddus were evaluating the election mess that Saturday morning. They sat together in Conyer's private locker room, which had been swept for bugs that morning.

Like Hunt, Conyer was a billionaire, but his fortune, made in construction and hotels, was a small fraction of Hunt's. Of course, he knew Hunt. Had seen him around New York and shaken hands a few times, but due to the vast gulf between their political opinions, the size of their fortunes, and the fact that they were in totally different industries, they were not friends on any level.

The political explosion this past week after the election investigation surfaced had surprised Conyer. He had no experience in politics and so had never been in the middle of a political shitstorm. He was discovering he didn't like it.

"What I want to know," he said to Kiddus, "is where this investigation is likely to go. What is the probable outcome?"

"The FBI has their teeth in it. If they can find evidence admissible in court that Anton Hunt tried to fix voting machines in swing counties in swing states, they'll give it to Justice. It'll get looked at by professional prosecutors, and unless they turn thumbs down at that level, it'll wind up on the attorney general's desk for a go-or-no-go decision."

"Will they find enough evidence?"

"No one can say right now."

"Hunt tried to get Hinton elected and failed."

"That is the fact that has to be proven in court. The Democrats in the House and Senate will do everything in their power to discredit any evidence that tends to support that finding. They'll accuse the FBI of being incompetent, the Justice Department of being biased, and you of being petty, mean, and vindictive, of trying to slander your political opposition."

"Jesus," Conyer said.

"It'll be the scandal of the century," Kiddus said, "and we're only seventeen years into it."

"What if the CIA or FBI finds a foreign connection?"

"If they do, that will be another can of worms. Suppose the Chinese or Russians had their fingers in this? Even if the FBI and CIA bring you proof positive, what are you going to do about it? Ask Congress to declare war on China? On Russia?"

"I see your point. But there are plenty of options short of war."

"Grafton is a hard man to control. He wants to make sure that if a foreign government tried to rig the election, they don't try it again. That's all well and good, but that argument would have put this administration in a terrible position if we had refused him permission to try to find that connection. We discussed that a month ago. If it came out that you refused to let the CIA check to ensure that no foreign government tried to rig the election, that revelation could have brought down your presidency. We're talking congressional investigations and a possible impeachment."

"Well, the fat is in the fire now," Vaughn Conyer said bitterly. "The pundits and Democrats are saying that I am trying to smear Hunt and the progressive movement, perhaps to cover up the fact that *I* rigged the election."

"There's no clean end on this piece of shit," Reem Kiddus remarked.

Conyer swore. "Well, we're here and we have to get out of this mess one way or another. How?"

"Our only option is to wait. See what the FBI and CIA come up with. They will either find evidence that Hunt is guilty or they won't. They'll find evidence of foreign involvement or they won't."

"If it's heads we lose, tails they win."

Vaughn Conyer had managed to get the Republican nomination and win the election because he had an instinctual grasp for how the average, working American felt about the issues of the day. He had never been an average, working American; he'd been born rich and taken huge risks, some of which worked out and some of which were disasters. He had been bankrupt and publicly humiliated. Still, Vaughn Conyer had persevered, never given up, had bulled through on brains and sheer guts, so he had gotten richer. He had won the White House against amazing odds.

He knew working people struggled too. He thought he understood them. He thought he knew how it felt when your job went overseas, when you weren't qualified for the jobs that were available, when you weren't hired because you were too old, when the bureaucrats and bankers who ruled America said No, when it seemed America had chewed you up and spit you out. Most important, he thought working Americans understood him. They expected him to stay the course and keep fighting. They knew he would. That was why they voted for him.

"We'll hang in there," Conyer told Reem Kiddus, then stood up and put on the cap he wore when he played golf.

CHAPTER SEVENTEEN

As I flew the pond I did some thinking. Why had Nick Liszt gone to Italy? Was Hunt going to short the Euro in a big way? The European Union had developed numerous large cracks. Greece was on the verge of bankruptcy, Italy was being convulsed politically and economically, and France was having a presidential election. Germany was having its own political problems due to the government's decision to admit vast numbers of Middle Eastern "refugees," over ninety percent of whom were males of military age. The Swedes were deporting Muslims as fast as they could load the buses. If I were a billionaire, *I* would short the Euro.

But Europe's problems and Hunt's financial shenanigans weren't my portfolio. Finding out if anyone was going to pay Hunt to fix the U.S. presidential election was my job du jour. And I had never had a task less promising. From my vantage point, the chore looked hopeless. Damn that Jake Grafton.

"Admiral, here is that report you asked for about what's happening at the Hunt Hedge Fund and family office." Sarah Houston passed it across the desk.

It was on the tip of Grafton's tongue to say that it took her long enough, but he bit it off. He was getting too impatient, which never solved anything. As he flipped through the report, which ran at least thirty pages, he said, "Anything interesting in here?"

"The family office is where the action is. Anton Hunt and the previous administration were donating money to left-wing parties trying to win elections all over Africa and South America. The administration funded the leftists with money from the Agency for International Development. Hunt used his private funds."

"Uh-huh."

"Hunt apparently went further than the feds. He gave or paid individuals in the countries where he and the AID were trying to influence elections, not just to organized parties or candidates. I don't know what the payments were for."

Grafton took his time with the report. He looked at each country, which was quite a list. Hunt and the previous administration had spent nearly a billion dollars in total to try to get socialist governments elected in all these countries. In some they succeeded, in others they didn't.

"They tried to buy worldwide socialism," Sarah remarked. Grafton didn't look up. "Hunt is still trying."

Three of the nations were in Europe: Albania, the Netherlands, and France. The sums involved in the Netherlands and France were small compared to the sums the various parties raised and spent, but in Albania the numbers were a large percentage of the amounts reportedly spent by the various parties. Two of the individual payments looked as if they went to Albanians.

For what?

"Hunt also has a huge bet on Greek debt," Sarah said. "As you probably recall, once it was in the EU Greece borrowed money to finance socialism. It was the most profligate borrower in the EU. When the EU was pressing Greece on its deficit spending, Goldman Sachs and J. P. Morgan Chase and some other banks created sophisticated debt instruments they called 'swaps,' which gave the Greeks money to stay solvent for a little while in return for promises to pay later. These swaps supposedly kept the debt 'off the books' as far as the European central bankers were concerned. Hunt owns about nine billion dollars worth of Greek sovereign debt bonds and swaps."

"Long or short?"

"Short, of course. He's the King of Chaos. For Hunt, the sooner Greece defaults on its debt, the better. And Greece will default. It's the classic case of a spendthrift living beyond his means by borrowing every possible dime from friends and relatives to postpone the evil day of reckoning."

"Postpone the evil day . . ." Grafton echoed thoughtfully. Then he said, "Thank you, Sarah."

Houston knew the protocol, so she rose and left the office.

Grafton called in an executive assistant, told him to mark the report Secret, make a copy, and hand-deliver the copy to Reem Kiddus at the White House. He called Kiddus to tell him it was coming.

In Rome the company had a man waiting for me at the airport when I cleared immigration and customs. We didn't know each other, so he used a secret sign so that I would recognize him. It was an eight-by-ten-inch piece of white cardboard with "Carmellini" printed on it that he held in front of his chest.

"I'm Carmellini."

"Hey, man. Santiago Gutierrez."

He was about five feet eight or nine, blocky, not handsome like me, had a delicious accent, and looked Mexican. On the way into town I asked.

"Nicaragua. My parents sold everything, sneaked across Mexico, hired a coyote to get them into Texas, and only then, y'know, did Mom squeeze me down the birth canal. Back then Texas gave babies born on the holy soil birth certificates, but they wised up and don't do that no more. So I am an American, born but not bred. I think Dad knocked up Mom back in Nicaragua, y'know, but I can't be sure. They lied to me about many things. He might have done it in Mexico. Texas, maybe not."

"Right."

"I was very young then, so I don't remember much."

"They told me you speak Italian."

"Better than the pope, that's for sure."

"How'd you learn Italian so well?"

"We had an Italian maid when I was growing up. She and I talked dirty all the time in Italian so my folks wouldn't find out."

He grinned at me. "Man, your face didn't even change expression. You're pretty good. Actually I learned the dago lingo in the army. In case we have to invade again."

"Handy. So where's Liszt?"

"Shacked up at an eight-room villa that Hunt owns on the edge of town. Sits on maybe fifteen acres and has its own winery. They buy grapes and squeeze them right there, barrel it, and wait. Private label."

"How do you know all this?"

"Man, they give tours three days a week. You can buy bottles of the stuff in the gift shop and get them shipped home."

I thought Gutierrez was lying again, but it turned out he was telling the truth. In the gift shop on Monday I decided to send a case to Sarah for her to remember me by, but when I looked at the prices I decided to send a bottle instead. No wonder Anton Hunt was a billionaire!

The place looked properly rustic. An old barn

with the faint aroma of horse manure, a winery that was gleaming aluminum and looked state of the art, and a cutesy gift shop built to look old with a parking lot for cars and buses. Warehouses full of wine barrels. Three horses to populate the barn . . . and a really neat old farm tractor that Mussolini might have owned for pulling stuff the horses didn't want to bother with.

Up on the little knoll amid big old trees was the villa, partially hidden from sight. If I were Anton Hunt, I would have retired here a few decades ago. Making money was more fun for him, apparently, than living the Roman country squire lifestyle.

Nick Liszt was in residence just now, along with a staff of four. Santiago had names and positions. The cook and maid lived in a little house behind the villa, the chauffeur and his wife lived in an apartment over the garage, and the gardener commuted. So did the guards—there were at least two armed men on duty around the clock. The guards didn't eat in the house.

What I really wanted to do was keep track of Liszt and learn where he went and whom he met. I talked it over that evening with the Rome CIA station chief, a career spy I had known for several years. His name was Campari, of all things. He looked as Italian as the grocer in my old neighborhood in Brooklyn.

"We have limited manpower. We can't follow him day and night."

"What about taps on the telephones of the hedge fund and private office?"

"Admiral Grafton already asked us to do that, and we got it done Saturday. You can listen in to the SCIF." As usual, the old fox was always two jumps ahead.

However, I didn't want to listen to conversations in Italian, which wasn't one of my languages. "If they say something interesting, let me know."

"I've been reading the papers. Has this anything to do with the brouhaha over the last U.S. election?"

"Yes, sir. Liszt has a cell phone and I have the number. Any way we can track his phone and listen to his calls?"

He nodded yes. "I have a good working relationship with the chief of the *Carabinieri*. The Italians are worried stiff about terrorism. Muslims flooding in. The security services are stressed to the max worrying about the Vatican, which is Target *Numero Uno* for the Muslim extremists."

"I'll bet."

"We also have a fairly good working relationship with the AISI, *Agenzia Informationi e Securezza Interna*, which is the Internal Information and Security Service. We trade intelligence on terrorism all the time. Still, this being *Italia*, and Italians being Italians, the internal politics in the bureaucracies are cut-throat. There is always another bureaucratic reshuffle in the works or being considered by parliament. We gotta watch our step all the time. Are the wheels in Washington thinking about the Mafia?"

"If they are, they haven't told me."

"There's a special anti-Mafia police force. I haven't had much experience with them."

"Let's keep them out of the loop. The fewer people who know anything, the better."

"Business as usual," Campari said with a frown. "All these Italian police agencies leak like sieves. And they plant false stories in the press through paid journalists."

"Our American politicians like journalists too," I remarked.

At my request, Campari sent Jake Grafton a message asking for more help. I figured when Liszt broke cover he would either be going somewhere in Europe or meeting someone. Unless we were willing to commit the people and money to keep track of him, we should probably quit right now. I didn't say that in the message that I drafted and Campari sent. One of the lessons I had learned working for Grafton was that arguing your case when he hadn't asked was not good PR. Irritated him, for some reason.

On my third day in Italy, Liszt left the villa in a limo. Santiago was watching through powerful binoculars from a villa we had rented a half mile away and saw the limo pull up to the door and Liszt get in as the uniformed chauffeur held the door. Santiago called me, hopped into his Fiat, and set sail behind the limo.

The *Carabinieri* were set up to track the location of Liszt's cell phone by then, and apparently he had it on him. I got a call from their liaison officer, a wonderful guy who spoke English with such a heavy accent that I managed to comprehend about one sentence in four. He thought Liszt was on his way into Rome, I gathered.

Santiago called me on his cell and chatted away as the limo rolled into the heart of the old city of seven hills.

I grabbed my CIA tourist camera with the long lens and got into the back of one of the embassy's small sedans, a Lancia. The driver was a young woman who looked twenty and might have been twenty-five. Her name was Cami Rhue. She said she was from Chicago and this was her first foreign assignment with the company. She was very respectful, called me "sir," either because I was comparatively ancient or she thought I was a big wheel. I didn't ask which.

The "subject" was dropped by his limo in front of the Galleria Borghese, an old villa that was now a museum of Italian masters from the sixteenth and seventeenth centuries. I hopped out with my camera around my neck and went charging in. Bought a ticket and began strolling the galleries looking for Nick Liszt. I had studied his photo and was sure I would recognize him, but he had never seen me. For all he knew, if he did gaze upon my handsome features, I would be just another young American male tourist. Although a big one. At three inches over six feet, I had my troubles blending in.

I found him standing in front of Titian's *Sacred and Profane Love*, studying it. After giving it more scrutiny than I thought it deserved, Liszt wandered along, hands in pockets, for all appearances another devotee of the arts. Meanwhile I was scoping out our fellow art lovers. Most were, I thought, from Europe or America, but some were obviously from sunnier places. A couple of burkas, several Japanese men taking photos of every painting, some Arab women in complete western designer outfits wearing make-up and lipstick. At least one Arab guy in a western business suit. The guards looked bored. I heard most of Europe's languages and twitters of Japanese and maybe Arabic. It was an adult crowd; it was too early in the year for the hordes of American, British, and German students who "did" Italy every summer.

I followed Liszt, trying to stay in the middle of the crowd. He never once looked my way, so I don't think he really noticed me or loaded me into his memory bank.

He was giving Raphael's *Entombment of Christ* close scrutiny when he turned suddenly and bumped into someone. A man. Just a chance encounter. But I saw the exchange. It was devilishly quick. He had passed something to the other guy. It was a miracle I was in the right place to get a glimpse.

I took a good look at the bumpee, who was moving away. He was of medium height, dressed in dark slacks, black leather shoes, a pale pink long-sleeve shirt with the cuffs rolled up, no hat, and slicked-back dark hair. Maybe Italian or Eastern European.

Nick Liszt wandered away in a direction that would take him to statues, so I stayed behind the transferee. He took his time strolling through the entire museum, another half hour, and I was sure he'd seen me. He looked around from time to time and couldn't have missed me at six-foot three. I got three photos of his back, and using medium zoom, no flash, managed a profile.

Then I got smart. As he went into one gallery I stayed at the door and aimed the camera. Got ready. When he turned to look over his shoulder to see if I was following along, *click*, I got him.

And he knew it.

He headed for the main hallway leading to the museum's entrance, walking swiftly and talking on his phone. I hung back. I was on my phone with Santiago Gutierrez, gave him the guy's description, and told him to stick to him like glue. Then I called Cami Rhue. "Meet me out front."

Four minutes later I dived into the back seat of the Lancia. I had Santiago back on the line by then. "You got him?"

"Yeah. He got into a black BMW sedan that pulled up for him. It's now headed southwest along the edge of the park. I'm four cars back, so they can lose me anytime."

"Did you get the plate?"

"If I had I would have told you."

I gave Cami a quick sketch, and she put the hammer down. Weaved through traffic, cut people off, ran a red light, and soon we had Santiago's Fiat in sight.

"We're coming up behind you. Let us by."

We were crossing the Tiber by then. Cami traded lanes repeatedly and forced other drivers to give way.

Traffic was terrible. We saw him six cars ahead, then he shifted lanes without a signal and shot off a roundabout onto a side street. Cami tried to change lanes, but a large delivery van cut her off and wouldn't let her in.

I told Santiago where the BMW went, then said to Cami, "Back to the embassy."

We were looking at blow-ups of the photos when Santiago came into the SCIF. "I couldn't find him," he said.

"That's him," I said, pointing at the screen

where we had the grainy digital photo displayed. The photo showed three-quarters of his face, his eyes aimed right at the camera. Campari came in and I told him about the incident.

"Sir, I'd like to know who this guy is," I said. "Can your contacts in Italian intelligence help us?"

"Maybe. Give me a print and I'll ask."

That evening Cami went to the airport and came back with Travis Clay, Doc Gordon, and Ski.

I briefed them, then said, "I think Liszt set up a meet. Haven't the foggiest idea who with. We gotta be there when it goes down."

"What's this all about, Tommy?" Doc asked.

"Damned if I know. But we're going to find out."

I said to Campari, "We may need some guns."

What he had were some well-worn Beretta M-9s and shoulder holsters. We each took one and checked it over. Loaded the magazines and stuffed them where they were supposed to go and chambered a round. Donned the holsters and slid the pistols in. I felt better, and I think the guys did too. Walking around unarmed makes you feel naked, like you left the house this morning without your pants.

Then I sat down, wrote a complete report of the day's activities on Campari's computer, and attached two photos of the guy who brushed

Liszt, the three-quarters face and the profile. Campari encrypted it and sent it to Langley.

The guys and I went to the hotel with Santiago for a good Italian dinner. I invited Cami to accompany us, but she looked at the motley crew and said she had other plans. The barkeep at the restaurant had a bottle of I. W. Harper on the back shelf, so we made a big dent in that.

Nick Liszt didn't poke his head out of the villa for another two days. I was beginning to worry that he wasn't even in there. The Italians said his telephone was, so I relaxed a little.

Campari got a message from Jake Grafton for me. I read it in the SCIF. "Photo is of Prokopis Pappas, a Greek political operative with the Syriza party."

That was it, the whole message. I showed it to Campari. His eyebrows danced, but that was all.

What I knew about Greek politics you could put in your eye. "Syriza, isn't that the majority party?" I asked Campari.

"No, but it got the most votes in the last election. Syriza won a hundred forty-five out of the three hundred seats in the Greek parliament, and formed a coalition with a small party to govern. Alexis Tsipras is the party leader and prime minister."

"Any rumors about election fraud?"

"Man, there are always rumors."

"What does the Athens station chief say?"

Campari frowned at me. "I haven't the foggiest. He would report to Washington, not me."

Ignoring my faux pas, I asked, "Aren't the EU and World Bank after the Greeks to stop the deficit spending?"

"Austerity, they call it," Campari explained sourly. "We would call it living within our income. But, Tsipras and Syriza are dead set against austerity. Claim it would work a horrible hardship on the Greek people, who are not fond of the idea either."

I reflected that the United States Congress also had no desire to live without deficit spending. "Spending borrowed money is a way of life," I told Campari. "Ask anyone who ever bought a house with a mortgage or financed a new car. Buy now, pay later."

Campari said he had other things to do. Guess he was tired of my philosophizing. He wandered away to take care of the local spy business.

My end of the spy business consisted of getting my troops organized and equipped so that when Liszt came out of his hole to see if he was casting a shadow, we would be ready. Unobtrusive, essentially unnoticeable, but present, ready. For what, I didn't know.

It bothered me that Pappas had seen me in the Galleria Borghese, but there was nothing I could do about that. At the very least, whomever Liszt sent his note to would know that Liszt had a tail.

Unless he didn't have a tail. I told the guys we were going to have to leave Liszt naked and rely on the Italians to track his cell phone. If it stopped moving, we would close in with our cameras to see who Liszt didn't want us to see.

"What if the limo just picks someone up on a corner?" Travis asked.

"We're screwed."

I figured the limo driver would have his orders and would pull out all the stops to ensure no one was following. Liszt, of course, would be glued to the rear window, looking.

Going to have to take a chance here, I decided. No guts, no air medal, as I had once heard Grafton remark.

Liszt appeared two afternoons later, or at least his telephone did. My guys and I were wearing small two-way radios and driving rental cars— the embassy sedans were too well known. We spread out over downtown Rome and waited. I was hoping that when Liszt stopped, I could get someone there within fifteen minutes.

Since Santiago Gutierrez spoke the best Italian, he was our liaison with the *Carabinieri*, who were tracking the phone. He gave us periodic updates of the subject's progress, which made me wonder how many expeditions Nick Liszt had made without his cell phone. We would probably never know.

318

The phone began circling Rome clockwise on one of the motorways. Then it quickly reversed direction and went counter-clockwise a while. Then into the city, only to circle a traffic island three times before darting away down a spoke street. All this went on for at least two hours. I checked my watch. A few minutes past four o'clock and rush hour was setting in. You've never seen a rush hour until you've seen the Italians do it.

Mama Mia.

At four-thirty the limo dropped Liszt on a corner by the Coliseum. He began walking along one of the avenues southward. I inferred that was what was happening because his cell phone was moving slowly, Santiago said.

Cami Rhue was the first of my team to arrive. I had a devil of a time finding a parking space, so squeezed my little ride onto the sidewalk and abandoned it.

"He's stopped moving," Santiago said. "The cop says there is a restaurant there," and he named it.

Cami was a half block away where she could see the restaurant door when I walked up. "Did you see him go in?" I asked.

"No."

"Go in and see if he's there."

We had all studied photos of Liszt and Pappas, so she should be able to spot him if he was in a booth or at a table or the bar. As she walked away, I hoped that if she couldn't find him, she would wait to see if he came out of the men's room. But she was a smart girl and didn't need to be told the trivial details.

I looked around for watchers. There had to be some if this meet was set up three days ago at the museum. At the very least, Prokopis Pappas was standing around somewhere nearby looking for me.

The temp was in the low sixties and there was a gentle wind blowing in from the Mediterranean, so my sports coat felt good. My shoulder holster under it felt even better.

I saw Pappas first and bent down behind a car. He was on the other side of the avenue from the restaurant, in a little park, leaning against a tree. He had binoculars, as if he were watching birds. I told the guys he was there.

I kept looking and saw several people who didn't have much to do or anywhere to go. One was twenty feet from Pappas eating something from a basket and drinking wine from a bottle. Another was fooling with a car parked half on half off the sidewalk. I used the zoom on my camera. Uh-oh, both were wearing ear-pieces. There was another guy behind the wheel of a parked car a bit farther along.

I wondered if they were part of Pappas's crew or were with another interested party. *Carabinieri*?

"He's here," Cami Rhue said on the net. "Still alone."

"Sit at the bar and engage some handsome Italian in conversation," I told her.

Several couples and two single men went into the restaurant. Then a car dropped a single man, distinguished, with graying hair and wearing an expensive suit and silk tie. He looked neither right nor left, but merely walked across the sidewalk, opened the door to the restaurant, and disappeared inside. This guy was not a tourist.

"Scope out the guy coming in, Cami."

In a few moments she said, "This is the one. He just sat down in a booth with our man beside him. They shook hands and are now engaged in conversation."

Moments passed as the tension increased. I saw Travis drive by the restaurant, apparently looking for a place to park. He passed and saw me, but he gave no sign.

"Let me know when either man is ready to leave," I told Cami.

She gave me two mike clicks in reply.

Five minutes passed, then ten. None of the watchers moved.

At twelve minutes, a man on a powerful Italian motorcycle drove up and parked right in front of the restaurant. He was wearing a full-head helmet with a dark visor and leather motorcycle togs. He began fooling with his ride, checking things as traffic rolled past. He paused for a moment to zip his leather jacket halfway down. Kept the helmet on. The bike was idling and I could hear the murmur from where I was watching.

I knew trouble when I saw it. "You see the motorcyclist, Travis?"

"Yes."

"He's armed, I think."

Two mike clicks.

Something was going to happen. I could sense it. I thought someone was probably going to get whacked.

There wasn't a damn thing I could have done about it, had I been so inclined. Walking up to the motorcyclist and thwarting an assassination would have probably gotten me shot, which was a risk I didn't choose to run. We were voyeurs, watchers, not actors in this drama. All we wanted was a good photo.

Sometimes a good picture is hard to come by.

Cami said, "I got a photo of the two of them. They didn't see me take it."

Holy crap! What if they had? I didn't tell her to—
Well, what if they did see her?

"Send it to me," I told her.

I snapped a shot of the motorcyclist. Through my viewfinder he looked trim, fit, of medium height. I liked his leathers and boots. So I took another pic for the archives, then one of his license plate.

My cell phone dinged. I got it out and took a look. Terrible picture. Liszt wasn't even recognizable, although the other guy was.

"Take another, Cami. Walk right up to the table and snap one that gets both faces."

I put the cell in my pocket.

Another minute passed. Then two. The two men had been in the booth for seventeen minutes when Cami said, "I got it, Tommy. Startled them. The guy who met Liszt is coming out fast."

Thirty seconds later he came out of the restaurant striding briskly. He was on his cell phone, probably calling for his car.

He never completed the conversation. The motorcyclist pulled a pistol from under his leather jacket, took two steps toward the man of distinction, and fired three times. *Pop, pop, pop.* The man went down on the sidewalk and his cell phone fell beside him. The motorcyclist took a few steps closer until only five feet or so separated them, and fired again. Once. Then he turned, walked, not ran, back to his bike, climbed aboard, raised the kick stand with his heel, and accelerated off toward the Coliseum.

I keyed my mike. "The guy got it. Travis, bring up your car. Cami, stick a gun in Liszt's ribs and march him out. Get his cell phone. Put him in Travis's car."

I ran in that direction, looking around. Pappas had disappeared. The man on the grass with the wine bottle was scuttling away. The man in the car was trying to get it into traffic. He got a break and veered off toward the Coliseum.

I got to the front of the restaurant just as Travis pulled up and Cami Rhue marched through the doors beside Nick Liszt. Perfect timing, as if we had rehearsed it. They circled the small crowd that was gathering around the fallen man, who was sprawled out and very still. Everyone was looking at the victim, including Liszt, who couldn't take his eyes off the body. I opened the car's rear door, pushed Liszt in, and jumped in beside him. Cami slammed the door and disappeared.

"Drive," I told Travis, who promptly obeyed. The faint *hoo-haa* of an Italian siren was just audible.

"Were you good friends with the dead man?" I asked Liszt.

He looked dazed. Didn't say anything.

"Save the tears for the funeral," I told him.

CHAPTER EIGHTEEN

"Where's your phone?" I asked Nick Liszt, who finally turned his head and focused on me.

"Your phone?" I repeated.

He patted his pockets automatically, then remembered and quit. "She—"

"Save it."

I told Travis, "The safe house."

"Okay."

We actually made decent time, considering the traffic. A police car with lights flashing and siren blaring passed going the other way. Liszt didn't say a word, just sat staring straight ahead. No doubt he had a lot to think about. For that matter, so did I.

The safe house was a caretaker's cottage on a vast estate. It belonged to some rich Italian dude who made cars that only multi-millionaires or Ponzi-schemers could afford. Santiago Gutierrez showed up two minutes after we did, and he and Travis took Nick Liszt into the place.

I stayed in the yard and called Jake Grafton. It was morning in Washington, so I tried his cell. It rolled over to an answering service, so I tried the office. Got Robin and told her I needed the boss desperately.

In seconds he was on the phone. "This is a non-secure line, sir." I ran through it as quickly as I could, trying to get in all the essential facts. Say what you will about Jake Grafton, he can listen hard and get it all.

And get to the grit fast. "So why did you grab him?"

"Seemed to me that with the photo and the assassination, we could sweat this guy big time and wring him out."

Silence. Two seconds, three . . . "Who got shot?"

"I don't know yet. Campari will know. I'll call him when we hang up."

"Make it plain to Liszt that he can leave anytime he wants."

"Yes, sir."

"Get what you can."

That was it. I called Campari.

"This is Tommy. Who got whacked?"

"Andreas Theotokis, finance minister for the Greek government."

"I've got Nick Liszt here at your safe house. He was meeting Theotokis, and when Theotokis walked out of the restaurant, he was shot. Is he indeed dead?"

"Dead as Plato."

"Tell Cami Rhue to send me that last photo she took. I need to see it."

"Okay. You checked in with Washington?"

"Yep. Expect a phone call within the next few minutes."

"The usual time of day. They never read the summary. 'What's happening in Italy, dude?'"

"Yeah."

I hung up and did some serious thinking while waiting for my phone to tell me it had received a missive from Ms. Rhue, which it did within two minutes.

I looked at the attached photo. Two astonished faces were staring at the camera. No wonder Andreas Theotokis, finance minister for the Greek government, came out of that restaurant with his tail on fire. Photographed with Anton Hunt's right-hand man.

I thought this stew might do with some simmering, so I strolled in and said hi to my two guys. They were sitting with Nick Liszt and you could have cut the silence with a knife.

"Mr. Liszt. As you may know, your dinner buddy Andreas Theotokis was murdered leaving the restaurant. I have no idea who ordered the killing, but the guy who did it rode an Italian motorcycle, for whatever that is worth. Four shots."

I paused to see if Liszt had anything to say. Nope.

"My boss said you may leave anytime you wish. We were worried the assassins might also be after you, which was why we whisked you away from the crime scene. If you wish to return, speak to the Italian police, get a ride home, pose for shooters, whatever, there is the door." I pointed at it.

"If you wish to stay and think things over, maybe we can get something to eat." I raised my eyebrows at Santiago, and he nodded.

Dinner was brought down from the big house. Santiago said, "We told the car guy who owns this place that we're movie makers working on the next James Bond flick. We'd like Bond to drive one of his cars."

"I thought Bond drove Aston-Martins."

"We're thinking of changing rides. He bought it. I shit you not."

Liszt looked as if he had been hit by a semi. Still dazed, with no interest in his surroundings or companions. I strolled out of the room, in no hurry at all.

Outside on the lawn I emailed Cami's photo to Jake Grafton. I wrote the following caption: Andreas Theotokis, finance minister of the Greek government, moments before he was cruelly murdered on Friday, visiting with Anton Hunt's man, Nick Liszt, in a trendy Roman restaurant. U.S. government photo.

I hoped Cami Rhue wouldn't mind missing out on a photo credit, but what the hey, she got paid every month regardless of how many pictures she took and didn't sell.

We had just about polished off dinner when Campari showed up. He had some secret stuff that Langley had passed along. I looked at it. Hunt had sold about nine or ten billion bucks worth of Greek debt short. The picture got a little clearer for me. Campari picked at the grub while I read, then left.

I let Liszt simmer until ten that night, then went in to the bedroom where we had parked him with a bottle of local red vino and two glasses.

"Who are you?" he asked accusingly.

"Tommy Carmellini. That name mean anything to you?"

"No."

"Oh, you're going to give me shit. Or you can't remember the names of the people you had your Mafia buddy Bordeno Vitalle send hit men after. Which is it?"

"No. I mean . . . who the hell *are* you?"

"I'm an officer in the Central Intelligence Agency."

"Got any proof?"

I showed him my Langley pass. He looked it over then passed it back.

"Okay," he said, shaking his head slowly from side to side. After a bit he said, "Are you going to read me my rights?"

"Nope. Just tell you. You have the right to walk out of here anytime you wish. The CIA doesn't arrest people. You don't have to talk to me. You can have a glass of wine regardless of whether you wish to talk or not."

"People will want to know where I am."

I tossed him my cell phone, which he caught. His reflexes were still good.

"Call them."

"Is this conversation being recorded?"

Actually it was not. The station didn't have the resources. I wasn't going to let him off the hook, so I just shrugged and asked, "Do you want a record?"

He didn't say anything to that, just held the cell phone in his right hand.

"By the way, I have a good picture on that phone that might interest you. It isn't porn or anything kinky. I doubt if a guy like you is into that. Just push photos and see what comes up."

He did. The last photo popped up first. Nick and Andreas Theotokis. I was watching over his shoulder. "We were thinking of passing that to the press," I said.

For the first time I got a flash of temper. "You can't do that," he snarled.

"Man, this ain't the U.S. of A. if you haven't noticed. We can do damn near anything we want here. And we're assholes. What would you think if I passed this snapshot to the Italian press? Might get some serious walking-around money that the company would never know about. Tell me why I shouldn't."

No answer.

"Maybe you'll end up as dead as your buddy Andreas. Maybe the shooter was hoping that you two would walk out of the restaurant together and he could do you both. A two-fer."

"Who killed him?" he asked.

"I don't have a name yet. Someone thought he had lived enough. It wasn't the shooter; he was just doing a job. Maybe that someone didn't want the Greek government dumping the euro and defaulting on its debt. What do you think?"

He didn't say a word. Sat silently, brooding. After a moment he sipped at his glass of vino. I took a sip to keep him company. Drinking alone is bad for your soul.

"Or maybe that someone thought your buddy had something to do with election fraud in the last Greek election. With your help."

That shot hit home.

"Election fraud, stiffing the debt holders, subverting the currency . . ." I sighed. "Anyway, if you decided to lighten the load, maybe grease the skids with the prosecutors back in the states, you might think about talking to me. It isn't you they want. You know that." I stood. "Think about it. If you're staying, you can sleep right here. We can probably find an extra toothbrush. Or you can go back to your hotel and make telephone calls."

I held out my hand for my phone. He passed it over.

"Good night."

I walked out, closed the door, and there stood Travis, who had been standing outside the door in the hallway, just in case. I waggled my eyebrows and he followed me to the living room.

"Liszt can leave anytime he wants. Don't let him steal a car or use a phone here, though. If he leaves, he walks."

"You're a hard man, Carmellini."

"I'll be back tomorrow."

Then I left. Took Travis's car. Traffic wasn't bad at that time of night and I took only two wrong turns on my way into central Rome.

At the embassy Campari was on the griddle. The ambassador had questions, the Italian police had questions, the Italian government had questions, the Greek government had questions, and back in the states the company had questions. I told Campari what little I knew.

Cami had left Liszt's telephone on Campari's desk, so while he talked to all and sundry, some in Italian, I played with it. Examined his contact list. Sure enough, Anton Hunt could be called with one push of a button, the one-key. I thought about calling him, but what would I say? Anton was probably getting the news about Theotokis from some private news service. I thought one Greek politician getting popped in Rome wouldn't make the stateside news. I couldn't have been more wrong.

I left Liszt's phone on Campari's desk and walked the five blocks to my hotel. A streetwalker solicited me, futilely. Up in my room I brushed the fangs and crashed.

Ho-hum.

Another day in the spook business.

In Washington Jake Grafton and Robert Levy huddled at 6:00 p.m. in Jake's office at Langley to assess the news from Rome. In addition to the telephone call from Tommy Carmellini, Jake had received an encrypted message from Al Campari, the Rome station chief, which went into greater detail about the evening's events in Rome. The Athens station chief had also sent a summary. Jake had the last ten summaries from Athens in a classified file and had read them. Theotokis was suspected of engaging in election fraud in the last election to try to get Syriza a majority in the Greek parliament. The effort fell short, but there was a lot of smoke, if no fire. The fact that Theotokis had been a staunch advocate for Greece leaving the EU seemed to give the rumors substance. Grafton also showed Levy the photo of Liszt and the murdered Greek politico.

"But there's nothing there that we can use in court," Levy said bitterly. "Could Hunt have been the one who paid to have Theotokis killed?"

"Theotokis was his ally. It doesn't figure." Jake drummed his fingers on his desk then asked Levy,

"How close are you to getting a warrant to search Hunt's house, hedge fund, and family offices?"

Levy shrugged. "We've probably gotten all there is to get unless this Liszt decides to cooperate."

"Tommy wasn't hopeful. The man helped arrange several murders, tried to have Carmellini killed, is up to his eyeballs in this mess, and is probably worried that Hunt will try to have him killed if he talks. What are you getting from your bent agent, Farnem?"

"He's talking, all right. He and Shipper did the ElectTech killings. He says Liszt agreed to pay him a hundred grand. He got fifty of it and Liszt still owes him the rest."

"Why is he talking?"

"He doesn't want to spend his life on death row waiting for the hot shot. The pistol he had on him was the one he did the ElectTech shootings with."

Levy sighed. "What we don't have is any direct evidence that puts Hunt in the conspiracy. Liszt is the only one left alive who could do that, and if he doesn't . . ."

"Heiki Schlemmer said the Armageddon file is on Hunt's computer. Or one of them. And he altered it."

"I remember."

"Well?"

"Jake, let's be honest. If we get a warrant and go in there and can't find the computer with the altered file and tie Hunt to it, Justice won't prosecute. Hunt's political friends are already on the nightly news giving interviews, blaming the government for a smear campaign against their friend and hero, all to slime the progressive movement. If we can't find that damned thing, we are screwed. CIA dirty tricks, a crooked FBI agent, no direct evidence, no prosecution . . . they'll rip our balls off and nominate Hunt for sainthood."

"Can you get immunity for Nick Liszt?"

"He hired Farnem to do the ElectTech killings. He tried to arrange others. The prosecutors won't let murder slide. He's looking at life without parole, at the very least."

Grafton looked at his cell phone on his desk. Punched at the screen until the photo Tommy sent came up.

"Where's this foreign connection that you set out to find?" Levy asked.

"We're working on it," Grafton replied. "Hunt had at least two countries, Iran and China, that were willing to pay if Hinton won the presidency and he could prove he made it happen. The sources are human intelligence and can't be divulged."

"How was he going to prove it?"

"Give them the Armageddon file before the election and let them see that the vote tallies matched."

"Did he do that?"

"I think so. It'll be months before we know, and maybe never."

"So we are left with Anton Hunt, the untouchable."

"I'll talk to Tommy again," Jake said slowly. "Maybe he can get something out of Liszt. He was probably the one who passed the Armageddon file to Iran and China."

"No torture, no drugs, no promises, nothing like that," Robert Levy said bluntly. "We'll have to put him on a witness stand and you can bet your pension that he'll be asked."

They left it there. After Levy had been escorted out, Jake sat looking at the photo of Nick Liszt and Andreas Theotokis on his cell phone.

I rolled out at seven and did my morning ritual. I even showered and shaved. It was nine when I got to the embassy, via taxi. Traffic was terrible, as usual.

Campari gave me the oddest look. He tossed an Italian newspaper on my lap. The front-page photo was the shot Cami Rhue took. The two men stared at me wide-eyed. The quality of the picture wasn't great, but there was no doubt who they were.

"Did you do this?" he asked.

"*Hell, no*. Jake Grafton would rip my balls out by the roots. There ain't no way on God's green Earth that anyone could keep him from finding out."

Al Campari grunted. "Somebody leaked it. In Washington, apparently. The wire services sent it to Rome. A guy I know at this newspaper said it arrived just in time for the morning edition. He called this morning, wanting to question me. I hung up on the son of a bitch."

I said a cuss word. If Liszt saw this, he wouldn't tell me a goddamned thing.

"And Cami didn't leak it?"

"She was flabbergasted. Denied it. I believed her."

"I need a car."

Campari made a vague gesture and I scooted. Ran into Cami in the hallway. "You, come with me," I said.

My cell phone rang as I drove out of Rome. Travis Clay. "That photo was on television a little while ago. We had the thing on while we were eating and Liszt saw it. He walked out the front door."

"He's gone?"

"He hasn't come back."

Ah me.

"How long ago?"

"Ten minutes. You said he could leave anytime."

"He's not sitting outside under an olive tree?"

"No."

"Okay."

Well, the bastard couldn't have gone far unless he hitched a ride. I put the pedal to the metal.

• • •

It turned out that Nick Liszt wasn't difficult to find. He was walking along a dirt road going off through the hills. Cami saw him as we rolled by on the blacktop. I slammed on the brakes, backed up, and took the dirt road. He was walking away from us. I passed and stopped, got out of the car.

As he trudged up he glanced at me and kept walking. I fell in alongside.

"Where are you going?" I asked.

No reply.

"Well, you picked a good day for the road," I admitted. "Pleasant temperature, sunshine, doesn't look like rain, no mud. All in all, a good day for a hike."

He didn't make any sign that he had heard. I was trying to figure out where his head was. Had he just given up and was going to walk until he died? Did he even have a destination in mind? If he did, this dirt road wasn't the quickest way to get there. Or anywhere, for that matter. On both sides were groves of trees, some vineyards, and pastures where cattle grazed. There were fences on both sides of the road and they had gates in them, so farmers could have access. Summer weeds were getting a good start along the fences, with some wildflowers here and there. This was rural, bucolic Italian countryside, and it smelled delicious.

Ahead and on the left was a farmhouse, set back from the road. Someone was tending a vegetable garden beside the house. They had probably been hoeing gardens in this area for three or four thousand years.

"I think your big mistake was not sticking to the plan," I said. "Silencing all the possible witnesses who possessed direct knowledge of election fraud and hunkering down. That was actually a good plan."

Thirty seconds later I continued: "I knew you and Hunt had panicked when you sent hit men to kill me on the road back to Washington. Your enemy was the bureaucracy. I'm just a miniscule cog in that great malignant machine. You can't kill a bureaucracy. No one can. Not the president, not Congress, no one.

"Why, I'll bet you don't even know today why Tanaka's plan didn't work. All that scheming, plotting, and fixing machines to deliver the Armageddon totals, and it was all for naught. Someone betrayed you. You and Hunt. Screwed you good. Do you even know who it was?"

Nick Liszt just walked.

"I'll bet the thing that irritates Hunt the most is not knowing which of the little people fucked him over. Maybe he thinks it was you or Heiki Schlemmer, but it wasn't. I suspect the dumb bastard will go to his grave without ever learning who rammed it up his butt."

We topped a little hill and a nice wide valley lay before us. The road wound into the valley, crossed it, and snaked up the other side until it disappeared in some trees. Liszt didn't break stride. Behind us at about fifty yards, Cami Rhue had the car creeping along.

"Would you like to know who had a big piece of you?" I asked.

It was like talking to a statue in the park, only he was moving. I guess I realized that it was hopeless, that Nick Liszt had crossed over to the other side. It was as if he were fatally ill. Nothing on this side of the divide held any interest anymore. Not wives, kids, dreams, hopes, ambitions, regrets that life had worked out the way it did . . . nothing. He had worshipped money and done whatever it took to get it. In the end, even money didn't matter. I talked about that for a while. This was my last chance to get anything from Nick Liszt. That was the only thing certain.

I talked and talked and talked. I was looking around, thinking, trying to break through his shell, but he was concentrating on putting one foot in front of the other. If he looked right or left, I didn't see him do it.

"Maybe you're thinking about evil. I'm no philosopher, but it seems evil is all around us. Maybe it's the human condition. The old people thought evil was the devil's work. I think evil is people's willingness to do things that they know will harm others. Lying, cheating, stealing . . . I've done some stealing in my time, and I regret it. Mostly diamonds and jewelry. I know how easy it is to cross over, and there is always a justification. I need the money more than they do. I've got to protect myself. We lie to ourselves all the time about evil. Yet preachers and philosophers say we can cross back over to the good side if we are willing to try. Help undo the evil that we've done. Some call that redemption, but I call it getting right again with our fellow man . . ."

Cattle watched us as we walked through the valley, then went back to cropping grass. They weren't concerned about evil. Puffy little clouds cast shadows.

When we arrived on the crest of another low hill, with farms, farmhouses, and barns scattered around and mountains in the distance, I stopped. Stood there as Nick Liszt walked away without a glance at me. In fact, I don't think he had looked at me once since he walked up to me.

Cami pulled up beside me and stopped. Liszt was fifty yards ahead walking steadily, his shoulders hunched, his eyes on the road.

I got in the car. "He never said a word. Let's go back to the safe house and tell the others they needn't stay."

"Too bad," she said.

"He's already dead," I said.

Standing in the yard of the safe house while the guys packed to leave and straightened up the place, I called Jake Grafton on my cell. He picked up on the second ring.

"This is an unsecure line, boss. Liszt walked away from the safe house after he saw that photo Cami took on television this morning. The Italians are giving it a big play. I found him and tried to talk him around. He refused to say a word. Just walked away."

"Okay," Jake Grafton said.

"Do you want the guys to keep track of him?"

"What's your recommendation?"

"Let him go. He'll never talk to us. The Italian police will pick him up eventually if he doesn't kill himself before they snag him. That's a real possibility. If they do get him, he won't talk to them either."

"Okay. You and the guys come on home."

I didn't say a word about leaking the photo. I learned long ago not to defend myself from accusations that weren't made. I would have given odds that Grafton knew who the leaker was, probably because he did it. I said goodbye and that was it.

I rode into Rome with Cami. Neither of us was in the mood to talk. I was still thinking about Nick Liszt. Maybe she was too.

CHAPTER NINETEEN

The publication of the photo of Anton Hunt's lieutenant with the murdered Greek politician Andreas Theotokis had the effect of a political hand grenade in Washington. Italian reporters soon identified the restaurant where the photo was snapped. The fact that it was taken in the restaurant that Theotokis was leaving when he was murdered was on the news channels in the states, and in Italy and Greece and all over Europe, in short order.

The Italian press turned over every rock trying to find someone who remembered the person who took the picture prior to the murder, to no avail. The sensation of the assassination a few minutes later, if indeed the photo had been taken that day, was the only thing diners and staff could remember, and that in great detail.

The man the press really wanted to talk to was Nick Liszt, but he wasn't anywhere to be found. The *Carabinieri* leaked that they had been tracking his cell phone for days, right into the restaurant, on behalf of the CIA. After the murder, the phone had gone to the American Embassy, where the Italians lost it. Rumors began circulating. Liszt was hiding in the basement of the embassy, he was dead, he had fled to Moscow, he was hiding in Tehran, he was with a caravan crossing the Sahara, he had been kidnapped by the FBI or CIA, maybe both.

In Washington, Anton Hunt's political allies began a careful retreat amid rumors of election fraud in Greece, Theotokis's alleged part in it, and the connection with Liszt. The FBI needed to complete its investigation, they said. Hunt needed to be indicted or cleared.

American radio and television talk-show hosts busily connected the dots. They didn't need to wait for a conviction or even a grand jury indictment. Everyone wanted to talk about election fraud and about Anton Hunt, the King of Chaos. His short bets on American banks before the last presidential election and on Greek debt gave off an odor.

Cynthia Hinton wasn't talking to the press. Senator Westland began to suspect he was out on a limb that was about to break off, so he left Washington to attend to political business in his home state. Senator Rutherford first accused the FBI of setting up Hunt in a smear campaign, but when that only drew ridicule she burrowed into her office and refused to take calls. A political assassination with real bullets wasn't a smear campaign.

If Andreas Theotokis had been the victim of a political murder. Without an assassin in custody, that was only an assumption. Maybe it had been personal, a convoluted story of kinky sex. Or the killer had shot the wrong man. Maybe, maybe, maybe . . .

The Greek press wrote story after story about Theotokis's political career, his home life, his shocked, grieving widow, his shocked, grieving mistress, and his devastated children. His political allies said dark things about their political enemies, and his political enemies said dark things about his friends. The debate on a Greek exit, Grexit, from the EU raged anew in Athens and caused seismic tremors throughout Europe.

In the White House, President Vaughn Conyer decided, for once, that this would be an excellent time to forego the joys of tweeting. His press secretary stated that the FBI hadn't consulted with the president or senior staff.

In the Hoover Building in downtown Washington, Robert Levy and his staff assembled affidavits and search warrant requests as prosecutors from the Justice Department watched and offered unsolicited advice.

I was back in the states sitting in Jake Grafton's office at Langley when he got a call from Levy, three days after the photo bomb exploded, saying that the FBI was on the verge of obtaining search warrants.

"I'd like to be a fly on the wall when the agents walk into Hunt's hedge fund," I remarked. "I'd like to see the look on his face."

Grafton looked at me speculatively. "You are still technically a member of the Election Fraud Task Force," he said. He played with a pencil. "Why don't you go see your buddy Maggie Jewel Miller and ask to tag along?"

So I did.

Miller wasn't overjoyed to see me. "You!" she hissed. "Who leaked that photo?"

"The Russians. I heard it on the news. They're scum."

"I heard a rumor that you were in Italy when Theotokis got it."

I held up my hands. "So were a lot of people, including the pope. The country was chock full of people. I didn't pull the trigger on that Greek. Cross my heart and hope to—"

She spun on her heel and marched away. Since she hadn't told anyone to escort me out of the building, I followed along.

I sat in on meetings. The FBI had hit Bordeno Vitalle's New Jersey operations like the allies storming the beaches in Normandy, trying to find any connections between him and his and Hunt or Liszt. Vitalle's associates were receiving vast amounts of unwanted attention and publicity. Bordeno had apparently taken it on the fly. His whereabouts were unknown. His brother Pete, who ran the wrecker service, wasn't talking to anyone.

I suspected that Bordeno might be sleeping in

a landfill, but I kept my suspicions to myself. Perhaps he was riding with Nick Liszt on camels crossing the Sahara on the way to Timbuktu.

I rode the train to New York City and shacked up in an older midtown dump that had a government contract to house federal employees in town on per diem. Some of the FBI types were there too, but I didn't see Maggie Jewel Miller among them. Perhaps she was at the Manhattan office of the FBI or with the federal prosecutor plotting the assault on Anton Hunt's castle.

Not a peep about this FBI alpha strike leaked to the press, which I thought was a miracle given the number of people who were in the know. Surely someone had a journalist sister or in-law or cousin whose career would soar like a hawk if she or he could pull off a big scoop.

The next morning I followed the special agent crowd to the New York Field Office of the FBI at Federal Plaza in lower Manhattan. The heavy hitters were there getting a briefing. The U.S. attorney for the Southern District of New York sat alongside the assistant director-in-charge of the FBI New York Field Office.

There was some difficulty with the warrant. The federal judge whom the enforcers had captured for a signature was giving them a hard time about some of the affidavits, according to rumor. While I usually discount rumors by half, bureaucratic snafu rumors can be doubled or trebled and still be short of the truth. No doubt the judge wasn't a fool and knew that Anton Hunt would have the best legal talent money could buy defending him, so if the judge was a bit sloppy about the foundation for a warrant, he would not only hear about it but read about it in the press. Cross every "t" and dot every "i."

We troops put on black pullover shirts with "FBI" emblazoned on the back. I put my shoulder holster on over it. I liked the look and planned on stealing the shirt when this adventure was over. Now in costume, we stood around drinking coffee and munching doughnuts that someone had brought in to work that morning. Or maybe the morning before. They were slightly stale.

Then we were briefed. The plan was simple: the employees would be herded onto the helicopter pad while the law's troops searched the offices for thumb drives, iPads, and personal computers, all of which would be confiscated in accordance with the search warrant. All the desktops would be taken also. These devices would be taken to a basement in the federal building where a team of experts were waiting to go over their hard drives. When each computer was declared clean, it would be returned as soon as possible to the hedge fund.

Meanwhile, a similar strike would be underway at Hunt's mansion and at his private office. If the Armageddon file was on a thumb drive or computer, the FBI intended to find it.

I couldn't imagine why anyone would leave such a file on a hard drive. Neither could the FBI. The experts thought that even if the file had been erased, the forensic tech experts could ferret out the remnants, if it hadn't been written over. I thought the hedge fund employees and Anton Hunt wouldn't see their computers again for weeks. I also thought the chances of finding the file were only fifty-fifty, at best, if indeed it had ever been on one of those computers. Or two.

To gain access to the computers, the feds were also going to confiscate the private server that wired these machines together. Grafton had already provided the server's software without any explanation of how the agency obtained it. That would give Hunt's lawyers something to go to the Supreme Court about.

No one had any illusions that a successful prosecution of Hunt would be easy. Prosecuting a multi-billionaire who would hire an army of Harvard and Yale lawyers to throw sand in the gears looked as difficult as pushing peas up Pike's Peak with our noses.

My fellow black-shirted cops thought the U.S. attorney for the southern district had a one-in-fifty chance, even if we found the Armageddon file on Hunt's computer. If we didn't, zip point zero.

Then there was Hunt's age. He had just turned ninety. Armed with affidavits from doctors, the lawyers could drag out a prosecution for years. In fact, it was a safe bet that Hunt would die of old age before he ever spent a day in a cell.

I helped myself to the last half of a doughnut and more acidic coffee. As I munched and sipped I thought about Harry Tanaka. Hunt would never be prosecuted for that killing—I was sure that Tanaka hadn't killed himself. He'd had help.

If Bill Farnem and John Shipper had put Tanaka's neck in a noose and lowered him to strangle, they weren't telling about it. One of the someones on my list who might have done it or had it done was Bordeno Vitalle, the missing mobster. Someone did, and that someone was probably invulnerable to prosecution due to lack of evidence.

If only I could have gotten something from Nick Liszt!

The good news was that Harry Tanaka had screwed Anton Hunt, and he was probably one of the few who had ever managed that feat. He paid with his life for that victory, but a lot of us die for much less.

Late that morning the search warrant arrived, duly signed by a judge, and both the U.S. attorney and the assistant director scrutinized every word. The thought occurred to me as I watched them that they didn't really expect to find the Armageddon file, and in fact, probably hoped it wasn't there. They were going through the motions, forced to do so by the political meltdown in Washington, covering their asses.

After they had each read every word in the search warrant five times, they gave orders to load the buses.

We troops were herded downstairs and climbed aboard. I sat right behind Maggie Jewel Miller. I resolved to stick to her like her shadow.

The two buses pulled up right in front of the main entrance, blocking one lane of traffic. We filed off. An agent had already removed the security guard from her telephone, so there would be no advance notice we were going up. Maggie got one of the first elevators and I elbowed my way on right behind her. She had the warrant in her hand.

She presented it to the receptionist while the agents fanned out. More came up the elevators and did the same. Employees were herded up the stairs and out onto the helicopter platform.

I waited with Maggie while an agent brought Hunt to her. He scrutinized the warrant as his employees filed past.

"Never," he shouted, "have I seen or heard of such a wanton abuse of authority in the United States." He waved the warrant, which Miller was trying to retrieve. He wasn't going to turn it loose, so she gave up. It was his copy, anyway, although he probably didn't know that.

He was maybe eight inches over five feet, slender, with thinning, graying hair. The bags under his eyes had their own bags. His jowls shook in fury as he ranted, "This is Conyer's doing. He is a sworn enemy of the progressive movement. He wants to enslave Americans, chain them to an obsolete constitution, deport all immigrants, ban Islam, rule as a dictator . . ."

I thought that was pretty rich coming from a former Nazi SS trooper, but I held my tongue, as did all the feds. He had obviously suspected this raid would happen sooner or later and had decided how to handle it. He was going to make any investigation of him a war on the political Left.

The other thought that crossed my mind was that the Armageddon file wasn't on a computer in this building.

As Hunt raved on about his liberal friends— former presidents and presidential candidates, senators and celebrities—Maggie Miller gestured to two agents to take him in the direction of the helo pad. She didn't want to listen to his shit while she tried to supervise the great computer grab.

I was right there on his elbow, exerting pressure. He was frail. Another agent got his other elbow. We didn't exactly lift him off the floor, but if his feet hadn't moved we would have. Straight to the security door and out into the gathering crowd on the helipad. The crowd was his employees in suits and ties and a few women in designer dresses, but only a few.

Now he had an audience, one that he paid extremely well. He owned them. The other agent let go of him but I didn't. I kept him moving through the crowd to the edge of the helipad. He was shouting away, ranting, fighting my grip on his arm. People were watching. A sea of faces, mostly white, mostly male.

He was getting pretty worked up and I began to think that he might stroke out right there. When he paused for air, I whispered, just loud enough for him to hear, "The Greeks have Nick Liszt. He's talking."

Anton Hunt heard me all right. He turned and stared into my eyes. "Let go of me, you bastard!"

I released my grip and said softly, "The Greeks are going to extradite you."

His eyes grew as round as quarters as the wind played with his wispy hair.

"Nick is telling them everything."

His eyes were upon my Kimber now.

"All the lawyers in America can't save your sorry ass from the Greeks. They killed Theotokis. They'll—"

The old man went for my gun. I was a little worried that he wouldn't be able to get it out of the holster, but after two tugs he managed. He pointed it at me and shouted something—I don't know what. People screamed. Out of the corner of my eye I could see men and women throwing themselves down. There's nothing like the sight of a gun in someone's hand to get people excited.

I grabbed for the Kimber's slide and pulled

gently. Hunt pulled back as hard as he could. Maybe he thought he could plug me and use an insanity defense . . . but who knows what he thought. If he was thinking at all.

I had a firm grip on the business end of the pistol by then. We struggled for the gun for several seconds as I worked him backwards toward the safety rail. He was jerking on the trigger of the weapon but hadn't touched the safety. Probably didn't know what it was or had forgotten.

His feet hit the safety rail and he tottered, still holding the gun with both hands. I stopped pulling, gave one little push, and turned loose of the gun.

Anton Hunt fell backwards, hit the far rail of the safety net, and went over. In the last glimpse I had of his face, his eyes were locked on me. He did one complete somersault as he fell and landed on his back on the shelf twenty stories below.

Splat! Hit on his back like a sack of garbage and didn't even bounce. He didn't move after that. My Kimber lay there beside him.

I turned around. There were a hundred people staring at me. I passed a sleeve across my face, wiping at non-existent sweat as I arranged my features.

"The old fart must have panicked," I said to a horrified woman standing there with her hand over her mouth.

"Very sad."

CHAPTER TWENTY

"You stupid son of a bitch!" the assistant director for the New York Field Office of the FBI shouted into my face. "How in hell did a ninety-year-old man who didn't weigh a hundred and ten pounds get that gun out of your holster?"

We were in the field office and the witness's statements were coming in. Anton Hunt had jerked the gun from the agent's holster and they had wrestled for it. And he fell.

I was sweating now. I tried to keep my face deadpan. "I don't know, sir. It happened so fast that—"

"You incompetent bastard! Why in hell does that idiot Jake Grafton even let you carry a gun?" He turned and gestured to his aides. "Get this stupid shit out of my sight. Of all the fucking luck!"

They hustled me out. Believe me, I was ready to go. In the hours that followed I drank a lot of coffee and ate a terrible sandwich, something dead garnished with wilted lettuce. They returned my Kimber to me. It was scarred up some from the impact after a twenty-story drop, but appeared serviceable. I would have to take it to the range and shoot it to make sure. Hunt's head had burst like a dropped cantaloupe and his backbone was shattered. Death had been instantaneous. Four hours after the head FBI honcho had a piece of my ass they kicked me out of the building. A sympathetic agent took me out by the basement entrance so the press wouldn't get a photo.

I went to my hotel and collected my duffle, then took the subway to Penn Station, where I bought a ticket on the Acela to Washington. While I was waiting for the train I fed myself a decent meal and had a drink. As I ate I watched some television, which was treating the demise of Anton Hunt as a major story. The liberals thought he had panicked due to overreaching by the FBI and the Justice Department, the conservatives thought he had panicked because he knew that the feds would find incriminating evidence of election fraud in Greece and maybe even in America on his computers. Some of his employees who witnessed the fatal scuffle were having their one minute of fame.

I bought a paperback novel to read on the train and queued up for the platform. While I was standing there I received a text message from Jake Grafton. "Come see me at home when you get back to Washington."

I typed, "Yes."

I had a couple more drinks on the train. Damn, the stuff went down smooth.

The novel didn't interest me. I sat watching America go by out the window. Modest houses crammed in cheek by jowl, kids playing under streetlights, worn-out cars on blocks, trash, old factories, graffiti, traffic on the overpasses and highways. All those people living their lives as I rode by on the train.

It was eleven at night when we rolled into Union Station in Washington. I snagged a taxi out front and rode in style over to Grafton's place in Rosslyn. Gave the cabbie, a guy from Syria, a two-dollar tip.

"Tell me about it," Jake Grafton said. We both had bourbon, neat, in our glasses and were ensconced in his den.

I told it.

He rubbed his face then said, "What would you have done if he hadn't gone for your gun?"

"I don't know. I was playing it by ear."

"How did you know he wouldn't shoot you?"

"I was watching the safety. If he had tried to flip it off with his thumb I would have pushed the pistol aside and used my fist on his face. That would have killed him right there. I never lost control of the gun."

He nodded. Sipped his drink and nodded some more. "They would have never convicted him of anything."

"Yeah," I said.

"How do you feel?"

I thought about it before I answered. "Dirty," I said. "Hunt was a ninety-year-old man. He thought he was God. Could make the decisions for everyone. What everyone else thought didn't matter. I knew I had him when he went for my gun. Until that moment he was in control of his fate. When he grabbed the gun he was a dead man. I played for that."

I sipped the bourbon.

"Harry Tanaka deserved a lot better than he got," I said. "He was a romantic and a dreamer, and America needs guys like that. Nick Liszt was a weak man mesmerized by money. Farnem and Shipper were too. And Heiki Schlemmer. Kurt Lesh and Nora Shepherd. Doing evil for money. Maybe I did some evil too. Played God. *But not for money!* I'll find out how the scales balance when I get to the Pearly Gates and St. Peter reads from his list."

After a bit Jake Grafton said, "This afternoon I approved a fifty-thousand-dollar payment for the Armageddon file to Mrs. Tanaka."

"April."

"April Tanaka."

"Thank you." I finished off the booze and put my glass on his desk.

"Want some more?"

"No. What I want is a vacation. A week. Me and Sarah. I plan on buying a pickup tomorrow and heading out. I want to see how many miles I can put on it in a week driving through America."

"New or used?"

"New."

"Wish I could go with you," Jake Grafton said.

The odometer on my new ride, which was a four-wheel drive with a crew cab and short bed, read 2,586 miles when I parked it at Langley after my week off. Stuff had piled up on my desk. The Greeks were still in ferment mode and no one knew who had paid for Andreas Theotokis' assassination. Congress was mulling a bill to update American election procedures. The reform bill included a provision requiring every voter in a federal election to present a photo ID, which was the political firestorm of the week.

The Earth continued to circle the sun. Summer arrived right on time. The baseball season was in full swing when we heard that the Italians had found a body in a river that they thought might be Nick Liszt. It had been in the water for weeks. They thought he might have jumped off a bridge.

I thought, too bad. But he was already dead the last time I saw him.

Books are produced in the United States using U.S.-based materials

Books are printed using a revolutionary new process called THINKtech™ that lowers energy usage by 70% and increases overall quality

Books are durable and flexible because of smythe-sewing

Paper is sourced using environmentally responsible foresting methods and the paper is acid-free

Center Point Large Print
600 Brooks Road / PO Box 1
Thorndike, ME 04986-0001 USA

(207) 568-3717

US & Canada:
1 800 929-9108
www.centerpointlargeprint.com